Perfect

Paul Pickering
ham in 1952 and
Royal Masonic Schools in Bushey, Hertfordshire and at Leicester University.

He is a freelance journalist and has a special interest in South American politics. Paul Pickering's highly acclaimed first novel was *Wild About Harry*.

'Even at its most comic – and this book is often very funny indeed – Pickering's portrayal of the Nicaraguan scene is grittily authentic . . . Pickering's masters are Greene and Waugh . . . a skilful comic novel and a powerful account of this dismaying conflict.'
New Society

'Paul Pickering's second triumphant novel . . . leaves the reader breathless with laughter and admiration at just how wicked his prose can get . . . a classic text of black comedy . . . his cocktail of moral confusion, chaos, blood, spilled guts and corpses smacks of the real thing.'
Time Out

'A wonderfully satirical comic vision.'
Northern Echo

By the same author

Wild About Harry

Paul Pickering

Perfect English

Flamingo
Published by Fontana Paperbacks

First published in Great Britain by
George Weidenfeld & Nicolson Ltd 1986

This Flamingo edition first published
in 1987 by Fontana Paperbacks,
8 Grafton Street, London W1X 3LA

Flamingo is an imprint of
Fontana Paperbacks, part of
the Collins Publishing Group

Printed and bound in Great Britain by
William Collins Sons & Co. Ltd, Glasgow

To Alice

I would like to thank Caroline Dawnay, Victoria Petrie-Hay and all the people who so kindly helped me on my travels around Nicaragua, both in Managua and on the Atlantic Coast, and who I feel would prefer to remain anonymous.

P. P.

PROLOGUE

An unforgiving sun beat down on the ragged procession of middle-aged priests tramping relentlessly towards the muttering, angry crowd at the crossroads by the new church. They came all in black, like a flock of scavenging crows, self-assured though careful. Yet as they drew nearer the pace slackened, slowed by fear. The crumbling canyon of that poorest of barrio streets permitted no shadows, no hiding place. The fierce noonday light would not allow the deception or luxury of retreat. In the stifling heat, in that city of volcanoes and revolutions, they were walking inexorably to their appointed Calvary.

Johnny lit a cigarette, fascinated. Even in the centre of Managua there was the enchantment he had imagined, a strangeness and confusion, a mixture of marvel and panic that had once awed the stiff conquistadores. Before him the blue of the sky, the dark, impenetrable green of a mango tree and the reds of the Sandinista banners glowed around the drab clerics like the simple poster colours in a naïve painting. The homely smell of tortillas competed with the ostentatious perfume of incense from the ever-advancing line of men. It was as if no stone of the barrio wanted them. They reminded Johnny of the story of another over-optimistic mission accompanying the conquistador Francisco Hernández de Córdoba. Those first monks to the New World had been irritated by the magical countryside and above all by the Momotombo volcano, then called Molocatzonpol by the tribes who lived on the shores of Xolotlán lake. Despite the Indians' warnings the fathers set out to baptize the unpredictable mountain with a Christian name (as was the fashion), and exorcize the devils that lived there. They climbed the smoking giant, winding through the fumaroles with a cross at their head.

"Exorciso te, creatura ignis."

They chanted as they went but when the arrogant party reached the summit Momotombo began to rumble and a pall of choking ash descended from the crater. None of the unfortunates was ever seen again. Around Johnny the shuffling feet of the crowd and the black boots of the Sandinista soldiers sent up clouds of dust. Behind them rose the modern brick and concrete structure of the Church of St Francis, the core of the fiery new liberation theology in Nicaragua.

At first it had looked as if the gathering outside the church was going to welcome the priests. There had been a holiday atmosphere and barefoot children had played stick-and-stone baseball under a giant hoarding of a smiling General Sandino, the national hero. But from what Johnny had been told, certainty came hard in a land where you could not trust the earth itself, where peaceful valleys suddenly swallowed cities and generations of dreams could be washed away in acrid tides of lava without explanation or warning on a summer's day. Now he was sure there was going to be trouble.

He was still disappointed Catherine had not come to meet him at the airport. It had been the three longest months of his life since he had seen her. Johnny loved Catherine very much. Instead, a car full of Perfect English volunteers, the aid group he intended to work with, had picked him up. The old Buick had one of its back doors held on with string. A furled banner was crammed into the car and, as they travelled in mostly tense and fidgety silence, he was told he would see her at the demonstration. After thirty hours on planes via Moscow to beat the US blockade he felt too tired for questions. It did not seem odd that a radical Catholic education group should take him to the famous church, but Johnny was not prepared for what happened next.

From where he stood he could make out a silver cross. A squat priest carried it, rocking back and forth in a hypnotic motion as if his stubby legs did not want to take him forward. Another swung the censer of incense but had the same reluctance to proceed too quickly. Behind them came a man he later realized was the Archbishop, flanked by a dignitary in a dark suit who was obviously American and impatient. The cortège pressed on and Johnny could hear the mumbled chants. Beside him a soldier casually reached over for his Kalashnikov AK 47 assault rifle which he had slung round the neck of the brass statue of St Francis, transforming the gentle pastor into a hunter and making the crudely fashioned animals and birds about him look cowed and threatened. Groups began to unfurl anti-American and anti-Vatican banners. Still the priests came on and a hand grabbed Johnny's shoulder. He had hoped it was Catherine but it was Blanca, a Nicaraguan girl who had cadged a lift in the car. She had bright red painted nails.

"That whore of an Archbishop has come to take away the Madonna from the Church of St Francis," she shouted in his ear as all around them the crowd broke into a deafening, though disciplined, roar. "I should have told you. In the days of Somoza, the Madonna used to be in the rich Church of the Atonement near the Plaza España. When the people overthrew the pig they hid the statue in this barrio and she protected us. So we put her in the new church; the free church of the people. Now the fat priests who pray for the Contras, who wish to kill our revolution, want her back. They are our enemies."

He had hardly time to consider what the pretty girl said. The crowd drained away from the centre of the crossroads and the procession stopped. A soldier passed out empty beer bottles and an old man near him ripped a poster of the Pope in half and urinated defiantly on the kindly Polish face. An excited gang of children, the eldest barely five, were embedding razor-blades in green mangoes. He glanced back to the fleshy face of the man bearing the cross. The only emotion he could discern was embarrassment.

The red and black flag of the Frente Sandinista was everywhere. Slogans thundered at the intruding priests. The motley international brigades, an echo of Republican Spain, whipped themselves up into a frenzy. Beside Johnny a lovely blonde girl with candyfloss hair shrieked obscenities at the Pope and the church of St Augustine. As he turned round she smiled at him and accepted a stone a child handed to her. He wondered for a moment if her violence was a reaction to her own softness as the urchin passed him a larger missile from a wooden bucket. Johnny had read about the collision course between Managua and Rome, how the Sandinista Youth had screamed insults at the Pope on his visit, how the priests who supported the revolutionary government had been threatened with excommunication. But he had no idea the conflict was so bitter or that he would be forced to take sides so soon.

"Look, the shits have brought the glass case containing the Host," someone cried. "They are going to try to say Mass in our church. Death to the fascists! *No pasaran!* They will not pass!" It was the slogan of the revolution, and was followed by the sound of glass breaking.

Johnny squeezed the warm stone in his hand as the fury around him grew. But the people had to work themselves up sufficiently before actually doing battle with thirty aging clerics. The soldiers encouraged them. The conservative priests in Nicaragua preached a doctrine of obedience first to God and then only to Caesar, which has never been popular with the military. Such men preferred the Church of St Francis, which Catherine had sent pictures of, with its huge murals of Christ as the guerilla fighter, returned in triumph to help the poor. Instead of an altar there was a cross-shaped paving stone on an ordinary table below a stage for a pop group. In one photo Johnny had seen, the seventeenth-century carving of the Virgin seemed out of place and more than a little confused.

"The Archbishop loves the Contras! Death to Imperialism!"

A youth on the roof of the church threw the first stone. Other grinning youngsters set fire to a painstakingly constructed lifesize Uncle Sam doll, which sported a tinsel halo (meant as a warning to the American priest with the Archbishop) as the Sandinista slogans rumbled back and forth down the alleyways, always finishing up with "*No pasaran, No pasaran.*" Those about Johnny started to jostle forward and at first he moved with them, but he was pulled back by a soldier on the directions of Blanca. "Slowly, comrade, slowly . . ." More had been planned. The stone was still in his hand as rocks and beer bottles arched through the air.

The procession now huddled around a donkey cart,

though the squat priest continued to hold the cross defiantly over the head of the Archbishop like a spiritual umbrella. Some tried to retreat up the street towards the comparative safety of the main road. But the children on the roofs were ready for them and mangoes studded with sharp steel came tumbling down onto the fleeing priests. The men who had come for the Virgin were trapped. Every now and again the American cleric urged them on, like a coach at a time-out in some divine basketball match. The crowd heard him and began to taunt "Gringo Fascist" and "Contra".

In front of Johnny, below the Suffer Little Children banner of the Perfect English group, he suddenly noticed Catherine. He shouted and tried to get to her but it was no good. She stood on tiptoe waving a Sandinista flag attached to the end of a makeshift cross, yelling for liberation theology and against Rome. He could hardly believe she was wearing the same dull olive green as the soldiers. As she jumped up and down she supported herself on the shoulders of a strikingly handsome man with short dark hair. He put his arm round Catherine and hugged her to him. The hug did not look merely comradely.

"Throw your stone, gringo. Throw your stone at the fascist priests. You hate them, don't you?"

The child's face was twisted into an adult sneer. Others were peeping at Johnny. A firecracker exploded like a gun-shot and he ducked, only to be laughed at by the boy. The next moment Johnny hurled the stone harder than he had meant to and it struck the man carrying the cross on the shoulder. He stumbled with pain but held onto the pole as if praying. All at once the missiles ceased and the crowd watched the bloodied procession in an expectant quiet. The priests had that dazed look of animals at the door of a butcher's shop.

Johnny's heart began to beat faster as the clerics chose to advance again. He did not want to be part of this. Then, just as he thought the crowd might finish them off, Sandinista police vans surged out of side alleys, sirens wailing. A cheer went up. Everyone knew they had not come to arrest the stone throwers. In a space thoughtfully left in the centre of the crossroads a *comandante* addressed the demonstrators from the back of a pickup truck.

"These servants of America will not steal your Madonna. They will not steal your country."

Sacklike black shapes, some limp and bleeding, were bundled into several vehicles and the victorious congregation packed into the Church of St Francis to celebrate Mass.

"The spontaneous action of the proletariat cannot be ignored," continued the speaker. A band struck up inside the overflowing church. For reasons best known to themselves they started to play a medley of old Beatles songs. The streets ran with beer dispensed by the militia, and pedlars set up foodstalls. The ugly scene of minutes before was turning into a carnival. Johnny saw the dark denim-clad man plant a kiss on Catherine's cheek and then she was lost among the exultant mob.

"The Virgin is safe," cried Blanca with genuine fervour, her red claws clutching his arm. "The people of the barrios have triumphed again. Don't worry Johnny, we will catch up with the rest at the House of Perfect English."

In the street the halo of the Uncle Sam doll the children had burnt had failed to ignite and blew about fitfully in a hot wind as if not knowing what to do with itself. The priests had either been taken away or chased off, leaving only patches of blood on the earth and the lonely donkey cart one Benedictine had hoped to take his Madonna home on. Johnny felt sickened and a little cheated. Surely this was not the New Jerusalem.

"Come along my friend. It's all over now. We won," she laughed and held out her small hand.

"Did we?" he said as they walked away from the Church of St Francis towards the House of Perfect English, on the other side of the city. "Did we?"

1

Johnny sat with Blanca on a tasselled hammock in the exquisite garden of the House of Perfect English. The battle won, there was to be a celebration.

"You fought for the Virgin? Congratulations on a great victory. Would you like a glass of wine? I'm afraid it's only Californian," an apologetic American carrying a tray full of brimming glasses endlessly repeated. "We're getting some French champagne from the Bulgarian Embassy, but that hasn't arrived yet. Peace be with you, comrades. Enjoy."

More people drifted in and Blanca giggled with amazement as one Left Bank epicure, whispered to be from the French terrorist group Action Directe, actually refused the precious ice-cold liquid in anticipation of his patriotic tipple. Ancient trees shaded a shimmering blue swimming pool and the sizzle of meat on the barbecue was accompanied by the lazy strumming of a guitar. About them scarlet hibiscus tangled among small palms, tamerind and frangipani. Heavy fruit hung from a papaya sapling like pendulous breasts. Only the shards of broken bottles cemented into the high walls around the luxurious property reminded the visitor that it once was owned by a senior officer in Somoza's National Guard and that a harsher reality lay beyond the gates. Johnny sipped at the Napa Valley Chardonnay and it made his teeth tingle. All he could see now belonged to Perfect English, a fashionable "new generation" charity based at Laguna Beach, south of Los Angeles, dedicated to changing things and not just papering over the cracks. But their hedonistic Nicaraguan headquarters were a little unnerving after being in one of Managua's most impoverished barrios. The place smelt of money, not of the brave new fusing of socialism and Christianity.

"Hi. Peace be with you, comrade. My name's Bob," a man with straggly ginger hair and tinted glasses of the sort John Lennon used to wear said to an English girl Johnny had noticed on the plane. Bob sat down awkwardly next to her as if about to make an improper suggestion. She also was suffering from culture shock in the well-heeled surroundings and made a remark about camels and eyes of needles. Her admirer, who was telling her he had been in Nicaragua for a year, looked hurt. He was obviously one of the faithful. There was no sign of Catherine.

"Oh, it embarrasses Perfect English too," said Bob, gesticulating towards the house and pool. "The Sandys are very good to us and cash does not seem to be a problem for Perfect English. It's a miracle, figuratively speaking."

"How come?" asked Johnny, butting in, curious about the miraculous largesse.

"Well, basically, Perfect English used to be the name of a Los Angeles publishing house specializing in avant-garde poetry. But by the seventies no one wanted to know. Then a group of radical Catholics approached them to produce an illustrated English grammar for missionary friends in northern Ghana. The stories in the grammar stressed the right of every man to life, liberty and the pursuit of happiness."

"Perfect English seem to be good at the happiness bit," giggled the girl from the plane, looking pointedly around. Bob continued, unabashed.

"The old Perfect English firm thought the venture would just cover their debts, but the response was phenomenal. The book helped trigger off popular demonstrations among church organizations in Ghana for land reform, and a copy was sent to the UN. Six months and a dozen educational prizes later they could not print the books quick enough. The original owners were bought out and it became an independent Catholic charity, thriving on the thirst of Third World peoples for English, the language of science, technology and power, and radical ideas." Bob's protruding Adam's apple seemed to have a life of its own.

"Now the medium has partly become the message. The priests who started the ball rolling see English as a valuable unifying tool in poor countries; a new Latin for revolutionary ideas, not just the linguistic monopoly of Imperialism. In Europe and America, Perfect English are cautious and conservative and the dollars pour in from people who are suspicious of giving to food aid in Ethiopia, but think a little learning cannot hurt. Perfect English have become a flourishing vehicle for liberation theology worldwide . . . Are you here with your boyfriend?" The girl merely smiled at the question and walked off to get another drink. "Of course, Engels predicted liberation theology," he was soon enthusing to someone else.

Johnny took a cigarette out of a silver case which had belonged to his father. He offered one to Blanca and caught sight of his own reflection in the polished metal. He was frowning. He put it down to the demonstration.

"Look Johnny. Look what I found in the road," said Blanca. She had black Indian hair and bottomless eyes with a haunting darkness, a quality as elemental as it was disturbing. Blanca was part of the family Catherine had lived with and had borrowed a pair of her Fiorucci jeans. She excused the fact that at twenty-six she was four years older than Johnny's fiancée by announcing she had once won the Barrio Central America Bianca Jagger Beauty Contest. He could well believe it as the red nails tweaked his hand. "Look Johnny . . . ."

Smiling, she opened a handkerchief on her lap and white circular wafers of the Host fell out, some onto the ground. He remembered seeing her stoop to gather up something from the broken glass in the road after the riot. Before he could prevent her, she stamped on one and bit through another she held in her hand.

"See gringo. Christ does not bleed. At least the Christ of Rome, the Christ of the Contras does not bleed."

He winced.

"Please Blanca, don't do that." Tradition pulled stronger than his new allegiances.

"Why not? It's only rice paper. Now it must have lost its magic."

"I'm sure it's still some sort of sacrilege." It was too hot to recollect the ins and outs of transubstantiation. Sacrilege. The word sounded odd as she wiped a crumb of wafer from her lips. It fell on her left breast.

"How superstitious you are, Johnny. Catherine is not so old fashioned. Have one of these. Have a bite. It tastes nice. Have one Johnny." She pushed a wafer towards his mouth and he could see the imprint of Christ crucified. "If this is Christ, Johnny, He does not bleed like a man. He does not taste like a man." She licked another wafer.

"Stop it Blanca," he said quietly and tried to explain. "At the school I went to they told us if you did such things you went to hell for all eternity. A priest used to tell us one instant in eternity was how long it took to empty the Atlantic Ocean with a teaspoon."

She laughed.

"Stupid priest. How would emptying the sea help anyone? The new church believes the only sacrament is helping the poor. Surely you know that. Only the poor are innocent. The new priests anoint the ground with their sweat and blood like Christ. They support the Sandinistas. They don't just sip sweet wine and pass around cheap biscuits that stick to the top of your mouth and promise riches in the next world. They bleed with Christ on earth."

The sudden, fierce passion in those eyes surprised him. She removed a pin from her hair and, sticking it deftly through several of the white opalesque wafers, thrust them under his nose. "I do not belong to the church of cannibals," she said. "I belong . . . ."

"Lay off him Blanca. He belongs here too," said a deep, kindly voice. "After all, he is one of us, aren't you Johnny? Peace be with you comrades." Johnny looked up and there was the denim-shirted man he had seen with Catherine at the Church of St Francis. Blanca's smile returned in an instant. She spun on a high heel and walked towards the barbecue where she flung the remaining wafers on the burning coals. She was not one to go to hell by halves.

"I'm Father Anselm," said the newcomer. "But just plain Anselm will do. As the lady says, we don't stand on ceremony in Nicaragua." Then Johnny saw Catherine come through the gate behind the priest and he wanted all of them to go away. He stood up, spilling his wine, and she hugged him to her, kissing him passionately but then breaking off with a peck on the cheek as someone sniggered. She pushed him gently back onto the hammock. The welcome seemed something of an anticlimax after so long.

"Oh Johnny, I'm sorry I wasn't there to meet you at the airport. But did you go to the demonstration?" He nodded. "Wasn't it like nothing you have ever seen?"

"Unique," he said, not meaning it to sound as critical as it did. She started to introduce him.

"I'm sure Bob has made himself known to you. This is the famous Dr Annie Window," she said, pointing to the blonde girl with candyfloss hair he had seen by the Church of St Francis. He could hardly believe it was the same Dr Window who had just written a charming and very successful analysis of Marx's love poems to his wife. She appeared much younger than Catherine. By the academic sat a surly, broad-shouldered female with frizzy curls who towered over her elfin companion. She had hands like a man and one of them was on Annie's knee. "Meet Annie's friend Tanya. Like Dr Window and Bob, another of your fellow countrymen. All three will be coming with us to the Atlantic Coast."

"Peace be with you." Everyone exchanged the greeting, except Tanya, who grunted into her wine, even then seeming as if she was being over effusive. It caused an ugly little pause and Johnny was just about to say how pleased he was to be part of Perfect English when a grinning Bulgar arrived with armfuls of champagne and a fusilade of corks was fired into the swimming pool.

"Here's to victory," shouted Catherine, taking a drink out of a glass and handing it to him. She looked so happy. He scarcely noticed the others as he gazed at her deep blue eyes. His mother said she had the face of a holy Virgin and it was true. She had been the most beautiful girl at Cambridge, if somewhat more worldly than Mama's description allowed. A luminous, self-assured sort of beauty only Americans seemed to possess. The subtle evening light was failing now and with the clanging of the bell by the gate more people joined the party. The sudden rush of darkness took him by surprise and the garden began to vibrate with all the noises of the tropical night. The occasional unmistakable sweetness of marijuana, the incense of the new church, drifted on the evening air. Small oil lamps and flickering candles illuminated long hair and silk blouses. Everywhere was laughter and the release of optimistic abandonment to the cause. More bottles were opened and a wave of merriment swept around the pool as someone fell in.

Johnny had met Catherine at a damp May Ball at Cambridge. She had come up behind him as he had stared morosely into the Cam, two punch glasses in his hand and the girl he had brought nowhere to be seen. He would never forget what she had said.

"My middle name is America. Do you want to sleep with me?" It had sounded so innocent. One look and he had been in love with Catherine America Hope, of the Boston meat-packing Hopes, ever since.

He kissed her again and she dug him in the ribs as the priest began to speak.

"Well done everyone. That is what I would like to say first of all. A lot of ordinary folk here still regard the Catholic church as a servant of the dictator Somoza, as a tool of the Contras. We must get over to them that our new church is their church. To win folk back we have to convince them that we fully support the Sandinistas, that we are not starchy and inflexible and always concerned with petty rules. Above all we must show we are concerned about them, the *campesinos* and the urban poor. That way we will take the church out of the Middle Ages. Peace be with you. Now have a good time."

As if to indicate the flexibility of the new order two *Internationalistas* had stripped and were enjoying an affectionate swim. The rounded brown lines of their strong bodies interlocked below the water. Johnny could not help thinking of the white, pasty faces of the priests at the crossroads and the brutality of the crowd. He was about to challenge Anselm concerning the violence when Catherine, guessing he was going to put his foot in it, shot him a cautionary glance. When they lived together at Cambridge they had almost thought as one. He had not been long enough in Nicaragua to disagree publicly with anybody, especially Father Anselm. Three Sandinista priests, members of the government, had been ordered by Rome to stop saying Mass because of their attacks on the Holy See. The moral flexibility of the new church did not include taking the side of the conservatives. In the shadows by the gate was a guard with a gun.

Catherine's arm snaked back around Johnny as Anselm talked to several expensively-suited Perfect English representatives from the charity's publishing division, who had brought in another shipment of glossy books. The turbulent priest was a lean but muscular man in his early forties. His broad, tanned face and strong jaw emphasized an open, straightforward manner. It was a physical Christianity and like many a nineteenth-century missionary he looked ever ready to do battle with the devil. He ran a hand through stubbly, close cut brown hair. He was no intellectual like his Benedictine namesake, who abhorred politics and devoted himself to the spiritual. A deep scar creased his left cheek. The former longshoreman had returned to his native California from Vietnam with a beret full of medals and a Messianic desire to do something practical with his reawakened beliefs. Johnny had read the countless articles on the man in the Catholic *Universe*.

The priest's blue eyes shone with an intensity hard to resist. He had become a delegate of the Word, a lay preacher in Los Angeles among the Hispanic community and had then been sent by them to help with the many refugee organizations around Mexico City. There and in Argentina and Chile he had cut his teeth on the new theology and had started to preach and write about it. A jail term in Brazil after leading a march of evicted peasants brought him fame. Once ordained as a Catholic priest he was a natural choice to head the emergent Perfect English programme in Nicaragua. His battered face and quiet confidence won hearts and one could forgive the eager disciples around the pool for being in love with him. Johnny only hoped Catherine was not among them.

"You should see the goodies we have got for you," an overzealous publishing rep was saying. "We have the notebooks and textbooks and pencils all in red and white as you asked. We got posters and stickers and best of all we have badges to give the kids when they do good. Not patches but heavy duty sheriffs' stars saying 'Perfect English'. How's that for an idea?"

"Fabulous," said Anselm turning one over in his hand. "Just fabulous." He passed it to Catherine. It was an elaborate affair, a shiny red heart enamelled on a brass star emblazoned with the words, "I speak Perfect English". It could only have been made in America. Johnny imagined it would be a *campesino* child's pride and joy.

"So by teaching the children you can influence the parents?" asked Johnny, sounding knowledgeable. He had heard something of Perfect English's methods at meetings of the Cambridge Supports Nicaragua study group, which he had been a member of for the past year. Textually, he knew the place quite well.

"Right, Johnny. Peace be with you!" said Anselm enthusiastically, and took it as a cue to launch into a lecture for his appreciative audience.

"Very simply, we have been teaching the children of the *campesinos* to read and write in both Spanish and English. By teaching the kids we can bring them and their dads and moms nearer the revolution and the Lord. The Sandys are so pleased with our results they are letting us loose to improve the literacy skills of the English-speaking minorities on the Atlantic Coast." There was a hush.

"As many of you know it's a difficult and dangerous part of the country, thick jungle with much Contra activity. Two Swiss doctors were murdered last month. The people there are mainly Miskito Indians, together with a few Creole descendants of black plantation slaves. The Miskito are the results of seventeenth-century buccaneers intermarrying with Rama and Sumu Indians of the Coast. They are quite different from the Indians on this side of the country. The Miskito hate the Sandinistas because of the mistakes made in the heady days after the revolution. They are formidable enemies and we have to help the government win them back from the

Contras. The Sandys hope we can get them to see the light with our expensive hardware paid for out of American pockets. That's why we are making this pilot trip."

Catherine took Johnny's hand and left Father Anselm talking to the rapt disciples. All around there were murmurs of agreement. She led him towards the house for something to eat.

She smiled, kissing his cheek. "Don't say I don't get you to all the best parties. It's the Garden of Eden, Anselm says."

"Before or after eating the apple?"

"Oh, Johnny, please don't be silly. Please don't be jealous. I was all set to come out to the airport when Anselm told me I had to go into town to pick up some kit from the army depot. It was his idea you should be thrown in at the deep end. Neat, eh?"

"But you kissed him."

"Only as a sister, Mr Morgan. Loosen up, Johnny. You're among friends, remember?"

In front of them an excited huddle had gathered around a seated nun. A photographer took a picture and men with *Barricada* party newspaper armbands scribbled her every word into notebooks. She was Irish and apparently had seen a massacre near Jinotega.

". . . the Contras came into our village and you should have seen it. They chopped off men's heads and hung them on poles just like Genghis Khan. Oh yes, they said Reagan himself was paying them in dollars." Pencils scratched as she slid slowly from the low chair onto the floor, hiccupping slightly.

"How did you escape if everyone was killed?" asked a dissenting voice. The men from *Barricada* looked around angrily at the unprofessional questioner.

"I was saved by the Lord's angels," said the sister, reaching for her glass. No one noted the divine intervention. In propaganda terms massacres seemed much more important to a new church and a new state. Even so the middle-aged woman's face and hands were badly burnt. She needed her angels.

Later, as they walked back from helping themselves to the

buffet, Johnny noticed Catherine's eyes dart to the side. She quickly turned away from a lone figure. He had spotted the same guilty movement many times at college parties, when she was avoiding old boyfriends. Under a tree was a tubby man with a round face not quite visible in the shadow. The checked golfing trousers were in questionable taste. Johnny tapped Catherine's arm.

"Who is the wallflower that you don't want to speak to? Another broken heart for your trophy room, or is he a priest?"

She pulled a face. "Hardly, that one does not have a heart. Everyone should keep well away. He's certainly not a priest. That dear creature is from State Security." He was about to ask more but she shook her head. The subject was taboo. The harmless looking individual was from a nastier world outside the high walls of paradise. Johnny did not see him go. Near the house someone helped the nun away. Anselm's voice was clear and calm while the crowd around him were worse for alcohol. The American was not a whisky priest. Johnny had not seen him drink even a beer all evening. Catherine said he was viceless. There again she said he was a prophet.

Undeniably Anselm was impressive. It was not often Catherine was so passionate about anyone for so long. Usually her saints lost their haloes after a couple of weeks. In her letters she had written of the first "complete man" she had ever met, of the humility and charisma of the priest. He had not thought much of it at the time. Most of her tutors at Cambridge had been complete men. Then a glass of wine was spilt at a draughty table in an indifferent restaurant at the wrong moment, or a change in the wind exposed their bald patch, and she came back apologetically to Johnny. In contrast, she had continued to kiss the feet of Father Anselm for months. But jealousy was not an emotion Johnny approved of. He had always considered it the prerogative of peculiar kings in Shakespeare or an admission of an older lover's failing powers. The man was a priest after all and it had been Johnny's notion in the first place to come and join Perfect English. Catherine was a year older than him and he had to stay and finish his finals.

"Now, who has any ideas?" said the priest taking out a packet of Royale cigarettes ("The only cigarette with a real tobacco filter" Johnny had read on a hoarding near the airport). "We want to devise some short, maybe biblical plays to get our message across. To get across ideas of change and the reality of socialist man. Any thoughts, Johnny?"

"What about St Paul's conversion on the road to Damascus?"

"Wrong Johnny, I'm afraid. St Paul was a tax collector. The Miskito hate paying taxes."

"Well, David and Goliath then?"

"I don't feel you are on the right wavelength regarding these people. One thing we don't want to encourage is rebellion. King David could be seen as a Contra and the Sandinistas as the Philistine Goliath. Remember many Miskito joined the Contras because of early Sandinista excesses. We want to remedy that. We have to learn to think politically." He sounded a little irritated.

"We could do some scenes from the life of General Sandino," said Annie nervously.

"That's more like it. Peace be with you!" exclaimed the priest.

"We could have him coming back to earth again," continued Dr Window. "I know it's silly but I've this picture of him returning to earth as a sort of Christ figure. The Somoza Contras and the American Imperialists could be dressed up as devils. He could, well, lay them waste." She spoke with the rounded vowels of a private education.

"I like it," said Anselm. "It's got to be a simple moral message."

"The nativity could be done with Sandino as a baby," added an American girl. "You could borrow one from a *campesino*."

"What about the parable of the talents as an explanation of capitalism?" slurred Bob. "We did the prodigal son once to show Che coming back to take power in Cuba," said another. Eager faces were ever more anxious to combine the Gospels with the forbidden fruits of revolution and Sandino. "We ought to have a special section about contraception and the suffering of women everywhere through the centuries," added Tanya with combative gloom. No one disagreed.

Johnny wondered what his sad-eyed mother, a devout Catholic of the old school, would have made of it all; the kind who still ate fish on Fridays. Johnny was an only child. His father had been an invalid for most of his life, stricken with TB. It had prevented him from going to Spain to fight Franco. Despite coming from an aristocratic though declining family of west country landowners, he was a socialist and told Johnny he must be too. To his father it was self evident and it did not interfere with a belief in God. His mother quietly loved her ailing husband as he talked for hours and put the world to rights in their rambling farmhouse; finance had forced them to close The Hall. Then one day they found him dead on the front lawn in the snow dressed in his pyjamas. Johnny's mother had not missed Mass since.

Anselm rested a hand on Johnny's shoulder and led him a little apart from the others as Catherine joined in the discussion. At the other end of the pool a girl opened the sliding glass doors and put a record on the stereo. "Street Fighting Man" blared across the water from speakers in the trees. The dancing began. It looked like the Caribbean retreat of a wealthy pop star.

"I wanted a private word, Johnny," confided Anselm. "I know we have written to each other and Catherine tells me great things about your political work, but sometimes folks out here find they just don't fit in. I can only take a small party to the Atlantic Coast. Excuse me for being so blunt but a lot of people want to go. What I am saying is, are you totally committed to the programme? I mean a hundred per cent?" The eyes were deep pools of shadow and a lot of the friendliness had gone out of the drawl.

"It would be pretty daft coming all this way if I wasn't sure. I was just brought up rather strictly regarding religion, both at home and at school, and all of this takes a bit of getting used to."

"There won't be much time for enjoyment on the Coast. Or for teenage romance. Are you certain you did not come out here simply to be with Catherine? We didn't pay your fare to come on vacation."

Johnny paused for a second so as not to betray annoyance. "I'm sorry I gave stupid answers before, Father. The flight was a marathon. I had to come via Moscow. With or without Catherine you can depend on me, three hundred per cent."

"Peace be with you. That's what I like to hear. I didn't mean to offend. It's just that earlier you looked a bit out of it." Despite himself Johnny blushed and the priest smiled, knowing he had won for the moment. "I'm satisfied, Johnny. Say, if you like you can sleep here tonight. It will be more private than where you will be living. You and Catherine can have my room."

They were magic words. After three whole months away from her nothing else seemed to matter.

The bedroom was at the opposite side of the house to the garden. The walls were white and so were the bed and the thick carpet in the huge room. The lacquered furniture and modern paintings were carefully chosen. His clothes fought themselves to the floor as she gracefully slipped off the green uniform. Her hair tumbled across her breasts and he lifted her onto the bed.

"Please Johnny, love me," she said. Typically, it was almost a command.

2

They had not fallen asleep until the sun began to stream through the windows. When he awoke it was noon and he opened his eyes to see Catherine standing at the bottom of the bed, dressed only in a rough green army shirt which ended at her hips. Her long black hair was still wet from the shower. The shirt was open and the light caught the silver crucifix on her chest. Everything was smooth and brown and bare except for a pert belly button and the dark forest of curls between her legs. He glimpsed her breasts as she stooped and picked up a pack which she put on the bed. It was part of a jumble of military kit in the corner of the room he had not paid much attention to. Then she walked to the wardrobe and lifted out something that made him sit up. It was an AK 47 assault rifle. The harsh lines of the weapon emphasized her nakedness. As she toyed with the sights her crucifix fell against the curved magazine. He wanted it to be last night again.

"Come back to bed. Where did you get that horrible thing?"

She dropped the rifle with a thud, like a discarded toy thrown from a child's pushchair, and sat down on the bed putting a long, delicate hand at the back of his neck and pressing him to her. Catherine stroked his hair gently and his arm went around her waist.

"No Johnny," she said. "I'm afraid there isn't time." She smiled. "We all have to go and learn how to use those dreadful guns on a coffee *finca* up in the north before they let us begin teaching on the Atlantic Coast. *Internationalistas* picking coffee have to bear arms in case of Contra attack, so that's where the army trains people to shoot. The Sandys say we need to be able to defend ourselves. I have to go right away, today."

"What about me?"

"You'll have to follow on in a couple of days with the others."

"But Catherine . . ."

"Look Johnny, they have never issued every *permiso* at once when Anselm's people wanted to travel about the country before. It was doubly unfortunate that we applied for them on a saint's day. Things here are still very old fashioned. We just have to do it their way or not at all. You can sleep where I was staying at Blanca's house."

"But I thought we would at least have a week or so together? Couldn't you delay going for a while and stay with me? It's been a long time, remember. I've counted the days. Haven't you missed me?" He had wanted to come and work out in the Third World. Yet if he was truthful to himself she was his major reason for being anywhere. He did not want to lose her.

"Of course I missed you, Johnny. I do love you. Last night was beautiful and we will be together again very soon. But I have to go, my *permiso* is stamped for today. You can't pick and choose your days off in someone else's revolution."

"I'm sorry. It's so good to be with you."

She kissed him on the cheek. "What did you think of the others?" she asked, but did not give him time to reply. "I'm afraid Tanya is a real ogress when it comes to men. Prone to look for answers in the bottom of a bottle. But she's very committed. Bob can be a bore but he works awfully hard and Dr Annie is delightful. Window isn't her real name, you know. We got bombed on rum together the other night and she told me that both of her paternal grandparents had affairs with Vita Sackville-West. She says she does not want to be renowned for their sexuality."

He brushed a droplet of water off her forehead as they talked. Her eyes were the deepest blue he had ever seen, almost violet, and had the effect of making her face look pale. Her too perfect nose touched his. It was Catherine Hope's only flaw. It had been a present from her mother for coming top of the class at Vassar.

"How's your family?" she said suddenly. "How's your

mother and that pig of a stepdad? I can't understand how such an artistic woman can be married to someone like that."

"She's all right. Her last project was to rescue all the orphaned ducklings on the village stream. I thought his nibs was going to have a seizure. He loathes anything young, poor thing. He only approved of my coming out here to get shot of me for a bit. My mother thinks it's a romantic quest . . ." Johnny's wiry, self-made financier of a stepfather was in a way another reason for joining the Perfect English programme. He was extremely rich and though generous and devoted to Johnny's mother, he deeply resented the memory of her aristocratic first husband. Since they had moved from the old farm to his stepfather's house the man had systematically purged every photograph and portrait of his father. Unable to discard Johnny, he had taken to making gentle fun of his commitment to his father's Fabian ideals. "We all have idiotic ideas when we're young, Johnny. But socialists aren't even fashionable anymore. About as much use as your mother's popery." Johnny had determined there and then that the Perfect English programme was going to be a success.

"My parents seemed pleased too. I was ready for a fight," said Catherine. "But Pop was very glad I was following in the family's female tradition of voluntary work. I forgot to tell you when I wrote that he'd got a priest waiting in Boston to bless me when I went home to get my things. I think he believed I was going with the Peace Corps. Father McCadam was not a bit happy. He'd heard of Father Anselm but was too scared to mention anything to Pop. My mother said she was encouraged that I had stopped running around with troublemakers and turned to the church again. She imagines because the Sandinistas are Marxist anyone Christian must be against them. She means well though."

Johnny had met both Mr and Mrs Hope and the one thing he was certain of was they were not fools. In her father's case he was convinced that beneath the civilized veneer his money had provided when he came from Chicago to the East, was the stony heart of a stockyard boss. Nothing anyone did ever seemed to affect him. Catherine had said he had not shown a flicker of emotion when told his brother had drowned in a boating accident other than to say, "Oh, God . . .", and ask if the boat was lost. If his daughter wanted to go to Cambridge and then chase around the world do-gooding that was all right. She would come home one day. Wasn't that what the Kennedy kids did? If in her youthful high spirits she kicked over a few traces, well what the hell? Not that he didn't keep a close eye on her. At Cambridge it was rumoured he had her followed by a private detective. Subsequently it came as no surprise that a notorious student drugs pusher had been found badly beaten up. No, the man shouldn't be belittled. Johnny was grateful Mr Hope liked him. On their last meeting he had called him "sonny".

"I'd like my children not to have parents," Johnny said thoughtfully, tweaking a nipple.

He gazed at the Kalashnikov on the expensive carpet.

"Catherine?"

"Yes."

"It is all right isn't it, all this?" he gestured around him. "It wasn't quite what I imagined. Not this bedroom or house, but everything. The party last night . . . I think I expected it to be a bit more straight-laced and, well, Catholic. We came out here to teach and now we are fiddling about with guns. We used to be so anti-war. You are sure of Perfect English?"

She kissed him and got up, retrieving the Kalashnikov.

"Please Johnny, not the guilt thing, not this morning. We talked all this over before we came out. The Left in Europe is asleep. Liberation theology is where it's happening. We only have these things for defence. You said yourself we'll be doing something useful for a change. Hey, can you get this magazine off?"

There was a knock at the door.

"Are you ready, Catherine? We're leaving in five. Peace be with you." The voice was Anselm's. In a whirlwind of purpose she was dressed with the rifle and pack on her back. He reached for her but she dodged away.

"You wouldn't molest a poor little soldier girl, kind sir?" she giggled, opening the door and darting back to kiss him. "I love you Johnny. Peace be with you, and your damp English doubts." Then she was gone.

The bathroom, he decided, originally had been designed for a pervert. It had mock Doric columns and everywhere were mirrors. After he had showered he examined his skinny frame. At school they nicknamed him The Leaning Tower of Morgan. Catherine was tall too. She called him her angel. Choirboy features of curly blond hair and blue eyes made him look a lot younger than twenty-one and with Catherine he was constantly being mistaken for a younger brother. He blinked at himself. He'd turned on the hot tap to shave and his reflection blurred with the condensation, becoming as hazy as his real knowledge of Nicaragua. Yet, if yesterday were anything to go by, seeing things too clearly might prove a handicap in this part of the world. His naturally dissenting nature had got him into trouble at school. Mother called it the Protestant in him. He had ruined allegiances and relationships in the past by looking for imperfections, picking at the seams until they fell apart. When he was a boy he once threw away a whole jar of tadpoles because they were losing their tails, not realizing they were going to turn into frogs. He smiled. Unlike Catherine he was probably never entirely convinced about anything. He would have to be careful.

But Johnny did share with Catherine a deeply felt desire to go out into the world and change things, to do good; an inclination which seemed lost on most of his contemporaries at Cambridge. When he had been an altar boy in the parish church and later at school, he had thought seriously of missionary work and of going to some far flung corner of the globe to do the will of God. He even once or twice toyed with the idea, at about the age of thirteen, of being a priest, but concluded he had been much too wicked already, mainly due to the fact he became quite dizzy with lust whenever he even thought of women's silken thighs. But it was his father's mild and cheerful socialism that really weakened his trust of the established church, though it never stopped him searching for a way to fulfil those early longings. Perhaps Perfect English was the answer.

A maid brought him coffee and rolls by the swimming pool. He had to go into town to hand in yet more forms for the *per-*

miso to travel to the Atlantic Coast and he hoped to pick up the one needed to go up to the coffee *finca*. Johnny wandered back inside the house to ask where one caught the bus and found a discussion group in progress.

"I'd show you but I've got to take a class," said an American girl who had welcomed him and Blanca yesterday. "The bus stop is on the corner by the military checkpoint. Just ask anyone for the 119 to the Plaza España. Here, take this map of the centre. I've marked the Ministry. You do speak Spanish, don't you?" He nodded. The checkpoint was easy to find. The bus was a revelation.

There was an orderly queue for the battered vehicle, at least until it came and he was shoulder charged out of the way by an old woman in black who cackled like a crow. The old Bluebird buses had been designed for thirty-seven Americans to ride in comfort and keep their God-fearing bodies to themselves, not for a teeming, shouting mass of two hundred adults plus baggage and the occasional dog, sheep, pig or chicken. Everyone seemed to accept the crush joyfully, as if it were an expression of national togetherness.

Johnny forced himself along the bucking steel tube past kindly smiles, apologizing all the way because he was so large and clumsy. Catherine had told him in her letters the buses smelled, yet this one certainly didn't. Such friendliness was a treat. A young man forced him into an old woman, fat as an armchair, and next to her a soldier was taking care the sharp sight of his AK 47 did not catch in the pink cotton dress of a pretty girl, as he moved with Johnny towards the rear door. Conversation was not possible over the noise of the engine, only contact. In Managua municipal transport was a sensual experience. Johnny became pressed up against an old man whose brown football of a head hit him in the solar plexus, the eyes turning to leer up at him, grinning with toothless gums. They lurched around another corner and he was nestled into the soft body of a schoolgirl. She had a satchel full of books and a haughty Spanish face. She swayed slightly and did not take her eyes off him. On the next bend her forehead touched his lips. In her bag was *One Hundred Years of Solitude*. She looked up at him. No words were spoken. Suddenly it was his stop and he jumped off, his close communion with the country ended.

He nearly tripped over one of last night's drunks as he reached the top of the hill on his way from the Plaza España. The man had jammed his head inside an old paint can to prevent it being stepped on. No one disturbed him. Other inebriates lay slumped under trees on a piece of waste ground. It was almost as if there had been a shooting. For a revolutionary state the Sandinistas were curiously tolerant of the desire for oblivion. Behind Johnny the suburbs of brightly coloured homes sprawled happily over the green landscape. Yet to an outsider the primal reds and yellows and blues had the same unreal quality as the volcanoes. Twenty or more could be counted from that hill on a clear day with the tricky Momotombo looming in the distance, billowing smoke.

In front of the office where he was meant to get his *permiso* he saw Dr Window curled up on the steps reading a book.

"Peace be with you," she sighed. "What a night. I still have a hangover. Have you got the forms Anselm sent you in England?"

"Yes," he replied, fumbling in his over-stuffed trouser pocket.

"Well, give them to me. There's no point in us all hanging about. We are meeting up at the bar by Lake Tiscapa. Show me your map." He opened it out and leant over her. She smelt of shampoo and Johnson's Baby Powder. "It's just here. You've probably read about its infamy under Somoza but it's different now."

"Peace be with you," he said as a goodbye. In her frilly white blouse she looked like a refugee from a romantic novel.

It was rather fun to explore the city and seek out the sights he had glimpsed in Cambridge Supports Nicaragua study group slide shows. From the illustrated tourist map he located the concrete Aztec temple of the Hotel Intercontinental. At a restaurant across the road, marked Los Antojitos on the map, two men with long hair, beads, draw-string trousers and sandals, whom he recognized from the party, gave him a clenched-fist salute. The straggling district resembled an ambitious Californian housing scheme the builders had given up on. There were many desolate spaces overgrown with bush and columbine hiding the ribs of a burnt home or the remains of a rusting tank; the remnants of earthquake or civil war when Somoza had considered it West-Point-good-sense to bomb his own capital. The sudden roar of anti-aircraft gun practice at the airport made him jump but did not stir the interest of a group of four-year-olds playing with the carcass of a rat. It was friendly fire. They did not even look up.

Johnny walked to the brown sea-like expanse of Lake Managua, which the map indicated was not recommended for swimming, and located the cathedral. He knew it had been battered by the earthquake of 1972 but was moved by what he saw. It was now an empty hulk abandoned and sad as the gull-picked skeleton of a beached whale. A huge picture of Sandino stared down from one wall, while inside a small mongrel with yellow teeth curling from the top of its gums growled at Johnny. Where the pews had been, homeless refugees from the north squatted over their belongings, marking out mean territories with the red and black Sandinista flag. They used the high altar as a toilet wall and amid the stench one man appeared to be praying, begging forgiveness for his brothers' presumption. It was an acrid reminder that any church is the work of man. Fidel Castro had boasted that if someone could prove the existence of God to him he would rebuild Managua's cathedral. To Johnny the resilient shell, the country's broken heart, was a confirmation beyond logic.

Next he loafed around the oriental market and finally strolled up to Lake Tiscapa, a water-filled volcanic crater in the centre of town. A flock of green parakeets skimmed in low as he sat down at a bar on the shoreline. A man was swimming, and the birds, banking along the rim of the old *caldera*, came screeching in again like fighter planes, as if daring the spirits of the dead, for whom the opaque waters were the last resting place, to snatch them out of the air. Johnny knew from reading the accounts of survivors that the deepest of Nicaragua's lakes could have told many stories if it gave up all the men the dictator Somoza had pitched in there from El Chipote Prison, still standing like a sore on the crater's rim. Even if the unfortunate survived the fall, though many who made the journey to Tiscapa had been badly tortured and past caring, the sides were very steep at the water's edge. It looked difficult to pull yourself out, impossible for a wounded man. Some said there was a current which dragged swimmers down to spin round and round for eternity with Chipote's victims in that nightmare pit. If a person drowned in Tiscapa the body was never found. Perhaps a lot was superstition. Yet, it somehow seemed wrong that the Sandinistas had tried to rehabilitate the hellish place, building bars and charging admission for a part of town to which the *Guardia* had found difficulty bringing people at gunpoint. Now there were little thatched beach umbrellas and new flowers and plants to rid it of its devils as though the bitter past, too, was a landscape garden. It made him shudder to think of being sucked into that cold whirlpool.

The bar on a bamboo platform jutting out over the lake had been erected with total amnesia concerning frequent earthquakes. The last had killed 20,000 people in a few minutes. His eyes strayed to the swimmer making for the middle of the *caldera*. The man was cutting effortlessly through the water with a fast but lazy-looking crawl, seemingly unconscious of the abyss below him. Directly across the lake on the crater wall skull-white stones had been arranged into the motto *No Pasaran* to exhort the people to repel the constantly forecast US invasion. But watching the vulnerable, lithe body of the swimmer the slogan could apply to those Tiscapa had gulped down and was not going to let go. Similar thoughts must have entered the young man's mind out there. As he approached the dark centre he suddenly turned, kicking out for the nearest shore, the easy rhythm of his stroke gone. He appeared to be fighting the water and it took him much longer to swim back to the shelving bank, only hauling himself out with great effort after several attempts. Johnny lit a cigarette. The swimmer's body was heaving, struggling for breath.

No doubt because of the lake's grim associations, there were only a handful of people in the bar. The waiter brought him a bottle of Victoria beer as he watched a fat, middle-aged man and his teenage mistress. She glared at Johnny enviously and as her escort said something he caught a flash of gold teeth. How long had she been with such a man? When her beau demanded a half-bottle chaser of Flor de Caña rum she squirmed out of reach of the pawing hands and put a mournful *ranchero* song on a jukebox, which was winking bright blue and red lights as it played. Her partner perspired as he gripped the slim waist. The armpits of his garish shirt, which advertised the delights of Miami Beach, were wet. On his neck were tight rolls of fat. The man grinned in his direction.

"Do you have dollars?" he inquired as they shuffled past. "I give you four hundred *córdabas* to the dollar."

Johnny looked round for somewhere to retreat to. The revolution might have landscaped the gardens but hadn't weeded out the blackmarketeers.

"I say, are you English?" said a voice behind him.

"Yes, actually."

A two-foot-long iridescent blue lizard shot like a lightning bolt up the passion flower vine shading the tables.

"Join us if that lout's bothering you. He bothered us. My brother keeps cleaner pigs," continued a tall man in ruffled Home Counties English. "My name's Arthur and this is George. What's yours, old man?" They shook hands.

"Johnny, Johnny Morgan."

Arthur had a startling strawberry-coloured birthmark that crept across an otherwise dignified face, as if someone had thrown a handful of the soft fruit and it had stuck. His white linen shirt was slightly frayed and he wore a regimental tie and the same old-fashioned light cotton suit as the man across from him. His companion, George, sported oval gold cufflinks. He must have been the first man in Nicaragua to wear cufflinks since the revolution.

"Take a pew," offered George.

"Thank you," said Johnny. He noticed on the seat beside Arthur a battered black briefcase which said "Tambey and Brown" in faded gold script.

"We're here on business," began George, as if any other reason for visiting the country would be absurd, pausing as a large black bird in the vine above him made an obscene chuckling sound. "I must say you don't look like the usual long-haired revolutionary layabouts at our hotel. In fact in those white togs you remind me of my son off for a game of cricket. He's a solicitor. Plays for the county seconds. Yes, we're here on government contract. Are you here . . . commercially?" The men had an unhealthy pallor.

"Not exactly," said Johnny. "I hope to teach. I'm with an independent Catholic education programme called Perfect English. They speak English on the Atlantic Coast you know."

George shot him a conspiratorial smile. "I have always been very fond of the Roman Church. Very fond indeed."

"What is it you do?" asked Johnny, trying not to sound prying. "Are you in aviation?" He pointed at a faded brochure for Managua's airport on the table by Arthur's large and bony hand.

"We help people on their way but we cannot always guarantee where they will land," quipped George. "We're undertakers, morticians if you like. Only don't call us funeral directors. It sounds vulgar. Rather as if we were policemen on traffic duty. Body handlers is even worse. That's quite indecent."

"I thought the Nicaraguans were pretty well used to funerals," Johnny said, a little puzzled.

"They've had enough practice, certainly," replied Arthur. "The last rites are undertaken here in a colourful, if primitive, way. It's all to do with the Spanish, Indian and probably Basque influence. No one measures up to the Basques when it comes to ornate burials. I once wrote a book about it. But we aren't an ordinary firm, my Lord no." He produced a card from his pocket with the Royal Warrant emblazoned on it. "Tambey and Brown of Windsor even had a hand in Queen Victoria." He took a tiny sip of beer and then whispered, "I say, what do you know about this Sandino cove? The fellow with the ten-gallon hat who's painted on all the walls like some damn fool sherry advert?" He held up a government pamphlet showing the guerilla hero in his eccentric hat and boots which laced up to the knee. "The interest is professional."

"Well, I'm afraid you're out of luck," said Johnny. "He was murdered by the elder Somoza in 1934. The Somoza family were the dictators here before the revolution."

"We know that," snapped George in mock annoyance. "We are perfectly aware of him being a cross between Robin Hood and the Tooth Fairy. The General of Free Men. That for years he was the darling of the Left and even poor muddled Chiang Kai-shek named a division after him. But when he got rid of the Yanks he renounced the machete and the gun. He was a devout spiritualist, you realize. Mad as a pocketful of hatters. So the elder Somoza, who, if my memory serves me, used to take bets on how long day-old calves could last swimming in a pool of freshwater sharks, invited him to dinner and a poetry reading. They then laid on a car to take him and his two friends home. On the way they were put up against a wall and shot. Dangerous stuff, poetry." George preened himself in the knowledge of research thoroughly done. "Am I correct?"

"Sorry. I didn't mean to sound a know-all," said Johnny colouring with embarrassment.

"But tell us how people feel about him now the socialists have hijacked the legend. Is he still as popular?" They obviously didn't appreciate he was straight off the boat.

Johnny looked over his shoulder. Objective discussions about the man whose name the Sandinistas had taken were fraught with problems. No two books or people he had talked to at Cambridge seemed to agree about Sandino. But he didn't want to be put down a second time. "Oh, I think he's every bit as popular as when he was running around the Sierras," he offered. "His silhouette is on every wall. In the minds of the people he is a sort of major saint. Some claim he has risen from the dead and soldiers in the northern provinces say he suddenly appears in the middle of a battle and leads the charge against the Contras. The government does nothing to discourage the stories. The progressive priests have his picture by that of Christ carrying an AK 47. They have been known to argue that he is the second coming. Christ armed . . . It's caused more than a spot of bother with the Vatican."

"But do they know where he is buried?" asked Arthur slyly.

"No," Johnny answered. "No one does. When the assassins had done their work the bodies were buried in quick lime. Peasants often scatter flowers in a field to honour his unknown resting place. Or carrots. Apparently he adored carrots. But no one knows where he is."

"We do," said George.

Johnny blinked.

"We do," echoed Arthur. "That's why we are here."

"But how? Surely he would have disintegrated, burnt up?"

"Shall we tell him?" said Arthur. George nodded. "You must remember this is hush-hush, but I suppose as you're English it won't matter. Serve them right for giving us awful rooms at the Intercontinental. We just want to get the job done and go home. It's always been thought Augusto César Sandino's last resting place was near the International Airport. Well, soldiers digging yet another air raid shelter discovered three mummified bodies and, being good comrades and not eager to do any more hard work, alerted the University history department. It appears in their haste the assassins did not use quick lime. They used sugar. In this hot and dryish climate the corpses rapidly had a protective coating. Their precious Sandino is as well preserved as a Fortnum & Mason sugared plum."

"Even the famous hat is intact," added his partner.

Johnny coughed. It was the Nicaraguan equivalent of finding the Holy Grail.

"That's incredible," he said politely. "But I don't quite follow how you come to be involved. Are you connected with the solidarity committees?" Arthur's birthmark started to pulsate.

"What do you take us for, Communists? No, my family, our families, have always been number one when it comes to embalming but we were brought down by our own success. Clobbered by death duties in the Wilson years, so we took anything that came along. One day, out of the blue, the Department of Trade, who were sucking up to the Soviets for some reason, approached us because the Russians had a problem with Lenin. In short, he was going mouldy and his nose was collapsing. Can't have a national saviour without a conk so they wanted someone to put it right. But we undertakers are a pretty free-thinking bunch and the Bolshies murdered all their good ones long ago. The upshot was we got the job. The trouble is, when the Russians find you can do something, they never leave you alone. But I must confess, sweet Sandino is more of a challenge than a chore."

Johnny was trying to imagine the impact producing the body of the blessed Sandino would have. It would at least establish a national shrine.

"Our research, especially of the cheaper Egyptian funeral parlours, shows sugar was often used. With the right conditions the skin turns into a kind of pastry. Sandino probably looks more like apple pie than anything else. It must be dreadful for the old boy. The scourge of the US Marines. As American as apple pie, what?" They both roared.

"I wouldn't talk about the find if I were you."

"Oh don't worry. We were given a long lecture on how superstitious the Indians and peasants are here. You know the stuff, lots of trinkets to ward off the evil eye, enough bits of the true cross to rebuild the city and strands of the holy beard to restuff every sofa in town. Our taxi driver yesterday had a gear stick which lit up and showed a picture of the Virgin Mary."

"It's their way," Johnny understated.

"It's more than that," added George. "The little magpies in this part of the world are constantly helping themselves to new protectors without letting go of the old. The icons just get bloodier to fit in with their increasingly murderous habits."

"But don't worry about us. We're not taking it lightly," said Arthur. "We know how to watch our political Ps and Qs. All we have to do is pop him in a glass box and then they can do what they like with him. Nothing wrong with having heroes, but personally I've always thought it a bit odd to keep them around after they've kicked the bucket. Couldn't really imagine anyone wanting to stuff Margaret Thatcher."

Johnny heard the sound of familiar voices coming down

the steps towards the bar. It was the chatty Dr Window with Blanca and several young soldiers. Tanya lumbered along in the rear. They shouted to him as George drained his beer.

"Got to be getting along now, old man. Didn't know you were so well connected." They both shook his hand quickly. "Don't go getting into any trouble," George murmured, nodding towards the oncoming group. Then they were gone. He wondered if they had been having him on. The bald black-marketeer and his mistress also melted into the background and vanished at the arrival of the military. It seemed an over-reaction to a few green uniforms.

"Peace be with you, Johnny," smiled Annie. "We're all able to go up to the coffee *finca* together. The papers for the Atlantic Coast will take a little longer."

"So you're going to be staying with my family?" said Blanca.

"Yes. Catherine told me I could take her bed when she went off this morning. I hope that's all right?"

"Fine. I didn't know she was going straight out to the *finca* at La Colonia. I thought I saw her stopping off to see a friend in Los Robles, the diplomatic district . . . Possibly she will go tomorrow." She grinned. He realized she was trying to unsettle him.

"Never mind, Johnny. I'm sure she will come back to Blanca's place if she's still in town," comforted Annie. But the doubt had been sown and a chill breeze blew off Tiscapa.

3

The small house where Blanca lived, indeed the street, woke sharply and simultaneously at six. It was not a road as such but a walkway where the spare pieces of land had been turned into air raid trenches and simple gardens by the all-powerful Sandinista block committees who, as Johnny had been there longer than three days, had issued him with a ration book. But the absence of cars and trucks and motor bikes did little to detract from the noise. A gentle overture to the cacophony proper started about five with an old (and Johnny believed) psychotic cockerel that lived in the back garden of the even more tumble down abode next door. Chanticleer, as someone had christened the bird, woke the magpie jays and the large black birds that croaked and whooped and chattered and whistled. Dogs barked as shouts echoed around the one-storey houses. Cries of bread sellers, warm milk women, fresh juice men, tortilla and empanada vendors all joined in, some with blaring radios slung from their necks, like a string of garlic cloves worn against the vampires of peace and quiet. The traders were a ragged army from the still poorer barrios where they didn't have the luxury of concrete walls and broken tiles but made do with a grant of government timber and a dirt floor, no water, no electricity and no hope. The very poor were rumoured to be the eyes and ears of the political police and sometimes there was a violence in the voices of the thin, pinched women with huge baskets on their heads. *"Hay leche. Hay leche,"* shrieked one outside the window.

Johnny was enclosed on two sides by a dirty curtain. Beyond the thin material was a narrow space and then only a foot away another curtain and bed. At the other end the room became slightly wider and by the door was a tiny cot which the cousin who worked as a night porter would squirm into at first light. It was the least cramped of three bedrooms in the prefabricated building which was home for twenty-three people; he had been surprised to learn one old aunt had her own house but preferred living in this human ant heap.

Johnny forced his head into the pillow to shut out the din and could smell Catherine's perfume. She was still using Givenchy. In contrast the dank cotton sheets betrayed the chronic shortage of soap. A fragment of rust fell from the bare corrugated roof as a prowling iguana or rat pattered above. He was no more comfortable with that theatre of poverty than he had been with the affluent House of Perfect English. It was the sort of thing Catherine would revel in. For him, after less than a week, the revolutionary novelty of living with the Pocaterras was wearing off.

The sounds outside were gradually matched inside, starting with the intimate, often disgusting, noises of early morning. These built into a crescendo and were masked to an extent by the radio and TV and record player, not to mention the boys' guitars and the doleful singing of the family's matriarch, Doña Resignación, so named because she was the sixth daughter in a society which only favoured the male. She had been severely depressed ever since the Sandinistas had seized all the Pocaterras' property, including a modest but profitable sugar mill. La Doña preferred Contra ballads, sung round camp fires by the Nicaraguan Democratic Front, the murderous remnants of Somoza's National Guard. Johnny had been quite shocked when he found out not all the family supported the Sandinistas.

"I don't care as long as I can still climb a mango tree. They will not take me alive, the Communist pigs," La Doña had said when he had puzzled over what a particularly bloodthirsty ditty meant. The mango tree was thirty feet high. Doña Resignación had climbed it right to the top and bombarded all below with harmless squashy fruit, intoning sedition as loud as she could over the tin roofs. She had nothing to fear as her small bulldog of a son, a man in his thirties, was a political officer in the militia.

Another record was put on the crackling gramophone. The song told of a gory Sandinista bank robbery before the revolution. The children sang along. A rhythmic squelching came from the bed next to his. Close to Johnny's feet the night porter had slunk into his lair. He turned towards the wall, wishing Catherine had stayed with him. Had Blanca really seen her in town when she and Anselm were meant to be at La Colonia? If she had remained with Johnny they would be making love like the couple in the bed beside him. I shall get used to Nicaragua, he willed himself as the two-backed beast crashed towards orgasm. Someone had started using the toilet. Nicaraguans loved their morning chorus. Both an Affirmation and a Laudate that they were still alive.

A dream he had in the hot night still nagged him like a headache. It had so disturbed him he had almost shouted out; the patched sheet on his bed was wet with sweat. Catherine had been in the Perfect English garden, lying back in a hammock wearing her red shorts and a T-shirt which said *No Pasaran*. He had called out to her but she had shaken her head. From the house had emerged the figure of Father Anselm with two Sandinista soldiers. "She does not want you or your doubts any more, Johnny. You are not part of Perfect English. She does not want you any more." The gates had slammed behind him and he had heard mocking laughter coming from within. Then he had woken up.

At his elbow the lovers paused for a brief moment and then continued. Privacy in the Pocaterra household was a state of mind needing the detachment of a Tibetan lama. The wooden frame of the bed began to knock against the wall. Johnny decided to get up. He drew back the curtain of his own cubicle and what he saw made him suddenly very angry.

Protruding from under the curtain next door was a foot and a delicate gold chain. He only saw the blur of flesh for a second but he knew that chain anywhere. He had given one to Catherine and she wore it on her ankle. She had not gone to the *finca*. She had got into another man's bed in the same bloody room. That was too much. In a dreadful slow motion, or so it seemed to him at the time, he ripped away the piece of stained red calico that screened the other bed.

"Baa . . ."

He had intended the word to be "Bastards" and in his confusion and embarrassment at the scene that confronted him he repeated the syllable.

"Baa . . ."

"Baa?" replied Blanca Pocaterra, her legs drawn up around the back of her astonished lover who was kneeling and looked pointedly in the direction of his Makarov pistol hanging from a nail on the wall. Johnny recognized him as one of the soldiers who had joined them in the Tiscapa bar. The man was furious but Blanca was grinning; they had finished. Teasingly she wiped a finger up from the tight black hairs which fringed the bottom of her belly, drawing it lazily over her breasts coated with sweat and wetness and licked it. Johnny felt a shudder.

"Baa?" she said again. Then her smile widened.

"Baa, baa, black sheep, have you any wool? This is our English teacher *compadre*. He has come to teach us the language of diplomacy. Yes sir, yes sir, three bags full . . ."

Johnny quickly drew back the curtain as they started to laugh uncontrollably and the bed soon began to bang against the wall with renewed vigour. Blanca, he realized, could be a pest. Her husband had disappeared some time ago and rumour had it that he had joined one of the Contra groups in the north-east where the Pocaterras once had lands. As a reaction she had become a militant Sandinista. She was of *campesino* parents but carried herself like an Indian princess. Her light skin and feline poise obviously earned the peasant girl a place as a maid in the Pocaterra household. When no one could be found for Doña Resignación's ugly second son, Blanca was coaxed to the altar and had been taking over the family ever since. From Catherine's highly selective feminism she drew a justification for her own natural ruthlessness and had athletically embraced the new Catholicism's much relaxed attitude to sexuality. There was something wicked about her from an era long before the conquistadores which Johnny found not unattractive.

The bed was still clacking against the wall ten minutes later with the brutal efficiency of a Lancashire milling machine as

Johnny entered the suffocating cupboard that doubled as shower and toilet. Even here the wall did not go up to the roof and his first day's efforts at ablutions were greeted with applause. Now he propped himself up against the decaying wall and gazed morosely into the pan. He could hear the breakfast noises of bread being slopped into milky coffee only a few feet away. Was he being petty bourgeois? After all it was a privilege to be among the people; no longer an armchair socialist. From all that he read and heard he had liked the Nicaraguans long before he arrived in the country itself, he had admired their bravery and determination, their beauty and wit; but he prayed for strength to cope with the dreadful Pocaterras. His thoughts turned back to where Catherine had possibly spent the last few nights and he felt another twinge of jealousy.

Above him there was a muffled giggle. An evil Cuban grenade dropped by his foot. The impish face of a young boy grinned down for a second from the top of the toilet wall. It was a practice grenade and the joke had been played before. A cockroach went to examine the weapon. The grenade's ring and pin were still in position.

"Mama, I have killed the gringo. I killed the gringo."

"Good, good," cooed his mother.

Johnny looked about him. There was no toilet paper, only the half sodden baseball page of *Barricada*. In the circumstances it was better than asking for some. The anti-aircraft guns around the airport crashed into life on their morning exercise. The cockroach disappeared back down a hole in the slimy brick floor. A rusty pipe above his head dribbled brackish water and he decided he could not face a shower under it this morning. Little bugs jumped on his feet as the water splashed down. He did not want to face the demented family much either.

"*Hola* Winston Churchill!" Doña Resignación's son made the same joke every day. The family always laughed.

"Winston Churchill wants to get in bed with Blanca and her friend. Lock up your ducks, Doña Resignación, or he will be after them next. The English are an inventive people."

Around the table clustered the innumerable Pocaterras. A

sea of coffee was spreading out over the cracked Formica and one of the children had been sick. The newest offspring spouted a jet of clear urine which did not inspire the slightest surprise. The anti-aircraft practice had stopped and the radio was turned up louder. No one mentioned the guns. As La Doña had admitted to Johnny, the first they would know of an actual air attack was that they would cease to know anything at all. It would be like an earthquake, she had shrugged. One never talked about earthquakes.

Johnny greeted everyone with a polite smile. Another guffaw erupted. The radio announcer was telling the story of a soldier on guard duty by the monument to Carlos Fonseca and the Eternal Flame, just across from the cathedral, who had shot one of the alligators in the ornamental pool nearby. A country boy, no one had explained to him about the reptiles being quite amenable or that they sometimes went for a stroll.

"See you later, alligator," said a child in English.

La Doña's son grinned. "Our gringo teacher has come to save us from the Contra alligators. Everyone knows it is a plan of Mr Reagan to drop ferocious alligators all over the city to eat us up in our beds at night. Get your guns *muchachos*," he cried, cuffing his firstborn, who ran out of the room to the family arms chest and came back brandishing an old .22. A small child pulled at Blanca's lover's holster as he emerged from the bedroom. Casually the soldier drew the clip of neat little bullets from the weapon before handing it to the boy. There was no shortage of guns in Nicaragua, only of toys. The family, like any other on the street except for those distrusted by the block committees, had their own private arsenal; the Pocaterras' prize possession was an American-made rocket launcher which had severely disabled an armoured car during the insurrection. It was brought out only when the men of the house had become completely inebriated and La Doña's son rather spoiled the story by admitting the *Guardia* driving the vehicle had already surrendered.

The children now turned their weapons on the Pope's picture which was drawing-pinned on the front door. Beneath it was pasted a sign saying "Death to the Contras". The room was almost bare expect for the long table, a settee and an aging Cuban TV set showing only SS-TV, Sistema Sandinista Televisión, a ghostly grey image on a greasy screen. "Bang, bang," shouted the children as they murdered the Pontiff. One little girl with the eyes of a saint tweaked Johnny's leg. "There is blood in there, gringo. Much blood."

Another child jabbed him in the jaw with the muzzle of the rifle and was slapped hard by Blanca as she made her entrance. All the children simultaneously burst into tears and huddled on the settee, a family heirloom. It had graced the Pocaterras' former town house, according to La Doña, until the earthquake in 1972 had shaken the solid building with its cool courtyard to rubble and swallowed the rest. It had happened at night and three of the family had died. In the morning all that was left was the settee, a few bottles of rum and a pet duck. La Doña had made the duck into soup while the family stood around the settee in the ruined city. Johnny bet even such a catastrophe had not subdued the Pocaterras for long.

Blanca sat on a chair, crossing her legs. They were very long and slender for an Indian and her dress short, no doubt borrowed like the gold chain from Catherine. The high-heeled sandals were Nicaraguan and she waggled a painted toe. Once she had been at the Pocaterras' beck and call. Now she worked for the Ministry of the Interior and Johnny was not quite sure what she did except hang around with Perfect English. The only work she had talked about was choosing a martyr for a new administration wing. The one stipulation was it had to be a woman. Johnny had not thought it was a particularly arduous task as the graveyards were full of brave young women with the legends DIED FOR THE FATHERLAND or RAPED BY THE CONTRAS or even DISEMBOWELLED on the tombstones. But for some reason these would not do. It had, she explained, to be someone attractive and acceptable. Rape was not deemed a sufficiently respectable or seemly death in her Indian eyes and she finally settled on a distant cousin, a nineteen-year-old, very popular girl who had drowned in the surf at the beach resort of Ponaloya.

"Johnny is going to teach us all nursery rhymes," she said and he smiled at her. Something told him to keep on the right side of Blanca. Several of the family declared they would go to Mass, or rather the altarless ceremony that passed for it, at the Church of St Francis, the church where the ill-fated procession had tried to rescue the Virgin and where Christ was portrayed at the twelve stations of the cross as *campesino* and guerilla fighter. Christ returned triumphant in the person of Sandino. Blanca had taken him back to look at it since. She did not go to church because she was devout, he had decided, but for the political advantage in attending. Just as there probably had been a reason for making noisy love to the Sandinista captain; a love which still hung limp on her wet hair. Many Indians, she confided, carried their enthusiasm for the old Catholicism with its dolls' house of saints and martyrs to the point of sorcery and married it with their traditional witchcraft, even calling favoured children Christos; a double-edged gift as in one remote village in the Segovias it had ended in a sacrificial crucifixion of a fifteen-year-old to guarantee the coffee crop. In Mexico that was commonplace. Blanca, on the other hand, under the influence of Catherine, maintained she had put aside superstition.

Her English had been energetically learnt under the previous government. She wiped a precious American lipstick on to her large lips. "No church for you today Johnny. We have to pick up your kit. Oh, I nearly forgot," she added casually. "My friend has a friend who is going to the States. Do you have some dollars?"

She was asking him to participate in the destruction of the economy of the country he had come to help by selling her dollars. Even the children in the room had stopped their bedlam and were looking at him, sentient of the most magical of all invocations, the word dollar. But it would be naïve, he reasoned, to change them at the government rate. Yet as he put his hand into the pocket of his trousers he felt it was wrong.

"Yes, I do have dollars, but not too many. Will fifty do?" he said reluctantly. In a flash he was clutching a rotting wedge of thirty thousand *córdobas;* the official rate was ten to a dollar. If he had cashed all the cheques in his pocket he could have easily been a rich man. Doña Resignación stood over him. He gave her a thousand and she took it without a smile. As they left to collect his kit from the army depot in town he saw she had climbed the mango tree and heard her singing hymns for the enemy.

Tanya, Bob and Dr Annie were waiting outside the forbidding barracks. Dr Annie looked up from a copy of Christopher Hill's *The English Revolution* and smiled. Tanya, dressed in window cleaner's overalls, grunted and glanced at her watch.

"You're late," sniffed Bob, stating the obvious.

"I'm sorry. There was the usual problem with the buses."

"We can't seem to make the man understand what we want," said Dr Annie. "Could you please have a try Blanca?"

From the gate of the fortified building a teenage guard eyed them hungrily as if they were undercover American agents he might possibly shoot. In the courtyard beyond, Johnny watched two massive women push a barrow full of uniforms, many he could plainly see stained with blood, to a makeshift incinerator.

Blanca strode forward. The guard was about to challenge her but she stood stock still and surveyed him with contempt, as if examining a seldom emptied dustbin.

"What is it?" she snapped. "Are you going to stop me from entering? My family and I fought for this rathole." The boy, chastened, went and sat down in the sentry box. An old man in civilian clothes appeared and began to argue. Blanca produced a laminated card from her pocket, which halted the official in his tracks. Johnny was even more surprised when Blanca, who was young enough to be the man's daughter, pushed him roughly into his office and slammed the door. A much more compliant senior citizen emerged and took them nervously towards the armoury. Blanca glowed with satisfaction.

"He's not a bad man at heart," she said casually. "He lived through the terror under Somoza. Like many deep down he is frightened of his own shadow."

"He certainly seems terrified of yours," said Johnny out of a mixture of respect and curiosity about what she really did. Blanca only smiled sweetly.

At first they could not find any uniform trousers long enough for Johnny but then an old seamstress who smoked a clay pipe cut a foot off each leg of some ominously soiled fatigues and sewed them on a pair which were the right size around his waist. "Must fit you good to keep out the snakes," she said with a throaty laugh. Then a youth brought in four Kalashnikovs. Tanya and Bob could hardly control their delight, like small children receiving special toys at Christmas. Dr Window immediately tried to take her weapon apart, doubtless in an effort to understand its mystique, even though no one had showed her how to put it together again. Johnny rested his against the wall and kept as far away from it as possible. Bob's eyes betrayed fantasies of hacking his way through jungle at the head of a Sandinista patrol, hell bent on teaching the Contra about the inevitability of history.

"*Bayoneta*," said one of the storemen, handing Johnny a small but extremely sharp Kalashnikov bayonet in its black metal scabbard. He took it. Dr Window shook her head when offered hers. The man insisted.

"But I don't want it really. I hate the sight of blood," she pleaded, her cheeks turning pink.

"This is yours," repeated the man. "It is in your name. If you do not take it then it must be lost. To lose military equipment is serious." He was not smiling.

"Take it," said Johnny quickly in English. "This chap could get you into trouble. You can always use it as a paper knife."

She gave in and took the weapon gingerly. "Thank you Johnny, but I do hate the sight of gore. An occasional demo is one thing but I'm not so sure I could shoot anyone." Tanya looked disgusted. Bob seemed fascinated with his own bayonet, sheathing it hastily as he saw the others staring at him. "It's a truly proletarian weapon, the bayonet," he muttered.

Three hours later, fully equipped, they walked away in triumph. Blanca insisted they take her to buffet lunch at the Intercontinental, an *Internationalista* ritual.

"Come on my little army. To you it will only be a dollar each."

"But what about our guns and these packs?" asked Tanya anxiously.

"Oh don't worry about those. We can leave them with the *maître d'*."

4

The rifle range at La Colonia coffee *finca* was merely a clearing among the dull green bushes with their holly-red berries concealing the precious bean, vital to the country's economy. There was no sense of urgency as a dishevelled officer, his tunic hanging open to expose a tattoo of an inky panther on his chest, examined Johnny's target with resentment and distrust. The oblong of cardboard had been roughly painted to look like a charging man with a predatory snarl on his lips. "Made in the USA" had been written on the paper soldier's helmet and, in case anyone should still be in doubt, the word CONTRA was stencilled underneath. But the officer was not worried about the lack of subtlety in revolutionary design or why the target was painted purple. What troubled him was the tight grouping of shots the young gringo had put in, or just to one side of, the six-inch bull's eye. It was so good it was suspicious. He held up his own target. The spread of shots was not nearly so proficient.

"You have fired a gun before?" he asked quietly in Spanish.

"Yes," Johnny answered.

"A Kalashnikov?" The man nodded at the battered weapon at Johnny's side.

"Never. I never even saw one until I came out here. They are a very fine gun." Proud of his Spanish, he smiled. The officer did not.

"If you have never fired this gun before, how did you do this?" He waggled a nicotine browned finger through a hole right in the centre of the bull.

"Well, my father showed me how to use a shotgun."

"A Kalashnikov is not a shotgun."

"Oh, and they taught me how to shoot at school."

"At school?" The man's brow puzzled into a frown. "I did not know that in England they teach you to shoot in school."

"Yes, that's where I learned how to use a rifle. In the cadet corps. They also taught us how to destroy a tank, throw a grenade and fire various types of machine-guns and automatic weapons."

The others, who had splattered bullets the length and breadth of their targets – apart from an apologetic Dr Window who had missed her own completely but, as she pointed out in mitigation, scored several hits on those nearby – looked on. Tanya and Bob seemed envious. Bob had only hit his paper Contra in the foot.

"If you learn to shoot at school, why do these and most other *Internationalistas* shoot like half-blind old women?"

The remark stung Bob, who had taken off his glasses, into a reply. A former computer programmer, he had discovered Perfect English while on holiday in America. In his native Bournemouth he had sampled every conceivable revolutionary tendency, working through them like dishes on a menu. Consequently he could become quite passionate about the Tolpuddle Martyrs and would explain the class position of armadillos if anyone would listen. On the long lorry ride up Johnny had surmised, after the first droning hour, that Marxism was not so much a sociological tool for brother Bob Town as part of an emotional disorder. Now Bob spoke to the range officer.

". . . Basically, comrade, you have to understand it is just the sons of the ruling capitalists in England and the United States who can afford to pay the millions of *córdobas* a year for private education. It is only at these bastions of privilege that the sons of the ruling class learn to shoot."

"Steady on," said Johnny, beginning to wish he had missed. "I was a scholarship boy."

But Bob's intervention had provided the confirmation the range officer wanted that something fishy was going on. He folded his muscular arms. "So, you are sent to a special school by your parents to be trained how to kill and destroy tanks. Do you know, I have been in the army for three years now and no one has shown me how to destroy a tank? I thought

England was a peaceful country. Why do you need to know these things? Was it to protect your *estancia* if your labourers rose up against you? Eh? Is that the reason?"

If Johnny had been speaking and thinking in English he might have been more cautious. But concentrating on perfecting his reply in Spanish complicated things.

"My stepfather only has a housekeeper and a gardener. They have been with us all their lives and the farms on our family estate have tenant farmers. They are very happy and making too much money to start a revolution. Ha, ha. We all get together and have a big party at Christmas. My stepfather doesn't see them normally. He works in a bank in London. It is just not the same system as in the Third World." He noticed Tanya and Bob were edging away from him as if he had caught some infectious disease, although Dr Window looked anxiously sympathetic.

"If everyone is so happy on their farms, why does your father send you to a school where you learn how to shoot?" asked the officer. "Or were they training you to attack the Soviet Union?"

"I wasn't learning to be a soldier. Teaching people how to kill each other is traditional in British public schools. No one takes it seriously. Anyway, we only did it twice a week."

"For how long?"

"Well, er, about five years I suppose."

"Our recruits only get one month's instruction before the front line." The man paused. "How do we know you are not on the side of the Contras? Planted here by the monarchist military academy you went to?"

Johnny glanced round for help, but no one spoke. "Tell him, someone. Tell him I'm a volunteer with Perfect English." There was a slight note of panic in his voice. The others nodded reluctantly. "I was secretary of the Socialist Society at Cambridge," he added to the puzzled officer, who looked for guidance to Bob.

"Another bastion of privilege," sneered the latterday Tolpuddle Martyr. "Another refuge of the boss class."

"We fire again," said the range officer. Five or six of the man's friends had wandered over. They were curious about the *Internationalista* who could shoot. Those they were used to only managed to shoot themselves or each other. There had been some horrible accidents on the plantations, one older man said gravely, shaking his head. Johnny took his place at the sandbag butts. "We fire off a magazine. *Fuego!*" commanded the officer. For a moment Johnny thought about missing and then squeezed the trigger carefully. A small orphan boy who tended the range scampered off to bring back the targets. Johnny's aim proved even more infuriating.

"Why you fire Pam one-two-three Pam and not Pam Pam Pam Pam like me?" said the officer glaring down at Johnny's target. "With the Contra you have to shoot quick."

"Because if you shoot like that you miss."

"But this is an automatic weapon."

"Yes, but that does not mean you automatically hit the bull." Johnny realized as soon as he had said it that the remark was a stupid mistake. "If you keep on firing, the rifle jumps about. My instructor used to say the only thing automatic fire was good for was following the movement of a target you cannot see . . ." He perceived from the officer's face that he was only amplifying the man's doubts about him. He thanked God he spotted Father Anselm and Catherine coming towards them.

Johnny laughed nervously. "Father, excuse me, could you help me? Hello Catherine. This man thinks I am a Contra spy because I hit the target." Anselm looked horrified and took him to one side.

"Don't let me ever hear you say that, not even as a joke. The army don't like *Internationalistas*. They have accused people of spying before just because they found a camera in their pack. It may seem an over-reaction but something as trivial as this could mean a year in jail for you, if it came before a court, and would ruin our programme. Let me have a word with the man."

The preacher was still making elaborate explanations and apologies to the range officer when Catherine looked at her watch and said it was time to go back to the huge barn where they were billeted.

"Don't rile them, Johnny," she warned when they were out of earshot. "This is not Managua. The Sandys can be very reasonable but if they decide you are a suspicious person it can be terribly bad. A lot don't agree with giving arms to foreigners."

"I'm glad we are only here a week," Johnny said changing the subject. "It's bloody awful and I don't see why we have to be segregated into men and women. I missed you last night."

"Poor Johnny," she soothed. "But it's only for a few nights. It's worth it to get out to the Atlantic Coast."

He hesitated a second before what he said next. "By the way, Blanca told me you didn't come straight here. She said you and Anselm went to a house in Los Robles."

"Oh Johnny, don't fall for that one. It's a Nicaraguan hobby to make lovers jealous of one another. We had to see someone influential to smooth your *permiso* for the Coast. You trust me, don't you?"

"Yes," he replied, but after that they walked in silence. The others trailed some way behind.

A spectacular sunset was turning the sage green hills first red and then purple as a clump of impressive trees – ironwood and teak and mango – loomed in front of them. In the middle of the trees, and seemingly built to the same scale, was an immense barn. Johnny and the rest had arrived last night after the long drive from Managua, through Matagalpa and Jinotega, to this outpost on the northern border zone of Nueva Segovia where Sandino had raised his first army. Now bands of Contras roamed the dreamy parkland and committed atrocities recorded with macabre relish on the front of the party newspaper.

"Bye-bye Johnny, see you tomorrow. I think I'm going to turn in and read. I'm not used to getting up at four in the morning."

Sadly he watched her go around to the far end of the building which marked the women's section, and then stepped through the nearest door into a cathedral-like interior. It was as if the place had been assembled by giants. Inside it was dark. Hurricane lamps cast a ghostly light. As his eyes became accustomed to the gloom, he looked up at the blackened rafters more than sixty feet above him. The barn appeared to stretch away for ever. Rough wooden platforms on six rickety tiers extended up to the roof with narrow alleys in between. On these levels crawled, lounged and scratched the coffee pickers, mostly Nicaraguan. The wood itself reeked of sweat and urine and the structure reverberated with the incessant chatter of the multitudes, making it seem like some hellish vision of the Tower of Babel.

Johnny took his evening meal of gallopinta, rice and red beans with a boiled plantain outside but the others did not follow him. The incident on the range had upset them. Reluctantly, after a last three deep breaths of fresh air, he went back inside.

He had been assigned a bunk space and a hammock made of fertilizer sacks several levels away from Father Anselm and the disagreeable Bob. They had put him right at the top of the creaking edifice, only a few feet from the soot-encrusted beams. Nearby a candle burned. In the flickering light he caught sight of a frightened face under a mosquito net and thought he heard a faint whimper. Shrill female laughter echoed up from the other end of the great hall. He hoped Catherine was better off than he was.

Johnny pulled his combat jacket over his face. Bugs dropped occasionally from the infested roof and more than once he had to shake little biting creatures out of his hair. Morning came electrically at four, when somewhere down below a generator roared into life. The petrol rationing meant the strings of bulbs were only lit for fifteen minutes in the morning. The rest of the time they relied on hurricane lamps and candles. He shuddered to think what would happen if there was a fire.

As he put on his trousers he noticed white blobs along the seams. Closer examination revealed tiny lobster-like creatures. The things were everywhere in the weave of the old blanket they had given him. He realized, almost with pride, that they were lice, and headed determinedly towards breakfast. His father had once read him a passage from Orwell on how he had got lice in Spain. Johnny felt a certain exhilaration despite and because of his surroundings. After all, lice were part of the "real life" he and Catherine had wanted to experience.

The wooden ladders swayed and creaked as scores of volunteers clambered down and made their way to a smoke-shrouded canteen in the corner of the barn. Here a line of sleepwalkers were receiving large breakfast helpings of rice, beans and boiled plantain with a spoonful of chili sauce. He took his own banana leaf platter-full from a grinning woman. The pungent sauce made his eyes water; the rest of the stodge on his plate looked and smelt of mouse droppings or a baby's nappy left too long on a radiator. Johnny suppressed a sudden spasm of nausea and took a bite of boiled banana. He walked outside into the cold darkness and sat on a tree stump. A voice interrupted his growing misery.

"Isn't it yummy? A gap in the fast food market that hasn't been exploited? I'm going to open a chain of rice and bean shops when I get out of here. It's not their national dish though, that's really disgusting. They call it Iguana in Pinol which is fried lizard in corn and pig's dripping. Oh, and some of the Indians near León actually chew dirt to extract a little worm. Now you cannot get a dish more national than that." The man spoke English with a breakneck New York accent. Johnny put his banana leaf on one side.

"If you're not hungry I'll have it," said his new friend, scooping up the platter. "Saw you come in the day before yesterday. What did they send you to this Gulag for? Was it a black market offence or just plain theft?"

"I beg your pardon. I'm a volunteer."

"Well I suppose stupidity is a crime. I guess I'm a volunteer too. A kangaroo court called a people's tribunal volunteered me. They volunteered about half the people in that barn. I was actually travelling through this godforsaken hole on holiday, having a wonderful time until some bitch yells rape and all my travellers cheques disappeared. My name's Tom, what's yours? I mean, do I look like a fucking rapist?"

"My name's Johnny," he said glancing over at Tom. A lantern had been lit by the door of the barn. If anyone looked like a rapist the spindly, deathly pale American certainly did.

A bell rang.

"What happens now? Yesterday I was taken straight out to the range."

"We have a parade," smiled Tom. "The day is just non-stop fun at La Colonia. After that we all have to pick coffee until lunchtime. Then I've managed to swing a week's guard duty at one of the out-stations. Lucky, eh? If you do that you don't have to pick. I always make a point of pissing on my beans anyway. Hope it kills some liberal in Greenwich Village. Anything is better than coffee picking. That's why I asked you about your crime, because they divide offences here into those against people and those against property. Crimes of violence against one's fellow human beings disqualify you from guard duty. But, for example, thieving is definitely against property. All property is theft, right? That's not so bad." Johnny had never met anyone so depressingly awake at four in the morning.

"But I thought you said you were here for rape? Isn't that the worst sort of violence and very much against a fellow human being?"

"Not in Nicaragua. It's kinda like a theft of a service. Like riding the subway for free. Your old lady is regarded as much of a piece of property as the family car. The only difference is that the husband usually kills you if you take a ride. In my case they just helped themselves to all my money and turned me over to the law. I can't even bribe my way out of here." Johnny opened his mouth to speak but decided the man was incorrigible.

Outside the barn was a concrete area for drying the coffee beans. It was also a parade ground. Tom chuckled as a girl blew a bugle and they went back into the building to collect their rifles. He had no idea where the others had got to. "Stick with me, kid," said Tom.

The Oldsters for Peace, an American pressure group, were the first out on the square and Johnny later learned the white-haired liberals had paid $1000 each for the privilege of coming to La Colonia. By them the serious looking Sandinista Youth formed up into platoons fifteen strong. The discipline and dressing of the lines was frighteningly exact. Without success he searched for a Perfect English banner or a familiar face in the growing dawn light, but it was useless. Yet not everyone was imbued with a volunteer's enthusiasm. There was a sluggishness of step and hunching of the shoulders by which one could identify the pressed men, those who had done something wrong. The bugle sounded again with flatulent imprecision and there was silence. An attractive girl of about sixteen stood before them and sang the party battle hymn. When they got to the phrase, *"luchamos contra el Yankee, enemigo de la humanidad,"* Tom turned round and winked, whispering "I'm a Yankee doodle dandy." But most of the other enemies of humanity sang along without protest. Johnny did too. There was something about the spectacle he found distasteful but it was not the time or place for dissent.

The girl harangued her *compañeros* detailing the atrocities of the *Guardia* before the revolution against the flower of the country's youth. She told how comrades had been murdered on their way to school. How others had been caught by the same agents of Yankee Imperialism and had spinning electric drill bits forced between their buttocks. Johnny tried not to look at Tom, who had made another vile comment.

She called the roll and then began to recite a long list of additional names, her slim shoulders shaking with emotion while everyone, including the cynical Tom, yelled *"Presente."* Johnny recognized the names of famous Sandinista guerilla fighters who had died in battle and the bizarre ritual reached a crescendo with a well-known character.

"Augusto César Sandino?"

"Presente! Presente! Presente!"

The shout echoed around the steep-sided hills like gentle summer thunder. Next, still trembling, the girl said Sandino was now walking with God and that they should all develop a revolutionary conscience and beware of the capitalists who lived in the Vatican. Many of the soldiers in front of her were even younger than she was. She repeatedly stressed the goodness of Sandino and how he cared for the poor, before taking a deep breath and going the whole way.

"Muchachos, Sandino is Christ come again to earth. He is Christ armed. We follow him to the hills against imperialist aggression in our fight for the poor. Our struggle is blessed."

Johnny heard Tom's giggle but no one else showed a flicker of amusement as they finished off by singing *"Qué es un Fal?"*, a song about how to strip and clean a rifle which could also double as a grenade launcher. Peace be with you, he thought to himself. Morning prayers at Ampleforth had never been like this.

"It does not surprise me you have found the worst company possible," said a Spanish voice which he knew immediately from the day before.

He looked up and saw the range officer. With him were another Sandinista and Father Anselm. The priest spoke.

"I have convinced the comrades of your bona fides, Johnny, but they do not think there is much point in your continuing weapons training as you are so proficient. Catherine and the others need more practice. They have gone back out to the range."

"You are to do guard duty with this one at one of the out-stations," said the range officer with a smile Johnny did not like. He was about to protest but thought better of it. He hated to be parted from Catherine again. "Perhaps there he can show us all how to fight the Contra," the officer continued. "First you will do a morning picking of at least a *lata* each. Then you will help carry the crop up to the top road as we have no more drying room here. An ox cart will take you to the out-station. But be careful, Mr Morgan, it is very strict there. It is where the first true International Brigade trains before they join our army."

Johnny never imagined coffee picking could be so difficult. For a start the slopes the bushes grew on seemed at times perpendicular. It was all he could do to keep his balance with two arms above his head stripping berries from the branches and dropping them into his basket or, more usually, onto the ground. The process was complicated by having to wear the Kalashnikov slung over his shoulder while trying to keep the awkward receptacle supported round his waist with a loop of sisal rope. A gnarled piece of bark was meant to brace the rope in the small of his back but it kept slipping out, sending the whole lot down around his ankles with depressing regularity. The only way he could seem to prevent this was to stick his stomach out as far as he could and lean back. Just when he was congratulating himself on mastering the knack he overbalanced and rolled for twenty-five yards before a concussive stop against the buttress roots of a large tree. He soon developed a healthy respect for the Nicaraguans who swarmed like ants around the bushes. However many berries he stripped off the twigs he never appeared to have enough to fill his *lata*.

Finally it was time to take the larger baskets of beans at the end of every line up to the top road. A soldier had been keeping a record of every *lata* picked.

"You have only picked a half *lata*? What is wrong? Do you know some *campesinos* can pick ten in a day? Even *Internationalistas* usually manage two."

"I'm terribly sorry . . ." he began, but the soldier made a peculiar pinched gesture of contempt with his nose and waved him on.

If anything, the next part was worse. They had to carry the bigger baskets of berries up a steep winding path to the bullock cart on a road which hugged the mountain ridge. As soon as his aching limbs hauled a basketful into the cart he was sent back for another. The stinging juice from the red berries ran down into his eyes. Johnny began to imagine how Sisyphus felt. In the end he did not remember collapsing on the wagon which wound slowly towards his new billet.

As Tom and Johnny helped spread the beans on the courtyard before the out-station's barn, a smart *Internationalista* came up to them. He was American. He had the fanatic mesmerized gleam of the truly committed.

"Tired?" he asked mildly in English.

"Absolutely," replied Johnny, straightening up and stretching.

"Nonsense!" barked the volunteer. "Tiredness is a bourgeois emotion, comrade. Ho Chi Minh was never pooped. After a few days you will be working as hard as a *campesino*. Now go and relieve the comrades on the top of the ridge and keep your eyes open. The Contras have 300 men in this region. If we are lucky we will get a chance to kick them in the butt." He turned and walked back to where others of his tribe were stripping a mortar.

A spur jutted out from the forest-covered ridge making a

natural and spectacular vantage point. Wearily they climbed up towards it, not speaking, as someone blew a bugle behind them. Johnny wondered if Catherine was thinking of him. He felt a whisper of jealousy, knowing she and Anselm would now be together without him again. He fought the notion that the priest had engineered his summary exile to the out-station.

They stopped half-way up, and drank water from Tom's canteen.

"How long have you been here?" Johnny asked.

"Two months."

"Ever thought of doing a bunk?"

Tom laughed. "Those murderous little wolf cubs from the Sandy Youth would get me before I'd gone a mile. They enjoy manhunts. It's just like when the old plantation owners went after slaves. Anyway, I don't have a map or compass, and if I did I don't know how to use them. To try to get across the Honduran border in Nicaraguan fatigues without papers or any way of telling which country you are in would not be a life-enhancing experience. I decided to grin and bear it. So now they even trust me with a rifle. I've got a month to go."

When they arrived at the top, two Nicaraguans showed them the deeply dug defensive positions consisting of several rooms underground, and explained they would be relieved every twelve hours. The out-station's white-painted barn nestled hundreds of feet below, obviously built before the civil war as it was in a suicidally indefensible position. The look-out point did not actually fill Johnny with optimism. Any attacking force would take out the guard post first. An idiot could see that.

"Much more of this and I'll be voting Republican," grumbled Tom. "Seems like I made a mistake. But look on the bright side."

"What's that?"

"The Contras might put us out of our misery."

5

Johnny lay against a sandbag dreamily contemplating the valley below between ranges of smooth green mountains which chased each other all the way to the Honduran border. Above, the sky was vast and flawlessly blue. This was their third day at the out-station, and he and Tom tried to spend as much time as possible on the ridge away from the barn, where a handful of young American and European volunteers were being trained to fight as combat soldiers in the often chaotic irregular battalion search-and-destroy sweeps of the border areas. The instructor in charge was a refreshingly cynical regular in his fifties who did not share his recruits' desperate enthusiasm to further the cause of world socialism. In fact he was deeply suspicious of anyone who wanted to help his country against the interests of their own. Up on the ridge he had told Johnny and Tom that he firmly believed the planet would be a lot better place if people stuck to the army they were born to instead of messing about in someone else's. Consequently the dapper officer from a formerly wealthy family in León pushed the would-be members of the new International Brigade through a crippling series of marches, night exercises and weapons training which would have brought howls of protest from any Nicaraguan conscript. The only trouble was that gringos brought up on Dr Spock seemed to love the lash. Delinquents such as Tom the officer could understand. Like him, they had no choice but to be there. In return for collecting various strange animals from his snares he gave Johnny and Tom long periods of easy duty. The appearance of a gallinazo bird, the sinister carrion hawk that the instructor had drily remarked should be his country's national emblem, signalled the return of Tom from the traps.

"We never seem to catch anything normal in these traps. Those weird things with long noses and two-tone tails give me the creeps, and I'm not sure what this one is at all. I'm not even sure if it's a mammal. At least the possums taste good. Care for a mountain fresh possum Johnny?"

"Great stuff. I don't mind in the least doing the cooking, Tom, if you promise to keep a look out. Is our instructor still making life as difficult as possible for his recruits?"

Tom peered over a low wall of sandbags. "Yes, he sure is giving them hell," sniggered the American, detaching the fattest possum from the pole the animals were slung on. It was a large, amiable looking creature with a pointed nose and big ears, straight out of a children's story book. Johnny hated killing them, especially as they were skilled at mimicking death. The first one he had tried to skin had leapt up screaming, bit him, and had probably not stopped running until it reached the border. Their hungry war against the possum had, however, become more ruthless. Tom now took pleasure stabbing each one fatally with his bayonet while it was still in the snare, on the grounds he hated all phoneys. It tasted like chicken and was infinitely preferable to rice, beans and boiled banana.

"Hey Johnny, do you know two of those dangerously insane volunteers down there training to fight U S aggression formerly served as Uncle Sam's Marines in Vietnam, shooting Gook? Do you think for them Nicaragua is some kind of guilt trip? Therapy almost?" asked Tom.

"Whatever they did before, I still don't think any of them would have a prayer against a former member of Somoza's National Guard," Johnny said seriously. "Purely because the Contra know the countryside. We would be even less use."

"What the fuck are you doing here, then?" scoffed the diminutive rapist.

"I'm beginning to wonder," laughed Johnny.

"When they set me free I'm going back to New York and spend the rest of my life in Manhattan. I won't even go to the Bronx. I've had my fill of foreign travel. What about you? Are you going through with this Perfect English crap?"

"I don't see why not."

"You mean you'd help a government which sticks you in a hole like this with people like me?"

"Oh, it's not that bad. They've made some silly mistakes . . . I know I have said some critical things about the Sandinistas but I do think their heart's in the right place. Otherwise they wouldn't let us teach English with a Christian message." Johnny's tone was a little too haughty.

"Christian message? From what you told me all you'll be doing is taking Sandy propaganda to natives whose relatives the Commies probably resettled the other side of the Pearly Gates."

"There have been a lot of exaggerations about the massacre of Miskitos," said Johnny, rather surprised at hearing himself defending Sandinista actions he righteously disapproved of. "The government admits it made errors and wants to put them right. We are going to help."

"You only know what they tell you. What they tell you and what you want to believe because of that girl of yours. She's the real pull isn't she? Tell a doubting Thomas he's right. Otherwise you are as dumb as the blinkered jerks doing weapons training."

"You want the Contras to win then?" Johnny retorted, picking up the skinned animal now white and bloody like a human foetus. He preferred not to talk to Tom about Catherine. There was something unclean about the New Yorker's attitude to the opposite sex in general which he disliked. What was more, he had avoided any mention of her closeness with Anselm. He just could not stand to be teased about that at the moment. Tom picked up the machete and wiped it on the ground.

"I don't want the Contras to win," said Tom. "I don't even want them to fight. I'm not exactly sure what the Sandinistas are fighting for in terms of the society they would like to create. What I do know from my misspent youth is gangs. If you join a gang, as a follower even, you are committed to that gang and against the others. If you think you can pitch for the Sandinistas and retain your independence and integrity you're a yo-yo. Even more of a yo-yo than the grunts down there."

"I suppose American foreign policy towards Central America is completely sane?"

"Is it my fault if we are always saddling up little right-wing tigers all over the world and are astonished when they won't let us get off? I hate that too. I want to go back to New York and do peculiar things with teenage girls. I just force myself on ladies, not countries." He grinned horribly. "Go cook the possum."

"Keep watch and shout if anyone comes up the path from the barn. We don't want to be put back picking coffee."

A wooden ladder led down into the roomy bunker which they had more or less converted into their private domain up on the hilltop. Tom had even gouged a few examples of authentic New York subway graffiti on the earth walls. He was a year younger than Johnny, wanted to be a technical dentist (because that's where the big bucks were) and was better company than anyone could have hoped for given the circumstances.

Johnny took out their precious frying pan from the ammunition box in which they hoarded provisions. The punishment for not sharing food was several days' hard labour so they had to be careful. The heat came from a minute wood stove they were allowed for brewing coffee. The only sounds of battle they had heard so far were from rifle practice down below with the instructor. The possum fat sizzled in the pan. He put in half the meat and the blood hissed with the fat.

"Hey Johnny, there is someone coming up the valley. Not from the barn. From the north. Shall we signal?"

There was no walkie-talkie, no field telephone except in the barn. The only way of attracting attention was either to wave a large red flag or let off a shot. With the possum starting to cook Johnny's empty stomach advised delay.

"What is it? A patrol or a truck?" If it was a truck it would be Sandinistas but it was just possible that a party of Contras would not know the barn had been recently reoccupied after lying empty for years. That's why they were on the ridge.

"There's one truck with some pipes on the back and two more full of soldiers. Now they're stopping. Hand me up the glasses." Johnny passed him the vintage pair of field glasses which had one lens cracked.

"I think it's all right. They're ours. I mean they're Sandys. There's the red and black flag. It's one of those multi-barrelled mortars. Those Katushas, Stalin Organs or whatever they call the things. The Contras don't have them do they, Johnny?"

"Not that I know of," he answered. "Tom, see if there's anything stirring down by our barn. If the Katusha commander's radioed ahead our chaps could be coming up here and we'll be caught red-handed with a possum in the pan. They'd be most upset. Keep your eyes open." His friend laughed and went to spy on the embryonic International Brigade and their instructor, who today was teaching them to use the 88 millimetre mortar.

Johnny listened, but all he could hear above the meat crackling was bird song. As he stuck his knife in the possum there was a hideous wailing sound as if a gigantic relative of the abused creature had come for revenge. It was followed by another and another and another and an explosion that threw him across the bunker, leaving him dazed and covered in partially cooked meat on the floor.

Instinctively he huddled into a ball as the awful detonations continued. An enormous fist seemed to be punching at the fragile skin of the earth from within and he was thrown repeatedly into the air as several of the bombs hit the ridge. The ground had ceased to be solid or predictable. His nose and mouth were filled with dirt. He could no longer hear what was happening and peered upwards through the debris in anticipation of another salvo. His legs were shaking and his teeth chattered. A bomb exploded directly above and he felt a flash of heat as the logs supporting the dug-out gave way and exposed an insanely cheerful blue sky smiling down on the dust and smoke, the smell of burning and high explosive. More of the roof fell in but he stayed exactly where he was, waiting for the next dreadful explosion.

The screaming of the Katushas came again but this time the crude rocket bombs arched over the ridge and dropped, as far as he could tell, towards the barn. The ground tremored once more and he thought he heard a bugle from below mixed with shouting and the dull metallic sound of the brigade's own smaller mortars returning fire at an enemy they could not see. The friendly bombs fell depressingly near. Then came an eerie silence as he crawled closer into a corner and watched the patch of sky.

After what seemed to be an age he heard voices. It was one of the Americans from the barn. A face looked down, and seeing the sorry figure of Johnny covered in earth and possum he drew the obvious conclusion.

"There's a body in here comrade, all blood and guts. He's definitely dead. A shell must have come through the roof." The head disappeared as rifles crackled from the valley below. "Let's get those fascist sons of bitches," an American said, followed by the unmistakable yelling of an infantry charge, punctuated only by the imperturbable deadly counterpoint of the heavy machine-gun on the other side. Johnny sighed. He did not need to see what was happening. He kept perfectly still and tried to imagine he was part of the earth wall.

A withering hail of automatic fire hit the ridge. One bullet ricocheted down into the dug-out, clattering into the ammunition boxes by which his rifle stood accusingly. He might as well have had a bow and arrow. The sounds of battle were getting nearer and nearer, when all at once a burst thudded into the dirt floor from a barrel pushed over the rim and a wild-eyed, uniformed figure sprang into the bunker, his machine-gun in one hand and a machete in the other. As his eyes adjusted to the sudden gloom a broad unfriendly smile spread across his grubby face.

"*Estúpido,*" said a voice above. "Are you trying to get yourself killed? What do you think grenades are for?"

"I have a gringo," shouted Johnny's new acquaintance, proudly prodding him with the long knife. "No, he is not dead, I think. He was just sleepy. I have a live gringo . . ."

"Bring him out."

Johnny emerged to a smoking moonscape which was now the top of the ridge. Huge tree stumps were still smouldering and the earth was covered in a black phosphoric snow. Tom was nowhere to be seen, and in the valley the barn was burning and had been overrun by more of the obviously highly trained troops who had taken the position.

He was surrounded by scowling men in full battle dress, one of whom was no more than fifteen. The man who had prodded him with the machete said something that made him feel cold.

"Hey Camilo. Do you want to kill your first gringo?"

Before he could scream two others pinned his arms and dragged him over to one of the tree stumps, pulling his head back and exposing his neck to the determined youth who was advancing towards him, machete drawn. Johnny struggled and tried to yell but no sound came from his dry throat. The fifteen-year-old raised the knife.

"Stop!"

It was a simple command but the Indian who loomed behind the boy expected to be obeyed. The knife fell slowly to Camilo's side. In a peevish gesture of rebellion he quickly jabbed Johnny in the ribs with the point.

"Well gringo," said the man who was undoubtedly their commander. "You can tell us what we want to know and we will shoot you quickly. Or we will blindfold this boy and tie you to that tree stump. A nice little game . . ."

"But," Johnny began in Spanish.

"No buts. Tell us which unit you are with and where is your base in Honduras and who your contacts are in Nicaragua. You are a Contra mercenary and we know how to deal with Contra mercenaries."

"You are not Contras?"

The man looked both angry and puzzled.

Johnny gasped for breath. "You're Sandinistas!" he exclaimed. "You see, I'm on your side! We are *Internationalistas* picking coffee. Ask the people down by the barn. You are Sandinistas and thought we were Contras," he kept repeating as if hardly believing it. "Ask the instructor down by the barn." He was caught in the middle of an embarrassing military mistake. But they still did not let him go.

Their commander spoke slowly. "The Contra often occupy the barns we leave empty. The Contra often wear our uniforms. Who told you this barn was empty, gringo? That is what we really want to know. We have already shot your gringo mercenary friends." The fifteen-year-old spat on him. He wore the badge of a Sandinista *militante*.

"Don't kill me, please," pleaded Johnny. "I'm on your side. Honestly. If you go down to the barn you'll find it's all a terrible muddle."

Shouts came from below the ridge and a man with a radio set on his back whispered in the ear of the commander. He hesitated, then came over to Johnny who, for the second time, braced himself for the slash of a knife. The man grabbed his shirt and pulled Johnny down to his face. Nothing was said. Johnny was being warned that if he was lying things would go badly. They pushed him along the path descending from the ridge, and he seemed to fall most of the way.

Outside the barn a little knot of Oldsters for Peace huddled with a hastily-made white flag. Johnny's weapons instructor stood with a grin on his face surrounded by uncertain looking attackers. The man's view of life had been confirmed.

"Congratulations *comandante*," he said, unbuttoning his top pocket and taking out a cigarette as the little party closed in on them. "A remarkable assault. The only small problem is that we are on the same side." The picture of Sandino on a remaining wall of the barn which was not visible from the ridge gazed down accusingly at the Indian commander. The instructor handed him some orders.

"I do hope you can read," he sneered. "I've sent out a call for help on the radio. With any luck we are in danger of being mortared by some other lunatic any moment." He blew a smoke ring. "I suppose they did not issue you with anything as complicated as a map?"

"We saw gringos on the ridge. We had intelligence reports of gringos in this valley from trusted *campesinos*. If we had got any closer we would have lost the advantage of surprise," said the Indian defensively.

"Yes, it will certainly come as a surprise to the area commander that his pet project, his International Brigade made up of American and European socialists, has been wiped out. Such a unit would have had incredible propaganda value, he said. Personally, I never thought they would be as good as our own troops and you seem to have proved it. But you should have an interesting time explaining why exactly you were moved to murder the army's most idealistic new unit. Comrades who had come to help us in the true spirit of Sandismo."

The Indian peered at the orders in his hands, searching for some flaw.

"Why did you tell your men to retaliate?" he countered. His darting eyes worried Johnny. Was he estimating the odds on getting rid of them all? But the instructor did not appear concerned.

"It may seem strange, *Indio*, but when several hundred pounds of explosive suddenly drop out of the sky on top of you . . . well . . . even someone of limited intelligence comes to the conclusion that he is being attacked by the enemy. By the Contra. But now we learn it is only one of our own comrades giving us a surprise. Perhaps you were bored?"

The Indian threw the orders on the ground. Generations of hatred showed for the man in front of him. "I am a loyal Sandinista who does not need a walking stick to get up the hill," he fumed. "You have made a mistake, old man, and are in the wrong barn in the wrong valley."

But there was doubt mixed with the anger in his eyes as he looked around him. One of his men said something about discussing it calmly and was promptly admonished. The instructor leant against an acacia tree carelessly blowing smoke.

"Don't worry over-much, comrade," he said in a mock conciliatory tone. "Don't worry. Most of the great military commanders in history were complete idiots. What you did today was very promising. Castro could not read a map. Alexander the Great was an alcoholic. You have done very well for an Indian. Your mother would be proud of you. Did your *mama* like military men?"

With a bellow the Indian went for his machete, but was grappled immediately by two of his men. "Easy comrade. The shit is trying to make you mad. He tries to cover his own mistakes."

"No one insults my *mama*," the Indian snarled. In the distance was the sound of a truck approaching.

"That is the relief platoon. I do not think it will be a good idea to talk of killing in front of them," said the instructor. The Indian stopped struggling and pulled away.

"You have not heard the last of this, *viejo*. It is not me but you who will be held responsible."

The argument continued to flicker between the two men completely divided by class, race and religion although both were supposed to be part of the same revolution. Each grew more confident of vindication as two new Jeeps followed by a rickety collection of trucks full of tough regulars came into view. The troops promptly deployed and surrounded everything. The men in the Jeeps were civilians.

"We salute you comrades. You have won a great victory against the Contra. The Minister here is proud of you. He has rushed to congratulate you," said a young man in the lead Jeep as it drew up beside them. He wore sunglasses and expensive casual clothes, and stood with his hands on the windscreen. The Minister said nothing. Two men with cameras and *Barricada* armbands got out of the Jeep with a large cardboard box of American K rations and what looked like a copy of *Playboy*. They quickly decorated the corpse of an Oldster for Peace with these props of US Imperialism and snapped him for posterity, no doubt to be depicted in their newspaper as a dangerous American mercenary.

"This *Indio* idiot attacked my post and for all I know massacred most of my *Internationalistas*," began the rattled instructor. "He shouldn't be in charge of himself, let alone a battalion."

"Do not listen to him. I had information there were Contras in this valley. The old goat has set up his camp in the wrong place," protested the Indian commander by way of explanation for the burning wreckage around them. Both were too angry to appreciate what the new arrival had said or what his men were up to.

"No comrades. No. No. No, comrades . . ." continued the handsome young ministerial aide slowly and carefully, as if talking to children. "We were in the area and have already had a full report from the barn radio operator who is also a loyal servant of the Department of State Security. Our minister, appointed by the people, has decided this is a heroic victory against the Contra. I know you military men are sticklers for detail but we are still in command of this piece of our beloved country. Let me not hear the words massacre or defeat. It seems clear that the comrade instructor here was relieved in the heroic defence of this barn by the comrade commander and his irregular battalion with its deadly Katushas. There has been much sacrifice. We shall take detailed pictures of the battlefield. Pictures to go around the world that will show we are ready for anything. Is this young man a survivor of the brave *Internationalistas*?" he said, pointing to Johnny. Heads nodded and the photographers from *Barricada* all turned their lenses on him. "Smile, gringo. What is your name?"

"Johnny Morgan."

"We salute you for fighting for principle in a country which is not your own," said the aide. "Please get into the other Jeep. You will be taken to Managua. We will radio ahead."

It was an order. Had he seen too much? Were they going to get rid of him? Were they annoyed about his not keeping a proper look out? But at that moment all he wanted to do was to be away from that awful place. On trembling legs, he walked to the second Jeep which was parked, its motor running, beside an ox cart. A thin man sat at the wheel. He turned to Johnny and tapped the passenger seat with a bony hand. A worried soldier got in the back.

"Am I going to Managua?" In the circumstances Johnny was not sure if he trusted what the ministerial aide had said.

The man nodded impatiently and tapped the seat again. The guard in the back looked away. He seemed scared of the civilian whose deeply lined face was framed by long black sideburns and crossed by a loose-lipped mouth. It could have been the twisted yet beautiful face of an El Greco saint, except for the large, brown eyes. They expressed one simple emotion: complete rage. Johnny hesitated, but this was not a man to argue with and the Jeep roared away as soon as he got in. Not one word had been spoken.

Coffee bushes sped past on both sides and soon they were

on the highway heading south. At first Johnny felt relief at being away from that dreadful hillside. He quietly prayed Tom had somehow survived the barrage; if anyone could it would be the street-wise New Yorker, and Johnny had not seen his body. The Jeep stopped at a military guard post in Jinotega and the soldier in the back got out. When he returned he handed a note to the driver and Johnny began to grow more anxious about his predicament.

It was an uncomfortable thought that he had been more than lax in his duties as a sentry. An international volunteer who, only a few days before, had done suspiciously well on the rifle range and had been accused of being an imperialist spy. The trouble was he was probably the only foreigner left in one piece who knew what had taken place. Was that why they were separating him from the rest, or did they plan something horribly permanent? He could not imagine the Sandinistas would employ such methods, and as they waited to pass a herd of goats he sneaked a look at the man next to him. He seemed capable of anything, except conversation.

Night had fallen when they slipped around a bend and suddenly below them were the twinkling, straggling lights of Managua. Johnny was exhausted. His eyes were sore and his throat dry. He thought initially he would be taken to one of the government buildings in the centre. His fears increased when they drove to the diplomatic area.

They drew up by ugly solid metal gates flanked on one side by a guard post, on which was mounted a machine-gun. The soldier in the back of the Jeep got out and produced documents for a sentry. The rusting jaws then opened and they roared through floodlit gardens to a single-storey white villa. Guards lurked by the bushes and the silhouette of a Doberman trotted around from the back of the house, the headlights of the Jeep catching its eyes and making them glow a demonic red. Another joined it. They surveyed the intruders with barkless contempt, glancing round to their handler, as if eager for permission to attack. Another guard examined the Jeep and this time shone a torch on the driver's papers, before opening a more ornate pair of gates in the wall of the house.

They inched into a courtyard. Johnny's captor switched off the engine and motioned him to get out, which he did with some trepidation. Thankfully the inner sanctum, illuminated by spotlights, seemed free of prowling dogs.

A twinge of pain drew his hand to a cut underneath his chin which had inexplicably started to bleed, as if his heart and entire body had been marking time since the ridiculous battle on the ridge. His head ached and a pulse thumped in his temples. He tried to collect his thoughts. Such security meant great power. The beliefs which had brought him to Nicaragua and the beautiful enthusiasms of Perfect English were part of a different world. He glanced around to find the silent man and the soldier had disappeared. Johnny Morgan felt very much alone.

6

"Hi there, Johnny!"

The voice seemed to come from the trees beyond the courtyard.

"Step down here, Johnny. Don't stand there like a sap," continued the not unfriendly but totally disembodied American-accented English.

The garden was if anything more sumptuous than that of Perfect English. Johnny made his way past a swimming pool with tubs of orchids around it to where he thought the mystery commands originated. Beneath a clump of trees was another smaller pool which appeared, at a glance, to be a repository for dry leaves. Then the leaves moved with a sudden rasping sound. Johnny bent down at the edge of the pool and gasped. It was completely full of money. Thousands of screwed up *córdoba* notes. He picked one out and peered at it amazed. It was for five thousand *córdobas* and as far as he could tell, genuine. He reached for another.

"Thief!"

From underneath the small fortune a crab-like hand grabbed his, twisting it round and causing him to topple over into the pool, into the jumble of paper. The currency came over his head. The pool was deep and it took him a few moments to push through the suffocating tide of *córdobas*, which rustled like rattlesnakes. Fear, not the fall, knocked the wind out of him and for a second he could not catch his breath, as in the last terrible moments of a nightmare. I must not panic, I must not panic, he thought. He forced himself up above the fusty paper and saw a rotund figure scuttling up a chrome pool ladder. He half swam towards it and manoeuvred a shaking foot onto a metal rung. As he hauled himself out the first thing he saw was a pair of two-tone golfing shoes and pink check golfing trousers.

Johnny had seen them lurking in the shadows at the Perfect English party. He froze as he remembered Catherine saying that the man was from State Security.

"Call me Bliss, everyone else does. Not Mr Bliss, but plain Bliss. It's kind of a nickname. In Sandino's time an American emissary was called Bliss Lane and by all accounts he was a real shit like me . . . Pardon my little joke with the pool. I'm paid mainly in *córdobas,* so I throw the worthless stuff in there. Shows I ain't part of the common herd. Come and sit down."

He led the way into a screened veranda at the back of the villa, overlooking the spotlit garden. For the first time Johnny was able to examine the strange man. The accent was as American as the clothes, but the features were definitely Latin. Bliss was in his forties and had the squat, dissipated look of a former boxer. His hair was cropped so short he appeared almost bald. The dark, close-set, piggy eyes had an unnerving intensity. But the most unsettling thing about Bliss was his smile, a broad, toothy grin as infectious as a clown's. The everlasting smile never slipped.

"How do you know my name?" asked Johnny, as Bliss grinned down at a file in front of him.

"I know everything about you, Johnny Morgan. I bet I know things you forgot. You will stay and have a beer?" The American took several bottles from a cooler by his chair.

"Let me see, Johnny . . . You were born on the fifteenth of April, 1963, in St Mary's Hospital, London . . . your father was called Richard, and he died of TB . . . it seems he wanted to go and fight in the Spanish Civil War. Your first dog was named Fido and your favourite flower is purple lilac. How am I doing, boy?"

Johnny was astonished. "I suppose you know I'm with the Perfect English programme, too. They sent me up to La Colonia to do my military training. I was on guard duty and . . . ."

"I know all about that, Johnny. My men at La Colonia radioed me. You certainly have covered yourself in glory." Bliss nodded at Johnny's blood-stained clothing.

"Oh that," he replied anxiously, wondering if the man somehow knew he and Tom had been illicitly cooking possum. "What will they do to me? Am I going to prison?" But Bliss did not seem to be remotely interested in Johnny's shortcomings as a sentry or a cook.

"I had you brought here because I wanted to talk in private. I understand you are friends with the American girl, Catherine Hope?"

"Yes, rather. Nothing's happened to her, has it?"

"Catherine's the daughter of an old friend of a friend of mine. I wouldn't let anything happen to her . . . You're a hero, Johnny Morgan."

"A what? But I don't think you realize what really took place." In the circumstances it seemed better to come clean. The man was a Sandinista. They were on the same side. He would understand. "To tell you the truth . . ."

The American sighed.

"Best leave the truth to the politicians, Johnny. It's all a question of perspective in the end. Just remember you're a hero. This country needs heroes."

He paused and examined the file of notes.

"So you came here with the rest of the rich unwashed, eh Johnny? Helping the poor Nicos to help themselves, right? Education, that's your line. I know all about Perfect English. Out in the villages teaching people who cannot rely on the present about the past subjunctive. Well you picked an odd country. Things tend to get turned on their heads here. You came to work for peace and are now in line for a military decoration for killing the 'enemy'."

"But I didn't kill anyone."

"Now that ain't helpful, Johnny," snapped Bliss. "I thought I explained. Forget what really went off up on that ridge and just go with the flow. Hell, it's not the first time the army's shot its own foot off, I can tell you. But, by God, it's the first time an *Internationalista* is coming out of it a hero. It's a pity you aren't American. From what I heard on my radio it's the first decent engagement the idiots have had for a month."

He took a sip of beer. "You see high casualty figures are good for everyone. Both the Contras and the Nicos want it to appear a huge war is being waged in the north. The Contras need it to get American aid. The Sandinistas need it to keep people's minds off the desperate shortages here. The Contras never disagree with our casualty figures and body counts, and we never disagree with theirs. In reality we have to scout around for accidents like yours to keep people interested."

"That's the most cynical thing I ever heard," said Johnny, knowing instinctively it was probably true.

"I want us to understand each other," said Bliss slowly as he felt and located a wallet in his large jacket; the ubiquitous American billfold with photos of the wife and kids to weep over in far-away bars. In Bliss's case they were surprisingly attractive children, Johnny noted, as the pictures were spread on a coffee table. Mrs Bliss stood at a garden gate. She had bushy red hair and a Pepsodent smile, looking all an American wife and mother is meant to be. "That's why I'm on your side, Johnny boy. I want to be reunited with my wife and kids one day. They're in Georgia. I miss them and she's talking divorce in her letters." His incongruous grin never faltered while he talked of his problems, as if the expression had been cut into the flabby, unhealthy-looking flesh.

"Why don't you go and see them then?" Johnny asked innocently.

Bliss chuckled; not a nice sound. "I wish it were that easy, Johnny old boy. But despite all this –" he gestured around – "despite all this the Sandys have got me by the balls."

"You haven't told me exactly what you do – er – Bliss."

"Well, it ain't simple. I was attached to the American Embassy here under Carter. You know what I mean by 'attached'?" He drew stubby quotation marks with his fingers in the air.

"Not the CIA?"

Bliss looked over his shoulder. It seemed only half in jest. "Let's call it The Company, Johnny. The Company, remember. Let me lay it on the line to you, Johnny. Catherine will confirm I always tell the truth. Or her good friend Father Anselm . . ." He paused for a moment to allow the remark to sink in. "Have you ever heard how the 'blood of the innocents' led to the revolution? You must have lots of Nico exiles in London."

"I'm not sure what you mean," said Johnny. He was more concerned about the link between the far from innocent Bliss and Catherine.

"So you don't know? Never mind, not many people really do." Bliss took another swig of beer. "When I was sent here in the late sixties, Johnny, Managua and the whole of Nicaragua were set for a boom to be masterminded by old Howard Hughes, who had a suite in the Intercontinental: jobs, factories, geothermal power, American aid, the entire gizmo. Naturally there were a lot of rackets and a couple of the boys bought into a little money-maker. They persuaded me to go in with them. We had a minority shareholding in the Somoza-owned national blood transfusion service. It wasn't exactly a racket, but we had to keep things *tranquilo*. Impoverished Central American peasants bleeding into plastic bags, which were then exported to the United States for their blood to be put into the arms of rich people sounds like exploitation, especially if The Company were thought to be involved. In fact, all we were taking out was plasma and putting everything else back into the shmucks' arms. We were scrupulous. Our plasma had a lower health risk than anywhere else in the world. We handled 1000 dingbats a day and shipped 20,000 litres a month. The donors were paid for the plasma and everyone was happy. Our cottage industry made twelve million dollars a year and we were on a one-tenth share when the liberal newspaper *La Prensa* and its editor Pedro Joaquín Chamorro blew the whistle.

"*La Prensa* denounced the traffic in the country's life-blood and threatened to name the other 'gangster' shareholders, specifically a Cuban called Dr Ramos and a lot of people at our station. Pedro had no idea how much of a fool he was being. It was about a year before the revolution proper and we were all primed to destabilize Somoza, who had been acting very strange, and sunshine superboy Pedro was the natural replacement. For once we were going to back the good guy, a staunch Catholic who believed in democracy and cared about his people and small animals. He looked like a John F. Kennedy in the making. Then out of the blue, as we worried about this blood business, Washington changed its mind and told us unless the Sandinistas were seen to lead the revolution the fucking Communists wouldn't lay down their arms afterwards. We got a telex which said 'Inhibit Chamorro'. No one had dared suggest ditching the interfering creep as it would have looked suspicious. But heaven had smiled on us. The boys took it to mean '*Adiós*, Pedro'. We didn't argue semantics. We took him for a drive and shot him."

Bliss was watching Johnny very closely.

"We made it appear like a National Guard job, counting on the fact that popular feeling would make Somoza flee. In fact, the guy's death was the spark which started the revolution. The kids took to the streets and burnt down the transfusion centre. Somoza sent in the tanks and then the shit really hit the fan. The whole of the opposition united behind the Sandinistas. It was beyond their wildest dreams! The motherfuckers only had sixty-four men and a horse five years previously. Yours truly and the rest of the station were in deep trouble. The Carter boys moaned that when they wrote 'inhibit' they did not mean Pedro's vital functions."

"So they gave you the sack," said Johnny quietly, somewhat alarmed. This was dangerous information. The man laughed.

"The only sack The Company gives you in those circumstances is one with large weights attached. Some decaying patriot in the Pentagon thought we had done it deliberately. That we were in the pay of the Commies."

"But how come you now work for the Sandinistas?"

"Well, naturally they were grateful for what happened, and promised to give me protection. It was the least they could do. If Pedro had been around, all our scenarios showed it would have been decades before they'd take power, if ever. Most of them were Maryknoll priests and you have no idea how reasonable they could be in those days. But when I said I would take my chances on my own, they started talking about putting me in the dock for the blood business. Imagine – a show trial publicly labelling me as the head vampire. Crimes against the fatherland's natural fluids and all that crap. Think of what it would have done to my wife! I want you to help me, Johnny, and in return I'll help you. You see, I more or less run their Security Service these days. The bastards trust me because I have no choice."

"I'll do anything I can. Honestly," said Johnny, swallowing hard.

Bliss continued staring at the table. "It was one big fiesta at first but now it's getting too hot. All the *comandantes* are envious of each other. The purges are just around the corner. They are all looking for scapegoats and I stand out like a pork chop at a synagogue. Then there's the civil war. Things can only get worse here, Johnny, believe me. Hell, I'm almost a friend of your Cathy's family. Tell Mr Hope I did good. He's got juice . . . the power. I'd like to go and settle in Costa Rica with my wife and kids, but unless someone put in a word I'd be dead on arrival in San Juan, even though my dough's mostly there. Do you know Washington cancelled my American passport and declared open season?"

There was silence for a few moments.

"I told you that story about the blood, Johnny, so you can understand how things really are. If we decide to make you a hero, you go along with it, *compadre*. Also, if I were you I'd be careful not to lose the lovely Catherine to that sex-crazed holy roller."

Before Johnny could open his mouth to ask Bliss just what the hell he meant, the driver of the Jeep and the soldier came round the corner of the veranda. Bliss put a finger to his lips. The conversation was over. They all got into the Jeep.

A police car with a red flashing light shepherded them through road blocks, where men gesticulated with illuminated batons and frantically blew whistles. They nosed slowly past the cathedral to the spectral white building of the People's Theatre, an eerie sterile oblong almost phosphorescent against the night sky. It was ringed with troops and crowds of people, and the militia were checking passes. It looked as if there was to be a big speech, a meeting of some sort. They got out of the Jeep, and then the firm hand of Bliss was on Johnny's shoulder, propelling him towards a fearsome line of soldiers and a side entrance.

As they turned down a flight of stairs into what seemed endless corridors, a rolling shout began outside. *"Sandino! Sandino! Sandino vive!"* Sandino lives. Bliss rapped on a heavy door. A grille slid back and a guard checked carefully before allowing them in.

"Like my office, son? Let me introduce you formally to Capitán Alegría Ramirez, your driver this afternoon. No, honestly, that's his real name. You know what Alegría means in Spanish, don't you Johnny? Behold Capitán Happiness." The two sullen eyes examined Johnny's as he took the limp hand. It did not strike him until he noticed the initials on the files that the DGSE, the Department of State Security, held court underneath the stage of the national theatre, like the Furies in Greek tragedy.

"There are other premises," grinned Bliss, tapping the side of his nose. "But only for bad boys. The very bad boys, eh Alegría? His mother called him that because she didn't want him to be as sad as her country was under Somoza." He wheezed with laughter at the man's hateful stare. "So, to bring felicity to his land, the Capitán started fighting the bastards as soon as he could walk. He killed more men than Pancho Villa. Fought bravely. One of the original Sandys. Would be up there now – wouldn't you Happy? – except the National Guard cut out his tongue. That's why he's not a conversationalist. All that time in the jungle planning seven-hour speeches on Socialist Man After The Revolution and you end up as a dumb waiter to a turncoat Yank agent in State Security. It's lucky he can't talk back."

Alegría moved silently to a desk somewhat less grand than Bliss's at the other end of a large room, which was bare except for a few filing cabinets. The man's papers were neatly stacked, the yellowing files matching the pallor of his face. On the wall above his head was a picture of Tomás Borge, the *comandante* who had described state coercion as an Act of Love. Bliss and Happiness were the fruits of that love.

A phone rang. Bliss picked it up, spoke briefly into it and turned to Johnny.

"Time to put you out of your misery," he said as he replaced the receiver. "Guess who is in the auditorium upstairs? Catherine is waiting for you, Johnny. We arranged it. We'll take you up there."

The guard opened the door and the three of them went along the corridor and came to a halt outside another door. Bliss unlocked it.

"She's in there, Johnny. You've got one hour. Make her ask her old man to put in a word for me. I want to get out of this place."

The auditorium was entirely white, even the seats. There was a sloping stage and behind it a cinema screen. Almost half of the seats in the rows near the stage had been cleared and long trestle tables had been set up. A huge sheet covered what Johnny imagined was a sumptuous buffet on the top table. It seemed they were preparing for a party, perhaps to entertain a foreign dignitary or possibly a Soviet delegation. His mouth watered at what might be under that sheet and he took a step into the hall. The light was harsh around the stage, and at first, as he wondered about the food, he did not see the slim figure in shadow.

"Johnny, thank God you're all right!"

"Catherine!"

Before he could catch his breath she darted forwards and threw her arms around him. He held her face in the palms of his hands and suddenly a tear ran down her cheek. One large glistening droplet seemed to wash away all the petty fears he had at La Colonia. He had never seen her cry before. Now she was crying for him. It was wonderful, in a way, she was so distraught.

"Johnny, are you very badly hurt?"

He thought of admitting it was only possum blood on his shirt, but it seemed a shame to disappoint her. "Only scratched," he managed to say before she tightened her hold on him and smothered his lips with hers, dragging him down onto the floor. His limbs would not answer any more. They kissed and kissed until she broke away breathless.

"I thought you were dead, Johnny. On the radio it claimed a coffee *finca* out-station had been attacked by a massive band of Contras, and aircraft from Honduras. We heard some explosions at La Colonia. They said many American *Internationalistas* had been killed and an English boy was with them, but it did not say which one or if it was you or if you were okay ... Then a Jeep arrived to bring me to Managua. Oh Johnny!" She pulled him towards her again. "Now you're a hero," she said, a strange, distant look in those wide eyes. The corner of her mouth quivered slightly. "Johnny, I love you. I have been very cruel ... You don't know how scared I was when we thought you were among the dead. Please forgive me ..." Not one line of her beautiful face contradicted the trembling sincerity in her voice. "I love you, Johnny. Do you love me?"

"Of course I do." They kissed again.

"Am I really a hero?" he asked. "To the others. Even Tanya?"

"One hundred per cent," she laughed, pulling him to his feet. "Anselm is going to get your picture put in *Barricada*. It will be marvellous publicity for Perfect English. Come on, let's sit on the floor here behind the table. We won't be seen if someone comes in."

"Bliss told me we have an hour," Johnny said.

"So you've met Bliss?" inquired Catherine.

"He wants your father to help him. How well do you know Bliss?"

"Everyone knows that creep. Bliss is an old service buddy of my father, or so he says. He's a real sleeze. Are you hungry?" she said reaching up to where the cloth hung over the side of the table.

"Famished, but we'd better not touch anything. What's under there anyway?" He'd not had a proper meal for ages. Perhaps he could just nibble a piece of bread. Surely they would not miss a sandwich or the odd tortilla?

Catherine reached underneath the cloth. "It must be good. There's a plastic cover to keep out the creepy crawlies." She grabbed a handful of food and held it out to him. They were irregularly-shaped biscuits and wafers, and what looked like tortilla chips. Another raid provided a different kind of confection in jelly-like chunks. He knelt and pulled back the cover a little way, eager for more conventional fare, and glimpsed silver plates and a crucifix. The tableware must have come from a church. He smiled. Deep down they were still all good Catholics; but a crucifix was a bit over the top for a cocktail party.

"Have a piece," Catherine said. "They don't look very appetizing but they taste all right. I suppose these are just a few canapés to have with drinks. They must be bringing the other stuff later. I don't think they will miss anything."

He took the crisp little scrap and it was surprisingly sweet but with a slight aftertaste. Still, it was food. He had another bit and another, until he went to get some more and the silver tray was empty. Catherine tried the jelly.

"It's Dulce de Membrillo," she pronounced knowledgeably. "A sort of quince paste. They make it in León. It's sweet but a little bit yukky. An acquired taste."

"If you were as hungry as I am you wouldn't quibble. For the past few days at the out-station I've been eating rats," he said rather proudly. Rats sounded far more the correct diet for the fearless revolutionary hero than the slow and endearing possum. "I say, had we better eat it all?"

"If we don't eat all of it we'll get the blame. If we eat it all they'll blame the caterers. It's an old Hope family motto: when in doubt take it all," she smiled and slowly fed him the last pieces of the sickly snacks.

There was a rattle of keys at the door, and Bliss burst in. An earnest looking Sandinista guard followed him with Capitán Happiness close behind.

"The Presidential party is early. Get out you two. You," he added in Spanish to the guard, "go fetch the exhibits. *Inmediatamente!*" he yelled as the man didn't move.

The guard shrugged and gestured at the table. Bliss stared at the ruffled cloth.

"Catherine . . . Johnny . . . you haven't touched anything, have you? Oh no . . . Please say you haven't touched anything. Why didn't you tell me they had brought in the centrepiece Alegría, you dumb bastard? Tell me you haven't touched the centrepiece," he pleaded, his small eyes bulging with disbelief, then fear.

"Centrepiece?" mumbled Johnny, licking the sugar off his lips.

Bliss appeared on the verge of apoplexy. The Capitán went over and threw back the table cover, exposing the empty silver trays. Only a few crumbs were left. Bliss put his head in his hands.

"It was only a few sugared tortilla chips," said Johnny as brightly as he could. "I was hungry. Can't we get some more?"

For once the smile had completely vanished from Bliss's face. "You mean you ate all of what was on those trays? Nothing in your pockets? No one put you up to this?"

"Yes, I told you, I was hungry," he said as Alegría roughly searched him.

Bliss drew back the cover further. Underneath was a carefully printed set of cards in English, French, Russian and Spanish. He handed the English version to Johnny. It was short and scientifically to the point:

"Fragments of hat and fleshy parts of facial and nasal tissue preserved in cane sugar. Only parts of mummified body of Augusto César Sandino discovered at Augusto César Sandino Airport not to be damaged by entymological ingress during storage." There followed signatures of verification. Bliss took him gently by the arm.

"Do you know what you've just done, Johnny, apart from ruining my career?" Alegría took out his automatic and Catherine screamed.

"You have just eaten their fucking national hero. You Brits can't keep your greedy grabbing hands to yourselves for a moment. Don't you realize, boy? You ate all that was left of Augusto César Sandino, all this godforsaken country has, because you were feeling peckish . . ." The main doors at the other end of the hall opened and a crowd of people stood on the threshold.

"You even ate the sonofabitch's hat," said Bliss, his voice shaking.

7

The heavy doors of the auditorium were slammed thunderously shut, and the sound of the chanting mob outside could no longer be heard. Bliss's henchmen had headed off the members of the government on the threshold, but angry men and women who had waited for hours began to push hysterically through a line of confused militia. A girl screamed that the body of Sandino had been stolen from the theatre, and for a moment it looked as if the crowd would pour vengefully into the hall. But fortunately the "spontaneous" demonstration was made up largely of off-duty soldiers who, accustomed to obeying orders, were soon streaming towards the Presidential Palace where ministers had promised them free beer. The theatre still had the barren but sadly expectant atmosphere as when a promising play is taken off before its first night. Unlike Bliss, the members of the presidential staff and bodyguard who faced him across the table were not yet angry, but stunned and confused that their planned triumph of showing off the remains of Sandino had been denied to them. With the group stood the two English undertakers from Tambey and Brown of Windsor, their faces practised masks of bereaved gloom at the sudden deplorable sacrilege, though Johnny thought he detected a slight wink from Arthur, the one with the strawberry-coloured birthmark. A soldier whispered in the ear of a tubby, fidgety man with a pencil-thin moustache who announced he was the presidential secretary and had orders from the Head of State to get to the bottom of things. Johnny felt the chill of guilt and tried not to look over at Catherine. He would, of course, own up for the lot. The soldier glanced sharply at him and continued his confidential advice to the civil servant. The little moustache quivered in disgust.

"We are civilized men," was the scandalized reply.

"But we are losing valuable time," said the soldier out loud, his hand on his short black Kalashnikov bayonet. "There may be a few pieces left in his stomach . . . We could get a doctor," he added as a reluctant concession. "I beg you, comrades, to remember we are talking about the body of Sandino here. The people will be outraged."

"There will be no killing. Those are my instructions. The *Presidente* wants suspects questioned, not disembowelled."

"But comrade," said the soldier with growing impatience, "these sacred national relics have not just been stolen or merely destroyed. They have been eaten. The father of our revolution has been eaten by a gringo. We should not be squeamish where history is concerned." Johnny involuntarily took a step away from the table.

"Much too late by now," interjected Arthur, who, to Johnny's relief, spoke an idiosyncratic Spanish. He glimpsed Catherine out of the corner of his eye. Bliss stood by her side. "Much too late now," repeated the undertaker. "The pieces are so delicate they were probably all mush before they reached the stomach. Try to put the matter out of your minds. No use crying over spilt milk. They should have been under better guard. Anyway, there was precious little left of the body after those termites got to it at the airport."

"That was sabotage," alleged another man in uniform. "That termite nest was purposely introduced into the compound. To me this looks like a case of Contra terrorism too. How do we know the fragments have not been hidden?"

"'Fraid not," said Bliss. "They were mistaken for sweet biscuits. This comrade had been fighting at the front and was very hungry. It was an unfortunate error . . ."

"And the girl?" asked the presidential secretary.

"She had nothing to do with it. Nothing at all. It was my fault," said Johnny bravely. As if on cue, Bliss hurried Catherine out through the side door, leaving Johnny with Alegría as his only advocate. Bliss was throwing him to the wolves. "I say . . ." he shouted after them in English. But the door was firmly shut.

"This is a crime of sabotage and an attack on the honour of our revolutionary state. It should be handled by the army," claimed the forbidding soldier who, piqued at being cheated out of cutting Johnny open, was determined to get him back to the barracks where there were no interfering bureaucrats. "How do we know he is not a CIA spy sent to destroy the remains of our beloved Sandino?"

"Ridiculous," sniffed the presidential secretary. "We were about to pin a medal on him for bravery."

"The CIA are very clever and constantly try to ridicule and debase our heroes. Did they not try to make Comrade Castro's beard drop out by giving him drugs?" Johnny thought he saw the smaller undertaker smile, but just for an instant.

"Why did you eat the remains of General Sandino?" asked the secretary. "Come along, don't be frightened."

"I – I ate the biscuits because I was hungry. Honestly I thought they were tortilla chips or something. I didn't mean any harm or disrespect to General Sandino. He is a man I have always admired."

"You ate the relics because he was your hero? Because you wanted to be like him? Is that the reason gringo?" sneered another bodyguard.

"I ate the things because I was hungry, that is all."

"Let me get this saboteur to the barracks and we will discover the truth," demanded the man with the bayonet, almost in anguish.

Johnny's cause seemed lost. Then a faltering voice spoke again.

"Please excuse me being forward at this unfortunate and sad occasion," said the undertaker who had spoken up for him. "But if you want a body of General Sandino, we can give you one. Before the termites went about their business, we managed to take a rather good plaster cast. We have certain secret and naturally very expensive techniques that can be employed when we have such a likeness – and I am not talking about making a mere waxwork. All we need is a cadaver of the right height and weight, and with accurate measurements and photographs we can work wonders with the face. Everyone expects dead people to look a bit odd, but it's amazing what we can do with the new plastics on the pliable skin of a dead man. All we need, gentlemen, is a body."

He cleared his throat and bowed politely at the end of his speech.

"We have the gringo," said the soldier. "It would be my pleasure to give you his, and national honour would be satisfied."

"No," said the presidential secretary, genuinely alarmed. Alegría had moved silently to Johnny's side. His pistol was still drawn.

"I'm afraid he won't do," said the undertaker after casting a cold, professional eye over Johnny which made him shudder. "Of course we could lop off a foot or two but the bone structure is so different. We cannot have a Nicaraguan hero looking like a sawn off Viking, can we? Even if the *Presidente* agreed, we at Tambey and Brown have a certain reputation."

"But what shall we do with the gringo?" asked the disappointed soldier. "We can't just let him go with the sacred relics inside him. Now they are part of him."

"Does he feel the presence of Sandino?" asked another voice.

"I feel sick," said Johnny.

"That will be the insecticide," piped up George, the smaller undertaker, in English. "Don't worry. It's not that fatal."

But Johnny felt a sudden chill of a different kind. He began to wonder if some of the insistent questioners would have liked to have had a nibble or two at the national hero themselves. They had begun to move nearer to him, and he was glad of the protection of the fateful table and of the watchful eye and automatic pistol of Capitán Alegría. Was it fanciful to think that they actually believed eating those brown fragments with Catherine was tantamount to consuming a communion wafer at Mass? Their comments were certainly leading along those lines, and Sandino was a good way down the road to acquiring full equality with the Son of God in socialist Managua. Perhaps they imagined that if one ate a piece of the old hero one took on something of his soul and power as well? The old Indian religions had preached such beliefs. Hungry eyes were on him as one bodyguard hunted for crumbs of the General beneath the table.

"Please believe me. I meant no harm. I did not know it was Sandino." Fear was in his voice. He was on the verge of tears.

"Listen to him snivelling," said the soldier. "It's time we taught these *Internationalistas* a lesson. Many of you are homosexuals and lesbians and drug-takers who would poison the minds of our youth movement and sabotage our moral fibre."

"That's not true!" wailed Johnny.

"Take him to the barracks. Better still, take him up to Chipote. Take him to the old jail for interrogation." There was a growing enthusiasm for the awful prison of El Chipote.

"Sorry old chap," said Arthur, grabbing his partner's arm as they made their retreat. "I'm afraid there is nothing we can do. We never stand in the way of politics. Professional ethics and all that. Toodle-oo."

The members of the presidential bodyguard moved towards him around the table.

"Stop," said the presidential secretary, holding up his hands. "We are all getting overwrought. We are not even in possession of the full facts. As it was the fault of the Department of State Security that this abomination took place, it is for them to take care of it. The *Presidente* wishes it to be so. I place this man in the custody of the Department, who will report directly to the *Presidente*'s office."

Alegría quickly seized the initiative and led Johnny briskly to the side door.

"We demand to be involved in this matter," protested the soldier.

"Then find us a body the same size as Sandino's," said the presidential secretary wearily. "Surely it should not be hard to come by one in your profession?"

Alegría grabbed Johnny's arm, forcing him at gunpoint down the stairs, along corridors and into a windowless room, empty but for a camp bed in the corner. He threw Johnny to the floor and then, lifting him by the hair, hit him precisely, pursing his thin lips in concentration. The blow had no particular force behind it but it struck Johnny exactly in the solar plexus in an explosion of pain which brought him immediately to his knees. The refined, almost delicate Capitán waited for him to regain his breath and his feet, and did it again. He seemed only casually to extend the bony white fist with a gold ring on the little finger to have Johnny's scream echoing around the room. He had tried not to cry out at first, but it was no good. On one of the walls was an old travel poster for Nicaragua from Somoza's day, showing a shy bull peeping round a bunch of gigantic carrots and a sophisticated-looking woman with a headscarf and sunglasses simultaneously water-skiing and big game fishing. "A Country of Delicious Surprises" ran the caption.

On the tenth blow Johnny wet himself and collapsed in a foetal ball on the floor. Capitán Happiness turned him over with his foot. Johnny would have told him anything, but Alegría was not asking questions and he did not require answers. He was beating Johnny for fun. Then it was over. Alegría spat on him and left him in the warm pool of urine on the linoleum floor where he remained, in his own wet filth. He wondered about the woman in the headscarf on the poster; he thought of his mother, then of Catherine. Bliss would make sure that she was all right. He pictured her back in the Perfect English villa trying to say as little as possible about what happened but still remain the centre of attention. People like Catherine Hope never suffered: some unwritten cosmic law seemed to protect them. Anselm and the rest would be sympathizing as they passed out the beers and made careful phone calls to ensure the "incident" did not affect their precious programme. There was little they could do for poor Johnny. To inform his embassy would only be used as propaganda by the counter revolutionaries. All they could do was pray.

Alegría did not come back, though Johnny's body seemed involuntarily to force itself into the corner by the camp bed on every occasion food or water was brought in. The food was filthy. Rice and beans and tortillas, which looked as if they had died before Sandino. The light was kept on day and night and once there was a scream from somewhere close by. He tried not to imagine what they would do to him.

On the evening of the second day, a commotion occurred outside his door and he heard a heated interchange going on even through the thick metal. A soldier was arguing over a *permiso;* someone had not got the right papers. Correct papers for what? Were they going to transfer him to an ordinary prison? To Chipote? He shuddered as he thought of the deep cold waters of the volcano. But the footsteps went away and the fear subsided. He regarded the travel poster and, in particular, the bull with the stupid, contented expression on its face. His own stupidity was the monumental arrogance that he could help the Country of Delicious Surprises. He fell into an uncomfortable sleep.

Before he realized exactly what had happened, Johnny was on his feet and walking. His escort this time were members of the regular army, tough Indian troops. Their long awkward machete scabbards made a slapping sound against the hips of dappled green uniforms.

They propped him up before the door of Bliss's office. One soldier held his shirt while the other meticulously brushed him down with his leathery hand. He then took out a comb and, standing on tiptoe, parted Johnny's hair with difficulty, swearing slightly under his oniony breath, but doing the job with all the determination of a Victorian governess. He spotted a mark dirtier than the rest on Johnny's stubbly chin. "*Putchica,*" he cursed and took out a handkerchief, spitting on it and wiping away the mark. The guard opened the door and Johnny went in.

Bliss was eating a huge beef sandwich. His face burst into a smile of mock surprise.

"Howdy, stranger. Where have you been keeping yourself?"

Johnny looked around the room. To his relief, there was no sign of Alegría.

"How is Catherine?" he asked, trying to clip the emotion from his voice. "I hope she has been treated a lot better than I have."

"Now let's get one thing straight," snapped Bliss, still smiling but without a trace of humour in his voice. "There are two ways you can go out of this building, either horizontal or vertical. Do you understand? I've been working my ass off to get you out of here standing up. We get you out of the mess at La Colonia. I try to make you a hero. I let you meet Catherine as a special favour and what do you do? You let me down. You have to do . . . what you did. This place ain't that sophisticated. They're old fashioned. They don't take kindly to foreigners eating national heroes." He took another bite of his sandwich. "It's not the end of the fucking world if you get kicked around in a cell for a few days. We could not be seen to be treating you with kid gloves. There are all sorts of rumours flying around this town. Until they've died down I wouldn't give a red cent for your chances in Managua. You have gobbled up the body and blood of their Lord Jesus Christ Sandino . . ." Bliss shook his head. "I don't know too much about Indian rituals, but if people start following you with salt and pepper, watch out. Within an hour of your little atrocity in the auditorium, small boys were selling sugar-coated tortilla chips on the street as *memento mori* of Sandino. The city is munching itself silly. But if they knew where to find you, Johnny . . . Yum, yum. Of course, some God damn atheists just plain want to kill you."

"What about Catherine? Is she all right?" he repeated anxiously.

"Don't worry, Johnny. She's quite safe for the moment. We have managed to keep her out of it, mainly by encouraging the stories about you. You're the star, Johnny. I knew you would want that. Do you know what? The lovely lady promised to get her father to help me out, but I had to swear on scout's honour to look after you, Johnny. I wouldn't be Catherine's best buddy if you ended up as a between meals snack for a bunch of religious maniacs. Walk out of that door if you want and take your chances with your consulate. But personally I don't think you would get very far. And if you left, Catherine wouldn't put in a good word for me, Johnny. So it just wouldn't be in my interests. She insists on staying.

What would her prospects be if people learned she ate Sandino, too?"

"Stop it," said Johnny. "Please stop."

"Then do as we say. The powers that be want you taken out of circulation for a while until the fuss dies down. Somewhere you can prove you are a good comrade. Until my say-so they'll withhold any exit visa. It cannot appear you are skipping the country scot free. People always do what we say in the end. Life can be as hard or as easy as you want. Your exile can be Gucci style or the Gulag. It's up to you. Don't forget the Sandys are fucking Communists." Bliss's smile was as wide as ever.

"I'm sorry, Bliss." Johnny felt dreadfully tired. "I'll stay and do what you wish. I got you into this mess." There was a knock at the door.

"Johnny, you look awful!" It was Blanca.

"Blanca, what on earth are you doing here?"

She handed some papers to Bliss. "Let me touch you, Johnny. They used to say touching Sandino could make you have many boy children," she giggled.

"Now listen, Johnny, and listen good," said Bliss. "You are to go with Comrade Pocaterra here. She will take you for a little holiday on the Pacific. You've never been there, so it will be educational." He gave Blanca a nod. "After that we might let you go to the Atlantic Coast and back to Perfect English. Don't worry. At least don't worry a lot. Do what we say Johnny, and in no time at all you'll be teaching the pickaninnies over there. Happy as a pig in shit."

Bliss held out his hand and Johnny shook it automatically. "Thank you Mr Bliss."

"Bliss is sufficient for any man."

8

A great ocean roller hesitated for a moment. Tons of sea-water teetered, green and foam-flecked at the peak and dark grey-blue underneath. Then it hurled itself towards land with a surging roar, breaking again and again. The foam hissed and seemed to boil as another immense wave rose up to follow. Johnny looked out across the Pacific from the veranda of a well-guarded beach-side bungalow as Blanca's long sharp nails clawed into his bare bottom: his trousers were around his ankles and a drink was still in his hand. Pleasure built up in his body, waiting for release. He cried out as the world melted and he attempted to pull away. But Blanca pinned him to her, draining every last drop of him as if it were precious, fastening her teeth around him and biting into his flesh. In pain he overbalanced and one arm flailed behind him into a wooden support which had been in the sun and sea blast too long. It snapped with a sound like a pistol shot and the veranda roof sagged, sending an avalanche of tiles onto the sand. Several came crashing through a hole in the roof, smashing glasses and bottles on a drinks trolley. Still Blanca stuck to him, as he tried to protect her head and his from the falling debris. Eventually, satisfied, she looked up.

"You are not just a lover, Johnny Morgan. You are an earthquake," Blanca giggled, wiping her mouth.

Almost immediately, she was leading him into her bedroom and beneath the billowing whiteness of her mosquito net. Sunlight danced on the sheets.

"Again, Johnny. Love me again," she kept taunting. "Come on, Johnny, you are a man. Love me again, my little Sandino."

Johnny had never for one moment imagined the protective

custody Bliss had ordered would be like this. Blanca had seduced him with patriotic fervour at the isolated bungalow near Ponaloya. In the month he had been there he estimated he had lost a stone in weight. Of course it had begun innocently enough with Blanca putting a sisterly arm round him, but now he felt increasingly guilty. He was not allowed to write to Catherine or anyone, but Blanca said Perfect English had been officially informed he was convalescing from his wounds. His affair with Blanca caused him to think jealously about Anselm and Catherine and the lack of communication made things worse. He closed his eyes. As a Christian it was hard just to lay back and think of Nicaragua and enjoy the view. There was a snip near his left ear.

"What was that for?" Johnny said, glancing round and seeing Blanca had cut off a lock of his hair with a pair of scissors.

"To remember you by, because I am a witch," she replied pertly. "It will be useful when we have seances and want to raise Sandino. I have a surprise for you, Johnny. You are leaving today. We will have to get your belongings packed and ready. In four days, Father Anselm will start north from Bluefields to begin the Perfect English programme. Two guards will drive you across to Rama tonight and you will get the riverboat to Bluefields in the morning. On the Coast you will be quite safe from those who think you desecrated our national hero. But be careful Johnny . . . the Miskito Contras do not take prisoners."

For an instant there was a caring look in her eyes and then she got up, placed the lock of hair in a little trinket box on a table by the bed and put her dress back on. She began a whirlwind of activity, piling his things into a borrowed suitcase. Blanca had managed to recover a few of his possessions from La Colonia and to these had been added items confiscated from jailed travellers. For the first time in his life Johnny had a pair of silver-backed hairbrushes. It was late afternoon and before long an old Pontiac with two plain-clothed guards honked its horn outside the bungalow.

"Give my love to Catherine," shouted Blanca, waving as Johnny got in the car. He had no doubt she meant it. She had a stainless steel soul. For Blanca there was no sin in the service of the state.

It would be marvellous to be free again, he thought as he stared at a smoking volcano from the back seat of the bumping automobile. He was determined this was going to be a new beginning, the great adventure he and Catherine had planned. He was going to put the past behind him. He wondered if he should tell Catherine about Blanca. Perhaps it would not be a good idea. He checked his *permiso* and the money Blanca had given back to him, then rummaged in his suitcase. Despite her warning, he was curious to see the Miskito Indians at first hand and had a sneaking admiration for the incorrigible tribe. The official line, much stressed by the Cambridge Supports Nicaragua study group, was the Miskito had been gentle, peace-loving farmers and fishermen until CIA gold transformed them overnight into the most bloodthirsty group of Indian warriors since the Apache. But now even the Sandinistas admitted it had a lot to do with their turning Miskito land into free fire zones without informing the Indian villages involved. By chance, Johnny had discovered much deeper antagonisms in a second-hand bookshop.

In the suitcase he found a small hardbacked book covered in brown paper with "Coffee Cultivation" scrawled across it in large letters. Luckily, it seemed no one who had been through his belongings had bothered to read it. It was, in fact, *The Observations of an Educated Clergyman in the American Isthmus* (1888) by the Reverend Clement Spadger. Johnny opened it at a marked page.

"In short, these Miskito are men of excellent and formidable parts, not aborigines as such, but the fruits of English, Dutch and French buccaneers intermarrying with Rama, Sumu and Carib Indians of the Coast. The union of European stock with these Indian Eves produces no weakening but specimens two yards high who could fill a door and often have blond hair and blue eyes. The Miskito are hated by the Spanish because they are good God-fearing Protestants, speak the Queen's English and fought with Drake and Sir Henry Morgan, not to mention Sir Horatio Nelson in his raids on Spanish Nicaragua. Several served in Drake's Golden Hind against the papist hordes of the Armada as powder monkeys for their English shipmates. A free and warlike people, the Miskito have always detested the tyranny of Spain and the poison of Rome . . . ."

The book was an undisguised polemic calling on Queen Victoria not to forget her duties to the Miskita Kingdom, established under Charles II to annoy Madrid with much use of coronets and ostrich feathers. Johnny had not even shown it to Catherine. Yet it was more than a cause for concern if the Protestant Miskitos' hatred for the Catholic "Spanish" from the Pacific side of the country was not just the fault of "a few excesses" by the Sandinistas but the expression of hundreds of years of enmity. Johnny was grateful to the Reverend Spadger for pointing this out.

The Pontiac bypassed Managua and pressed on through the night, stopping occasionally for the drivers to change over. Johnny was rocked to sleep at last in the large, comfortable car, waking only as they halted again sharply.

"Rama," grunted one of the guards.

The sun was strong and Johnny, surprised, realized it must be late morning. The landscape had changed from one of rolling plains to low jungle. The biggest building in the collection of shacks was, as a rotting sign proclaimed, Madame Amy's Restaurant and Rest Rooms. The Chinese owner, Amy, grudgingly made them coffee under the watchful gaze of a shiny plastic Buddha over the counter. As Johnny took his cup a brilliant blue butterfly landed on the Buddha's stomach. A scribbled menu said "empanadas" but when he asked for one the elderly Chinese lady put her tongue out at him. When he inquired if she had any food at all, she shook her head. She returned to her knitting while he examined a glass case crammed with preserved foodstuffs. A can of "Amoy Chinese Fried Dace" nestled next to a rusting family-sized tin of "Sweet Peace". But these were relics from a more plentiful past that Amy had no doubt preferred and prayed would return. Her cold glance told him they were not for sale. "No," she barked. Her dreams could not be bought.

They went to sit outside at a table in the sunshine and one

of his guards purchased Johnny's ticket for Bluefields from an office next door. Other travellers began to congregate for the riverboat to the sea, the Bluefields Express. The guards dozed as Johnny examined the dregs of his coffee. He was looking forward to seeing Catherine, but as he tried to picture her face he kept imagining Blanca's.

"Sinner repent! Repent of your evil ways," boomed a voice in English. A crutch banged against the boardwalk as Johnny jumped and sent the coffee cup into his lap. Before him stood a one-legged cripple dressed in black, holding a Bible. For a moment the man stared deep into Johnny's eyes with a slight, knowing smile on his lips, and then turned to the growing crowd in the street.

"A bad man," whispered one of the guards in Spanish. "A lover of the Contra." To the guard, English had not yet become the new Latin. The crooked man was preparing to preach on the uneven cobblestones which sloped down to the river. Hawkers were peddling oranges, iguana eggs, tortilla chips and drinks. Behind the cripple towered a giant hoarding showing an American bomber going down in Technicolor flames. *"En el Rama van a morder el polva los invasores,"* ran the caption. Rama would grind the invaders to dust. The preacher stood before it unimpressed. He balanced himself on one crutch and scratched the stump covered in threadbare flannel, which ended just above the knee. There was a hush of anticipation. He was no longer a cripple but the Word of God in Rama.

"Repent sinners or face the Eternal Fire! Down that river lies a town replete with more wickedness than both Sodom and Gomorrah, which the Almighty destroyed. Think carefully about your journey, my friends. Is it worth your Immortal Soul to be transported down river and tempted by those fleshpots? The devil waits there. Is one night of passion worth the pains of the Fire? Beware, sinner, the harlot."

A black woman took a huge basket of fruit off her head and, bending down, wiggled her immense bottom at him. The other negroes in the crowd laughed, as did the Miskitos. Sandinistas in green uniforms did not. A low wooden trolley, like an oversized skateboard, suddenly shot out of an alley propelled by two strong arms and a torso and topped by a round head with the biggest mouth and largest teeth Johnny had ever seen on a human being. The man had no legs and was fastened to the trolley with a strong leather harness. The trunk of his body fitted into a shiny black leather "shoe". With incredible skill this creature, seemingly loosed from a hell the minister had been describing, bore down on the woman's bottom. Howling with laughter the group jumped to the safety of the hotel boardwalk which, being a foot off the road, was inaccessible to the strange vehicle. Snapping teeth just missed the soft posterior and sunk themselves instead into the leg of a grey-haired black man half asleep on the wooden step. A young, unsure Sandinista conscript on guard duty picked up his rifle and moved slowly towards the minister. The bitten Creole let out a yelp and a stream of indignation followed in the patois of the Coast.

"What the fuck do you know about harlots, preacher? What you want to be disturbin' folks sleepin' for? Why you set your Gabriel on us? You know I'm a Christian. Let go of my leg, Gabriel, you devil."

"Gabriel's no devil. Gabriel is the servant of the Lord. Gabriel is the hammer of vengeance on the anvil of sin," said the preacher. "It is far better, Gladstone Pike, to have a sore ankle than a sore soul, and the next time you slump into the gutter after a night of drunkenness and debauchery, swollen with lust, covered in the filth of evil women . . . remember my vigilant Gabriel will be there. He patrols the gutters of New Sodom ceaselessly, chastising wickedness."

"Stealing people's hard earned *córdobas* too, thieving little bastard," someone shouted. Gabriel had let go of the leg as he heard his tireless work being described. An angelic smile spread across his face and he put two calloused hands together in the attitude of prayer. His features were disturbingly handsome with the pirate heritage of fair hair and blue eyes, one covered in a white cataract. The tranquil mood persisted even when the woman whose bottom he had been trying to bite threw an orange at him. His master launched into "Rock of Ages". Gabriel had not noticed the Sandinista edging closer to the preacher. The crowd joined in and the

Rest Rooms shook as the preacher banged out the time on the wooden panelling with his crutch. Periodically, a good-natured insult was screamed above the singing. Gabriel's head swung in ecstasy with the music. Little girls scampered up and giggled as they popped orange segments into the "monster's" mouth for a dare, but the man thanked them with a smile and bowed, growling only when one attempted to put in a tree frog. Between verses the leather straps which held Gabriei's trolley creaked as he leant over to lick a morsel of fruit from the cobbles. The crowd appeared to know the evangelic duo well. The street had become a bantering cathedral.

"You are creating a disturbance," said the Sandinista precisely in English, drawing himself up to his full height.

Another soldier who was checking a man's papers called out, "*No compañero*. Leave the preacher be." Johnny's guards were watching with the professional interest and detachment of State Security. A silence came over the crowd which moments before had been enjoying the fun. The Sandinista looked uncertain. The people's scowls showed the hispanic youth was resented. The one they called Gabriel had an apocalyptic gleam in his eye.

With a whoop he disappeared through a gap in the houses. The soldier rested the butt of his rifle on the ground as he asked the preacher for his papers. His postures of authority had the jerky indecision of an adolescent learning to dance. The preacher said nothing. Another bus arrived from Managua, pulling up on the hill which sloped down past Madame Amy's to the brown and sluggish river. The quiet became eerie. Voices carried from the bus a hundred yards away. The smell of stagnant water clung to the buildings. A family of blue and yellow macaws landed on the corrugated roof of the hotel and in a mango tree, as if the jungle had already had word of the confrontation.

"Where are you going, comrade?" demanded the young Sandinista of the preacher.

"Bluefields," said a now still, small voice. "Bluefields, to do the work of God. We travel doing God's work."

"That town is not the place for your sermons. You'd just get yourself into trouble. There are lots of our *compañeros* resting in Bluefields from the war against the Contras. They might be insulted by your preaching. We have hospitals for people like you. Come with me . . ."

The preacher let out a howl. It was the scream of every nightmare, a distillation of the indignities visited on that crooked figure. But the baleful wail had hardly died on the damp air when it was followed by a sound in one way as horrible, but somehow joyous. It was a battle cry.

"Aayeee . . ."

The interfering conscript half turned and saw Gabriel's wooden trolley flying at him down the steep incline towards the river. The sharp-toothed jaws gaped open. The soldier threw himself backwards and landed among several baskets of oranges, his rifle clattering into the gutter. With considerable *élan* Gabriel brought the trolley to a perfect sideways stop, sending pebbles scattering. He hauled himself back up to his master's side, proud as a charioteer. A young girl ran up with a hibiscus flower which she slotted through his earring. The soldier struggled to his feet and tried to recover his composure, glancing around.

"My gun . . . Who has taken my gun?" he said to gales of laughter as the preacher shrugged and Gabriel looked innocent. The rifle had been spirited away among the crowd. Even Johnny's guards laughed and a Sandinista in authority came out of Amy's to admonish the recruit for losing his rifle. As the angry officer shouted, the unfortunate soldier pointed repeatedly at the preacher and Gabriel. But just then two long blasts on a horn caused everyone to stampede towards the dock, picking up chickens, baskets and children, sweeping Gabriel and the preacher in the human tide away from the officer and down to the river, where the Bluefields Express was approaching on the wide expanse of the Río Escondido, trumpeting its arrival again and again. After the passengers from Bluefields tumbled off, his guards bid Johnny "*Adiós*" and he followed the throng onto the rusting hulk.

On the precarious gangplank a man took his ticket. Gabriel's face peered down moon-like from the roof of the bridge. As soon as the last person stepped aboard the twin diesels started up and the boat pulled swiftly away. The crippled preacher seemed oddly pleased that he was heading at full speed for Sodom and Gomorrah. The Express blew its horn once more as Rama receded.

A happy-faced black man with a baseball hat made room for Johnny on a bale of newspapers on the shaded lower deck. The sun was very hot and he was glad to be out of it. The boat moved quickly with the stream, passing a burnt out tug, moored at a small landing, with two gaping holes in its side.

"Mister Contra did that," beamed the man next to him. "They the rebels," he added. It was the first time Johnny had heard the Contras referred to as rebels. A helicopter hovered to watch their departure and then swooped past the boat twice. Each time it came overhead people cried out and waved. He was not sure if it was a cheer or a jeer. By the rail a man dozed with a black and white monkey on a chain.

The river bank slipped away and slowly the tall jungle hardwoods crowded closer together and the clearings with their Swiss-Family-Robinson houses and hordes of screaming children vanished. Soon they were between impenetrable green walls of mangrove jungle, backed by layers of old rain forest hung with liana and punctuated with giant tree ferns and brilliant orchids. The river narrowed at one point and the green tangle pressed in on them. Here and there Johnny saw purple blossoms and wondered whether the beautiful narrows were where the ambush on the tug boat had happened, leaving it holed and burning to limp back to Rama. Curiously, the people about him became more relaxed the thicker the barrier of vegetation became and the further down river they got. It truly was another country.

The Bluefields Express sounded its horn, and Johnny's attention was drawn to a canoe full of men scuttling out of its wake. A small Sandinista patrol boat throbbing with rock music and manned by heavily-armed soldiers roared past them, turning at breakneck speed and somehow managing to stop next to the canoe. The Creoles in it were obviously in trouble.

"No good 'Spanish'," explained Johnny's elderly companion, gesturing towards the Sandinistas. "They take us to prison if they find any rebel writings. No good. They take us to prison in Managua. They put us in irons. All for speaking the truth, man. Whatever you do in Bluefields, don't speak the truth."

It did not seem the time or place for a political discussion. "How far are we from Bluefields?" Johnny asked. "Why is it called Bluefields? Is it because of the blue flower?"

"Not exactly, boss. Bluefields she named after a bad pirate, a Dutch feller. But who knows, he may have been called after a flower when he was a good little baby. Bluefields is not too far now, thank God. We nearly half way. My name's Joseph. Why you come to Bluefields?" he said, taking Johnny's hand.

"I'm with an educational programme."

"Get away from me, man," Joseph said with mock seriousness. "First they bring in the education, then they bring in the guns when we niggers don't learn good. Next time they smack this black bottom I'm lightin' out for the rebels." Johnny glanced around him. "No need to look over your shoulder, youngster. Bad men always fly to Bluefields. There's no spies and stoolies on the Express. What's your name? You going to be a pirate or a stoolie?"

"My name's Johnny. You don't like the Sandys?" He laughed nervously. The diminutive sounded faintly ridiculous.

Joseph did not laugh. The big man by the rail had woken up. So had his monkey. They were both watching him.

"You mean the Spanish? The *piricuacos*? The dogs from beyond the mountains?" The Creole held his wrists together as if for imaginary cuffs. "Better watch your mouth when we get to Bluefields or they will take you too. You'll find not many folks have good words for the Spanish, Johnny."

"But things must be better than under Somoza?"

Joseph smiled and spat. "I didn't know there was a Somoza until he was dead and the Spanish soldiers come and tell us we all got to be Communists and fight their war. All I know is I used to pass by the church shop and buy Pabst Blue Ribbon beer for three *córdobas*. Now you can't get Pabst, the shop is closed and the preacher in jail. You get their Victoria shit if you're lucky and it cost you thirty *córdobas*. I live in Old Bank, Johnny. You come down there and see me. You ask for Uncle Jo. Then I tell you stories to make your pretty hair curl. Just this minute I don't trust that monkey. He may be a stoolie."

The monkey looked offended and hid his head. Joseph elaborately rolled himself a cigarette. The dissenting words had come to an abrupt halt, yet Johnny felt strangely at home on the boat.

Several more hours slipped by. He thought they would never get there. All at once, the horn blew and unmistakably Johnny could smell the sea. Now the boat was cruising between islands in a large bay past shores of mango and palm. A flight of pelicans skimmed overhead. A colder salt wind was coming in from the Atlantic. He bid goodbye to Joseph and pulled himself up, helped by willing hands, onto the roof of the Express as it steered slowly into the lagoon of Bluefields.

Clouds of mosquitos blew towards the boat from the town, a shambles of white, blue and green gingerbread houses with rusting red galvanized roofs. Crowds waved from a dock as fishermen paddled pangas for a muddy shore. At that instant the town and sea were bathed in the golden light of a tropical sunset. Johnny scanned the figures on the quay for Catherine, his heart pounding. He ached to see her.

9

The red, corrugated iron spire of a white wood church stood out among the coconut palms on the darkening horizon. Johnny lit a cigarette and watched as two Jeep-loads of troops examined the passengers who came off the Bluefields Express. The soldiers grabbed two Creoles and slammed them into the wall of a shack marked "Customs. Welcome to Bluefields." The suspects' legs were spread wide as the Sandinistas searched the men, prodding them viciously with rifle barrels. All the worried faces on the dock and the boat were black, except for the occasional Miskito. They avoided looking at the unsmiling, fair-skinned boys in the Jeeps from that revolutionary Nicaragua beyond the mountains. The soldiers were tense and watchful. Their empty, arrogant stares betrayed a fear and distrust of the people shuffling by. There was a tell-tale lack of complaint when a Creole teenager being frisked was, for no reason Johnny could detect, pummelled to the ground with a Kalashnikov butt. Bluefields was in the war zone and, from the attitude of these Sandinista troops, everyone who lived there was the enemy. Johnny breathed a sigh of relief when he had passed the check-point without difficulty; a search might have revealed the seditious writings of the Reverend Spadger.

"Johnny!"

In front of him stood the considerable bulk of Tanya, who seemed to have become even fatter, wearing a grubby uniform. Around her neck she had a Palestinian scarf.

"Peace be with you, comrade," she cried, giving him a hug and insisting on carrying his case. "Come on – Catherine and the others are at the school we use for rehearsals. The Sandys didn't want us to greet you down by the dock. You can see why. How does it feel to be a hero, Johnny?"

"Hero? But I . . ."

Tanya cut short his reply.

"Come on," she repeated, and strode off around the potholes. A fetid smell blew from the jungle inland and a warm, persistent rain began to fall. They had only gone a few yards when there was a momentary glimmer on the horizon to the north, then the sound of an explosion.

"What was that?"

"Contras," replied Tanya, unperturbed. "They keep chipping away at the defences."

The whoop of Gabriel could be heard from the port as Johnny hurried after her past a row of dimly lit bars. A bottle sailed over the wild west saloon doors of one and smashed in jewel-like fragments on the rubbish-strewn street. A woman under an electric light beckoned him, stroking her leg. Others lurked in the shadows. These were the temptations the preacher in Rama had warned of. The first one reminded him of Blanca.

Outside a collection of prefabricated buildings, Tanya stopped and handed Johnny's case back. She twisted her face into a revolting conspiratorial grin.

"Now, promise to wait here for three minutes. Have you got a watch?"

"Yes, but I'm afraid it's given up the ghost," he apologized. Sand had crept like sin into his father's old wristwatch while at Ponaloya. It was not an expensive timepiece but had immense sentimental value for Johnny.

"Well then," said Tanya briskly, "just stand here and count up to 180. Peace be with you, comrade." Before he could prevent her she had vanished through a door, leaving him counting in the rain, feeling silly. If a Sandinista patrol came along he could hardly say he was playing hide and seek. Another flash lit up the horizon, followed by a lingering rumble. Under a street lamp fifty yards away he saw a soldier coming towards him, and, racing through the numbers, Johnny stepped inside.

He felt his way in the gloom, then suddenly the lights were switched on.

> See, the conquering hero comes!
> Sound the trumpets, beat the drums!

Mistrusting his own eyes, Johnny blinked. At the end of a long room packed with people seated in rows was a stage, above which was hung a makeshift banner that said, "Hail to the heroic *Internationalista* Johnny Morgan wounded at the front!" The possum blood stains on a shirt he no longer possessed were obviously still serving him well. Johnny dropped his suitcase, speechless. Everyone was clapping, while on the stage he could see the Perfect English group. A figure ran towards him up the aisle.

"Johnny!" shouted Catherine. "Johnny, I've missed you so terribly. We all have. Come with me and sit down." She kissed him on the lips. Then flinging her arms wide added, "This is for you."

She led him to a seat by some senior military men in pressed uniforms. Most of the audience appeared to be school children or soldiers. She gave him another kiss and climbed back on the stage. Anselm, dressed in a Sandino outfit, was smiling down at Johnny.

The applause ceased and a slick series of playlets, originally discussed that first evening at the House of Perfect English, were crisply acted out on stage, culminating in an adaptation of The Prodigal Son. The climax came when Bob, who had feathers in his hair – presumably to resemble a Miskito Indian, although it made him look more like Hiawatha – said to Father Anselm, "Father, I have sinned against heaven and in thy sight. I am a poor Miskito. I have taken gold from the Imperialist and have gone to war against you. I have fought with the Contra. I am no longer worthy to be called your son."

On one side of the stage Dr Annie, in the guise of a tart with a Stars and Stripes hat, beckoned Bob with a bottle of Coke and a handful of money, but the Prodigal Son shook his head and turned to Sandino. Then Tanya and Catherine rushed on stage and showered him with streamers, Perfect English books and boxes of gifts. "My Miskito son was lost and now he is found. He is a Sandinista," declared Anselm, conveniently avoiding the second part of the parable. "Let us kill the fatted calf."

As the clapping died away, the priest addressed the audience. "Peace be with you, comrades. I hope you enjoyed our show, and now I want you to put your hands together to welcome another son who has returned, our brother in Christ ... our brother in Sandino ... Johnny Morgan, who has been convalescing from wounds received fighting the Contra at the front."

The applause reverberated off the old tin roof. Johnny was not sure he liked the reference about "our brother in Sandino". How much did the priest know? To his horror Anselm was gesturing to him to get up on the stage. Friendly hands slapped him on the back, pushing him forward. Johnny stepped up onto the boards. As he did so Anselm took off the wide-brimmed Sandino hat he had been wearing and placed it on Johnny's head.

"From now on, Johnny, you will take the part of Augusto César Sandino," declared the priest.

At once a group of Creole children holding red and black ribbons jumped up from their chairs and surged towards Johnny. They began to dance around him, binding his arms to his sides.

"This is the Bluefields maypole dance, Johnny. So you don't leave us again," said Anselm into a microphone. The audience cheered and there were cries of "*Sandino! Viva Sandino!*" His hands tied, Johnny could do nothing but stand there and accept the adulation. He had never experienced anything like it in his life.

"Read, comrades, how our brother Johnny was part of a newly formed *Internationalista* brigade who fought to the last man," exhorted Anselm, waving an old copy of *Barricada*. "Now a dinner has been prepared in Johnny's honour at Chez Marcel. Untie our hero. Come, let us really kill the fatted calf."

A group of aid workers and soldiers from the audience grabbed Johnny and carried him out of the hall on their shoulders, bumping his head on the door so he nearly lost the precious sombrero, and then bore him aloft through the dark streets in a gentle drizzle. Johnny concluded that he must take Bliss's advice and go with the flow. If they insisted he was a hero he wasn't going to argue.

The restaurant was at the back of the town and had a small, badly illuminated sign proclaiming "This Is Diners Card Country". Johnny was set down again on his feet and a waiter led him to a table laid for about twenty guests. Someone had gone to the trouble of creating a bourgeois French restaurant in that besieged outpost. There was even a fisherman's net full of dry starfish and a mural of the Cap d'Ail painted with the sad exactitude of exile. Anselm sat next to Johnny and introduced several stiff-backed officers who, the priest informed him between handshakes, were paying for the dinner. In deference to Johnny and the programme they spoke grudgingly in English, the language of the Coast for hundreds of years, though it was only too clear, like any occupying army, they preferred their native tongue, Spanish.

"We want you to have this," said one Sandinista, who had stitches in a wound above his right eye. His words were halting, with a heavy accent.

"Take it, Johnny," urged Anselm.

Was the priest using him to show Perfect English off to the military and to the other aid organizations? Johnny wondered. The dinner guests, who had all been at the theatre, were a mixture of volunteers and Sandinista soldiers. Johnny unwrapped his present.

"Only for the brave," laughed an officer. "It was General Sandino's favourite. We call it Old Momotombo."

In Johnny's hand was a bottle of mahogany brown rum with a smoking volcano on the label. Johnny thanked them sincerely for the Flor de Caña Gran Viejo export, 100 per cent proof, and put it down on the table. But he was immediately poured a thimble-sized glass of the stuff, which tasted surprisingly smooth, and then another. Waiters brought beer and dish after dish of lobster and prawns. For the next hour it seemed the infectious enjoyment of the House of Perfect English had been transplanted to the war zone. Johnny met another girl who was coming with them, an American called Sarah. She looked like a policewoman, with a bun of brown hair and broad shoulders, and it turned out she had in fact worked for the Los Angeles Police Department before becoming disillusioned and training to be a doctor. Sarah was to be Perfect English's medic. Bob started discussing the real purpose Marx had in writing *The Eighteenth Brumaire of Louis-Napoleon Bonaparte* with the endlessly patient Dr Annie. Catherine smiled lovingly at Johnny across the table.

"A toast to comrade *Comandante* Carlos Fonseca, fallen in battle," called out one of the officers, raising his bottle of beer. They stood, and afterwards Johnny's small glass of Old Momotombo was promptly refilled.

"We will now drink to salute those killed in the fourth attempt to retake the fire station at Masaya."

As he spilled some of the sticky liquid on the seventh toast, Johnny began to marvel just how many had died fighting Somoza during the civil war. For an instant he felt like crying; then for no reason at all he started to chuckle to himself.

"Now we drink a toast to all those of the 117th irregular battalion who have perished giving their lives against the Miskito Contra."

Johnny was only half listening. He pushed back his chair and swayed unsteadily to his feet, staring longingly at Catherine. She was so beautiful.

"The Miskito," he said, raising his glass. "They fought with good old Drake against the Armada when the Spanish . . ." His voice trailed off.

There was a sudden deadly silence. Anselm put a hand on Johnny's shoulder, forcing him back into his seat.

"What Comrade Johnny is trying to say is that the Miskito must be formidable enemies. It is a British tradition from the time of Sir Francis Drake – the greatest British sea captain, who finally perished, his expedition repulsed by the Spanish, a little further down this coast – to drink to their opponents, however vile and hateful they may be." Then in an attempt to mollify the irate Sandinistas, Anselm repeated what he had said in his politest Spanish.

Catherine came round the table to Johnny's side and

tugged at his arm. "We'd better go," she whispered in his ear. "To the army, the Miskito are not a joke. They are irredeemable." The angry looks from the senior men near them confirmed what she said.

But Johnny took another gulp of rum. *"Viva Sandino!"* he shouted. Down at the bottom of the table some of the younger officers took up the chant. *"Sandino, Sandino . . ."* One staggered to his feet.

"Hail, Sandino!" he yelled. "Tell us what you would do to the Miskito. Tell us, Sandino!" There was not a trace of irony.

Johnny realized the man was addressing him. He held onto the table, which seemed to be moving. He felt a sudden, overwhelming desire to tell the truth. The wide-brimmed hat slid over his eyes and he pushed it back.

"Now look here . . . Just because I'm wearing this hat doesn't make me Sandino. I admit I ate what . . . I did . . . there wasn't very much of him left. It doesn't mean I am the man. Every time I eat lobster doesn't mean I become one. Nip, nip, nip," he said, miming claw movements with his fingers for emphasis at the astonished soldiers who began muttering among themselves. "No, I am not a lobster, or Sandino. Actually, comrades, the only thing I felt afterwards was sick on account of the insecticide . . . ."

"The comrade is not himself," apologized Anselm, lifting Johnny out of his seat and steering him towards the door. Catherine followed them.

"Get off me, Blanca," said Johnny to Catherine. He lurched into a table.

"He called her Blanca. Sandino had a wife named Blanca," said one of the officers seriously. "It's all true. The gringo and Sandino are one."

"We're not! I mean I'm not," Johnny protested blearily. "He's not Jesus Christ you know . . . ."

Anselm's strong hand fastened over Johnny's mouth. "Blame Old Momotombo," laughed the priest mirthlessly, dragging him into the street. They propped him against the wall outside while the uproar continued within.

"Oh, Johnny," mused Anselm, shaking his head. "What are we going to do with you? I'm afraid this was all too much for you, wasn't it? You should have been more careful with that rum."

The Sandino hat rolled into the gutter. Anselm picked it up.

"You just wanted me out of the way from the beginning," snarled Johnny, suddenly very angry at being manhandled. The priest's saintly manner made things worse. "Just so you can go off into the jungle and live in a mud hut with Blanca . . . I mean Catherine. Whatever happened to vows of chastity? Call yourself a priest! You were telling those bastards I was Sandino so they would eat me and you could be alone with my Catherine."

Anselm ignored him. "Can you get him home?" he asked Catherine.

"I think so."

"I'd better sort things out with our hosts."

The next morning Johnny saw Catherine's lovely face looking down on him. She was fully dressed. He felt deceptively well.

"Dear Johnny," she smiled. "I have just seen Father Anselm. He's been putting a stop to the rumours about you eating Sandino by claiming they were started by counter-revolutionary elements in Managua, who want to discredit Perfect English and our attempts to bring the peaceful Miskito back to the Sandinista fold with our education programme. The officers finally agreed and one said you couldn't have become the General because Sandino could take his liquor. But please, please be more careful . . ." she laughed. "Didn't you realize I would have told Anselm everything that happened in the auditorium? At first he thought it best to welcome you as a hero and take the Sandino business on the chin by giving you the part of the General in the plays. There just wasn't time to tell you beforehand." She stroked his hair soothingly.

Johnny was glad it was all right. He reached for Catherine and pulled her onto the bed. Soon they were making violent, passionate love.

But the sudden movement was enough to make him fully appreciate how Old Momotombo had come by its nickname.

Johnny felt he could no longer breathe. The entire top of his skull seemed to have blown off while a molten lava flow was trying to push his eyes out from within. Even if he kept perfectly still the dreadful eruptions of pain became steadily worse. If Old Momotombo had indeed been Sandino's favourite drink, the man must have had a death wish.

An hour later, Catherine left to go to rehearsals, leaving him shivering on the bed. If he tried to sleep his dreams were full of vengeful, giant possums with immense fangs, smiling like Bliss and discussing the best way to cook a Johnny. When he managed to drag himself to the theatre he found rehearsals were over and no one was particularly anxious to talk to him. Anselm forgave him with a big, brotherly smile. No mention was made of the intricate diplomatic lengths the priest had gone to.

"Been wide-eyed and legless myself a few times, Johnny. Let's forget about it. I don't want to hear another word."

Even two days later, as he carried a box of Perfect English books he was to deliver up a cobbled hill where Anselm had told him the local Catholic church was, Johnny still had a headache and his swollen tongue felt as if it had passed away in his mouth. A shout made him wince.

"Johnny! Mister Teacher-man. It's your friend from the Express. Uncle Jo. You remember me don't you, Johnny?"

"Hello," he replied, forcing a smile. "Do you know where the Catholic church is?"

"I sure does. Then we go and pass by my house in Old Bank, the other side of Beholden. I show you." Johnny gratefully followed him. The quaint names given to the districts, possibly by British planters, now sounded out of place. They avoided three soldiers guarding a man completing a revolutionary mural showing happy Creole fishermen embracing the Sandinistas. Parts of the picture had been drawn by a master artist with a code to indicate colour pencilled on the board. It was Revolutionary painting by numbers.

Johnny delivered his box of books to the church and he and Uncle Jo walked on. The cobbled road soon petered out. On either side of the earth track houses stood on wooden piles under palm trees. A group of children were kicking dust at a family of piglets being suckled by an immense sow lolling in one of the kitchen gardens. Black people sat on their porches and waved happily to Johnny, laughing as the whoop of the now-familiar Gabriel echoed through the district. The crippled preacher's enforcer was about his business. In the sleepy sunshine Old Bank looked idyllic. Through one window Johnny saw a framed photograph, long since cut from a magazine, of Martin Luther King.

Uncle Jo sat down on the steps of his shack and began picking at his disintegrating plimsolls.

"Before all this revolution nonsense I used to have Saturday night shoes, church shoes and ordinary shoes, and that is a righteous fact. Now my one pair of shoes ain't got no sole. Do you know what the Spanish defence committee man said to me? He said I must be used to going barefoot. Man, do they expect me to take my woman out barefoot and dance barefoot? That's the revolution for you."

The old Creole offered to share a reefer with Johnny and together they ate scraps of salty fried fish cooked by Uncle Jo's carefree wife, who did not seem at all alarmed by the state of his footwear.

"So you going up the Coast, Johnny? Up past Pearl Lagoon, eh? That's Contra country. Maybe you meet with Mr Palmerston." Uncle Jo's shoulders trembled with laughter as he nibbled a piece of fish to the bone.

"Mr Palmerston?"

"Don't ever ask for him, Johnny. No white folk ever met Mr Palmerston and lived to tell the tale. People will say to you every rebel Miskito comes under the discipline of the Misura or the Misurasata Contra in Honduras. Don't believe that shit. Palmerston operates on his own, a pirate like his daddy and granddaddy before him, and man is he bad. He's killed more Sandys than all the other rebels put together. When the British come to this Coast we used to have Miskito kings and he says he will be next. Them Spanish are so frightened of him they don't even mention his name. He enjoys killing people and anyone will do. There's some wicked stories about Mr Palmerston."

They chatted and drank and smoked all afternoon, and

Uncle Jo told what Johnny imagined were extremely tall tales, accounts of pirates and treasure in the creeks and lagoons of the incredible Coast. As the sun began to go down, Johnny realized his hangover had at last disappeared and he was feeling at peace with himself in Old Bank. Then all at once he was conscious of soldiers running along the path towards the house.

"You are with the Perfect English group? Father Anselm sent us to look for you. Come with us now."

Despite Johnny's protests, he was taken to a truck and immediately driven away. It stopped with a screech of brakes outside the town hall and he was ushered past a guard at the door and into the concrete basement of the administration building. Anselm and the others were huddled in a crowded room.

Then the gunfire started.

10

The fighting ebbed and flowed around the town for most of the night like a tropical thunderstorm. Privileged, Perfect English huddled with army wives and frightened bureaucrats from Managua in the administration building. The chatter of machine-gun fire and the low whistle and clump of outgoing mortars made even the thought of sleep impossible as what had started as a skirmish developed into a full-scale assault. Tins of emergency rations were opened and made into a greasy stew on an ancient stove. Anselm, ever helpful, knelt and prayed with a woman whose son was among the defenders. Finally, when there had been silence for more than an hour, the priest sent Johnny and Bob down to the quay with a soldier to make sure the boat due to take them north had survived. The dock area had been the focus of the fighting. Johnny was glad to get out into the fresh, dank air.

"I envy you having been in combat," said Bob as they walked along in the darkness. "What's it like? I suppose you saw some blood? People getting killed?"

"If it's all right with you I'd rather not talk about it." Johnny had been so grateful to be alive after the fiasco at La Colonia he had hardly noticed the carnage. The only blood he remembered was that of the possum.

"War is the inevitable consequence of capitalism," continued Bob. "But I suppose we cannot make an omelette without breaking eggs. It's our duty to defend the revolution. We must witness terrible things during our struggle. I expect we will see some bodies down by the dock."

"I expect so," said Johnny.

"Of course, it doesn't bother me. Not at all. I once saw a seven-car smash on the Exeter bypass. It was sickening. But it didn't affect me. I suppose you're not squeamish when it comes to that sort of thing?"

"What sort of thing?"

"Dead people . . . guts and stuff."

"No, not a bit," lied Johnny. He was determined not to lose any more face after the other night, even though he privately dreaded what they might see.

They reached the quay, and the soldier they were with told them to wait while he went inside the customs house. Johnny noticed a line of corpses picked out in the lights of a military Jeep. A guard sat nearby and a candle burned in a glass, no doubt out of respect for the dead. Johnny crossed himself. To see the sad remains of men in that dark hour before dawn was enough to remind the most leaden soul of a fleeting mortality.

"Look, the bullet hit him right in the chest," whispered Bob, pointing at the nearest body.

"Yes," said Johnny. There was a nauseating smell of gasoline, excrement and burnt flesh. Under a tarpaulin something was smouldering.

"I'm going to have a closer look," announced his companion enthusiastically. "I understand if you'd rather not. I think as revolutionaries we should know the full horror of war."

"Go ahead," replied Johnny, trying to sound casual but feeling a little breathless.

He edged after Bob who bent down and, taking hold of the tarpaulin, jerked it back, much to the surprise of the guard watching them. For what seemed an age they peered down at the seared and twisted biological wreckage that once had been a man. Johnny suddenly could taste the stew of the evening before. He saw Bob start to wretch. Then, almost simultaneously, they rushed to the other side of the jetty and were violently sick.

A furious shout came up from the water.

Below them a uniformed figure rose from a rowing boat they had both failed to notice.

"Oh Lord. Sorry," said Bob, with a nervous laugh.

"Mother of God forgive me. I am going to kill you gringos . . ." Johnny glimpsed the flash of a bayonet in the first light of dawn. The soldier's uniform was completely covered in vomit.

"I kill you!" he cried in Spanish, making a lunge for the ladder.

"Help!" Bob screamed. Johnny ran. The bellowing officer, brandishing his weapon, sprinted after them towards the administration building.

"Not so fast, you guys." It was Anselm.

Johnny, closely followed by Bob, hurtled into the strong arms of the priest. It seemed he and the rest of the Perfect English group had decided to come down to the boat after them.

"Oh, I see you've met Capitán Fernandez. He's coming with us as our guard captain. Is anything wrong?"

Instinctively, Johnny and Bob had put the priest between them and the furious Sandinista who answered in English.

"Give them to me, Father . . . I will kill them. All night we fight the Contra . . . we lose many men. Afterwards I am so tired I have ten minutes' sleep in a rowing boat. Then . . . then these gringos think it a good joke to spew all over me. A joke, eh gringos? I kill you both . . . ."

The bayonet was now only inches from Anselm's throat. The priest shook his head.

"Please put that knife away, *Capitán*. I am sure it was an accident." Anselm gently took hold of the man's hand. Tanya was sporting the outsized Sandino hat while Dr Annie was dressed in a costume she had eccentrically decided was easier to wear than carry. It was a large red feathered bird meant to represent the Socialist Phoenix and it presently trembled with fear. "Give the bayonet to me," the priest persisted. Capitán Fernandez jerked the knife away and Catherine screamed. But, taking a step backwards, the enraged Sandinista returned the blade to the scabbard in his belt. He put his hands on his hips. He still looked murderous. A muscular man in his early forties, it wasn't fear that made him relent.

"You are lucky there is your priest to protect you," he shouted. "But answer me this, priest. How is it possible that two of your so-called helpers throw up on me at the same time by accident?"

"We were looking at the bodies," offered Bob, clutching at some straw of dignity.

"You were doing what?" said the *Capitán*, now sounding more amazed than annoyed. The unfamiliar language seemed to have softened his anger a little.

"Yes," said Bob. "Basically, comrade, we saw the line of corpses and there was one still on fire or something under a tarpaulin. So we had a look at it . . . and then we were sick. We didn't mean to be sick on you, comrade. I am very sorry. I had only ever seen a traffic accident before."

"*Madre*, give me strength!" exclaimed the *Capitán*. He turned to Anselm. "Forgive me, Father," he said after a moment. "The boat taking you north is undamaged. We should be able to leave in a few hours. As for you," he snarled at Johnny, "and you," he glared at Bob. "I . . ." But as vomit trickled from the sleeve of his uniform onto his boots the Sandinista's upper lip began to quiver and, instead of losing his temper again, he stalked off in the direction of the customs house. Johnny breathed a sigh of relief.

By early that afternoon the troubles of Bluefields were far behind them. With the rest of the Perfect English group, Johnny stood on a rubbish strewn beach beside their packing cases of books and equipment. The tiny settlement to the north of Pearl Lagoon had no name on his map. It was a collection of driftwood shacks built daringly out on a narrow sand bar just above sea level. Suspicious faces peered around broken doors as Johnny and the others carried their possessions up the sands, ready to transfer to canoes which would take them further north. Everyone worked like a Trojan. Now Perfect English was on the move, at last there was a real optimism. It was only slightly spoiled for Johnny when, as he lifted a crate, he spied the figure of Capitán Fernandez scowling at him from up the beach. But Fernandez, who had changed into clean denim, turned to harangue the fifteen lost-looking teenagers who had been assigned as Perfect English's personal bodyguard in Bluefields. Beyond the hamlet Soviet-made Hind helicopters whirled in and out of a small clearing between the jungle and the sea.

"Everyone all right?" shouted Anselm, standing on a box to address his own troops. He seemed as ruggedly happy as the cowboy in the Marlboro cigarette adverts. Catherine gazed at the priest with open adoration. The man was in his element and had done twice the work of anyone else unloading the boat.

"You have all met Capitán Fernandez by now," Anselm said. Dr Window giggled. "He and his men will come to the villages with us. The choppers you hear are bringing in two large columns and if we stick to our schedule we will always be between them as they advance north. They will keep us safe. There is one thing, though . . . While we are in the villages I will not be saying Mass because we do not want to offend any of the Protestant Miskito. But I will be available to pray with anyone who wants to, or to hear confession."

Anselm's speech over, Johnny walked into a hut that served as their temporary base while canoes were made ready. Catherine followed him in.

"I'm sorry I made a fool of myself this morning," he said. He wished he hadn't hidden behind Anselm when Capitán Fernandez had gone for him and Bob. The priest had been so depressingly cool and brave.

"It could have happened to anyone," Catherine answered. He searched her large, sleepy eyes for any trace of mockery. Instead she frowned.

"This is difficult for me, Johnny. Anselm asked me to talk to you."

"About this morning?"

"No, about us, about us sleeping together, Johnny. We have to be especially careful in the villages."

"But I thought Anselm was all for the pill?"

She laughed. "No, Johnny. He means, as we will be living on top of one another, all in one hut, we should abstain from sex entirely. It would create less tension with the rest if we didn't sleep together. And as we aren't married Anselm says the Miskito might not understand."

"I think I do," retorted Johnny angrily. "I understand that the priest wants to keep us apart . . . that he wants to come between us."

"Don't be silly, Johnny. Father Anselm is an extremely good man. He has given us a chance to do something really to help Nicaragua. But I don't love him like I love you Johnny. We can make up for it afterwards. I love you, Johnny." She touched his arm.

"Well, you have a peculiar way of showing it," he said and, aiming a kick at a crate of Perfect English books, pulled away from her and stormed outside to the beach.

The priest was watching a coaster lower a panga into the water. The crippled Protestant preacher was dropped unceremoniously into the flimsy canoe while a familiar cry came from the boat. Gabriel and his wooden chariot appeared to have been fastened to the deck for the voyage and the crew were now trying to transfer the difficult and dangerous cargo to shore. Johnny was almost glad to see the spiritually delinquent pair again.

"Preacher, tell your monster that if he bites me I will throw him to the sharks. Tell him, preacher," shouted a sailor on board the coaster.

But the preacher merely smiled and defiantly held up his Bible as Gabriel's jaws snapped at a forearm. There was a shriek and a whoop so loud it could probably be heard far out at sea.

"Right, get the crowbar under him. Tip the little shit over the side. Tip him over. Let the little monster drown."

Johnny watched as they detached Gabriel from the deck and ran with him towards the rail. The boat was only twenty yards off the shelving beach but the water was deep and he doubted if Gabriel's chariot would float for long. The crippled preacher was shaking his fist and threatened to upset the panga. Near him something broke the surface and vanished with a ripple. Were there sharks in the lagoon?

"God shall tie a millstone around the neck of any man who lays a hand on His children . . . on His unfortunate, defenceless children." The preacher turned to the shore as if in silent plea. Johnny looked at Anselm. He was not going to let him steal the glory this time. Also there was something compelling about the utter resignation in the preacher's hunched shoulders that made Johnny kick off his shoes and race towards the waves.

"One . . . two . . . three . . ." he heard the sailors chant as he dived into the water and saw Gabriel's trolley flip over before splashing into the lagoon. He swam as fast as he could and had covered half the distance when he looked again. The board was floating upside down. The preacher was trying to paddle his panga towards it with his Bible. Bubbles came from around the trolley. With a gasp Johnny was there.

"Please God, do not let Gabriel bite me," he murmured, steadying himself against the overturned board and shuddering as something brushed against his leg underwater. He tried to ignore his fear and with all his strength heaved the sinking trolley the right way up. Then he was face to face with the broad head and perfect white teeth of Gabriel, who coughed water and grinned from ear to ear.

"Thank you, friend," said a soft voice Johnny did not associate with the monster. It was followed by the familiar ear-splitting battle cry.

"Get away from him, gringo!" cried a man on the coaster, levelling a rifle he had brought on deck. "I don't see why I should have to look over my shoulder every night I want to get drunk. Get away from him, gringo!"

Johnny swam around the wooden trolley and began to push Gabriel slowly and defiantly towards shore. A short burst of fire hissed into the water to the right of them. Gabriel rowed with his arms. Another sailor yelled for the stupid gringo to move away. Johnny looked back. A patrol boat had come alongside the coaster. Soldiers were boarding and a heated argument was in progress. The sailor who had fired and several others waved their fists at the beach where Johnny and Gabriel landed. Like an unsteady crow, the preacher, whose Good Book had not failed him, hobbled up the sand towards them. Anselm came over reluctantly. Gabriel gave a final triumphant shriek and one of his over-large hands tightened around Johnny's. He was being thanked again. Then a group of women appeared from the huts and Gabriel and the preacher were hurried away.

"We should not interfere. You cannot stay out of trouble,

can you?" Anselm said quietly, putting a hand on Johnny's shoulder. "The preacher and the one you rescued are known Contra sympathizers. So was the coloured man at whose house you were found last night. What are you trying to do to us, Johnny?"

"I suppose I should have let a severely disabled man drown?" he countered. The silence which followed told him in no uncertain terms that the answer to the question was "Yes".

The jungle was astonishingly beautiful at close hand with layer upon layer of subtly changing greens, ascending to a noisy canopy. The line of canoes formed an almost soundless procession, with two paddlers in each sending the light dugouts forward against the stream. The channel was too overgrown to use engines. The paddler behind Johnny, named Benjamin, occasionally tapped him on the shoulder and pointed with a stubby clay pipe at a heron or an alligator motionless at the water's edge. Then they branched off on a tributary where the vegetation joined overhead. At one point they paddled for what seemed like a mile completely enclosed from above. There were no gaps in the green wall to either side, left or right. Johnny was enchanted with the place until it struck him the Contra could be a few yards away and he wouldn't know it. Under another section of overhanging vegetation a log had fallen across the waterway and they had to pull themselves through a gap only a foot or so wider than the boat. A large brown snake was coiled languorously on one trunk. As they had to lift the canoe partially out of the water to pass another log Johnny was especially careful where he put his feet, peering quizzically at the rotten wood fringed with brightly coloured fungus and small purple orchids.

Perfect English came to their first village, which the paddler called Silmilia, almost without realizing it. They were challenged by a guard who seemed to appear out of thin air. His young face had been transformed with black and green camouflage paint into a terrible mask. But he was expecting them. His movements were easy and relaxed as he waved them on with his gun barrel and blended back into the forest.

The deep channel widened. On the banks were neat high-gabled houses covered with banana leaf thatch. Children ran to the water to greet them, rangy yellow mongrels at their heels. Women and men came too. They were smiling. Were these the truculent, warlike Miskito? Above them the red and black flag of the Frente Sandinista hung lifeless in the damp jungle air.

The side of the panga hissed along the muddy bank and was pulled in by half a dozen pairs of willing hands. A striking Miskito girl with a scrum of offspring clutching at her blue skirt passionately embraced Benjamin who, in Johnny's estimation, looked too old for her. The boatman smiled and gave a wicked chuckle.

"My wife. You stay in my hut if you like?"

"Thank you. That would be very nice." It sounded better than being cloistered with Anselm and his disciples.

Benjamin's wife put up a hammock for Johnny as the sun went down. She brought him fermented palm wine. Anselm was still busy – in the light of hurricane lamps he worked away, making progress notes in a large blue ledger. Yet for the first time Anselm's halo had slipped. It was nothing to do with any jealousy Johnny felt over Catherine. Today it had been quite clear the priest would have let the helpless Gabriel drown. On a table next to Johnny a candle flame flickered and vibrated in the clammy air. His mother had always told him that meant the devil was on the prowl.

11

In the morning Benjamin's inquisitive children came and gently prodded Johnny awake. They insisted on taking him down to the misty river to inspect a fish they had caught. Barefoot, one four-year-old ran ahead excitedly as Johnny followed, yawning. A macaw in the forest screamed at the dawn, making everyone jump, and then laugh. Unfortunately, the children's prize catch had wriggled out of the flimsy fish trap, and they compelled Johnny to wait while they sought another. He had always liked watching children, and leant against a tree as the little army fetched poles and baited hooks. The settlement was coming slowly to life with the grunting of the hairy brown pigs and the yapping mongrels. Anselm's voice carried among the huts; there was to be a playlet that morning according to the schedule the priest had drawn up and Johnny was to act Sandino in front of a Miskito audience. He feared it might be an ordeal. But this village was much better than he had expected. The shacks were all fairly new and well built, probably put up by the government after the army massacres of Indians on the border. At least these Miskito were all right now. He took deep breaths of cool air and felt in his pocket for a packet of cigarettes. There was a movement on the path.

"Penny for your thoughts?"

Catherine took him by surprise, not just by her arrival but by the way she was dressed. Johnny was not sure whether to laugh or cry.

"Whose idea was it to have you playing the Virgin Mary? Surely not Father Anselm's?" he said. The words sounded more sarcastic than Johnny intended. Catherine put her tongue out at him, then grinned.

"Wait till you see what you're playing, grumpy."

"But I'm playing Sandino. Anselm said."

Catherine shook her head. "Oh no you're not, Comrade Morgan," she teased, pulling the blue nun's headdress around her exquisite face. "The revolutionary process continues while you go fishing. We just had a meeting. It was decided that wearing Sandino's hat seems to have a bad effect on you . . ." She giggled, "Also, Capitán Fernandez will be watching and it might irritate him if you were always on stage. So Dr Annie reassigned the parts."

Johnny could see Catherine was enjoying this. "Who am I playing?"

"More a question of what than who."

"I don't understand."

"You soon will. You're to be the Jackboot of Imperialism. It's a play you haven't seen, but it doesn't call for much acting ability. The costume completely hides your identity. After rescuing that Contra yesterday most of the others believe it's type-casting."

"I won't do it," he said angrily. "I was told that I would play Sandino . . ."

Catherine put an arm around his shoulders. "Oh come on, Johnny. It's not so bad. Perhaps you'll get to play him in another village. It's no big deal. Come on. Don't be a baby. I was only fooling about the type-casting. Don't you think I make a convincing Mary?"

He gazed at her and remembered how he had seen her the first time beside the River Cam. There was no denying she was beautiful. It seemed in life certain things were presented for one to behold, to marvel at, but never quite to have. Yet Johnny would always do anything Catherine asked for just one more smile.

Rows of grinning children were being lined up by their parents in front of a makeshift stage. Catherine led Johnny over to the eight-foot-high black cut-out Jackboot of Imperialism on a wooden frame. At the top of the painted plywood silhouette was hung the Stars and Stripes in case anyone was in doubt who the oppressive piece of footwear belonged to.

Some of the children had been roped into the performance and were energetically sowing pretend corn, weaving pretend cloth and catching pretend fish watched by adoring mothers and fathers. It was Johnny's task to move the boot in front of them and lift it up and down, making as if to pummel them into the earth.

"It's not very subtle, is it?"

"We have had several meetings where we all discussed the political implications of this play. You were recovering from your ordeal at La Colonia at the time," said Anselm in his long suffering voice, no doubt intended to be heard by the others.

"Oh, stop moaning, Johnny," added Tanya, sulkily.

Anselm showed him where to hold the boot and Johnny gave in. It did not improve his mood.

"Look Johnny," said the priest. "These people are not sophisticated. In the other villages this will be the climax of the education programme. Even if the kids don't learn anything else, we want to get across the political and religious message. That's why we are here."

Johnny did not answer.

"Come on comrade, you're on. Get out there," snapped Bob. For a moment Johnny considered throwing the boot at Anselm but there were the expectant faces of the children. He could see Benjamin through a crack in the boot; the paddler was smiling in anticipation of entertainment. Political message indeed. All at once Johnny felt such a fraud.

Reluctantly, he picked up the boot, stepped out into a sea of small bodies and proceeded to act out stamping them into the mud. His anger gave the boot a particular vigour. He nearly cut one child in half. A little face looked alarmed, screamed and ran to her parents in the audience. Then a shout almost made him drop the unwieldy prop.

"Jackboot of Imperialism, stop your oppression in the name of Christ and Sandino."

The voices of a very North American heavenly choir singing wafted across the clearing from Anselm's powerful sound system. The audience gasped as the figure of Sandino in an over-large hat and leather leggings strode up to the boot.

There was a titter of laughter. Unfortunately Tanya had won the right to play the revolutionary hero. They must have gone completely potty.

"Get off," she hissed at Johnny.

"Shan't," he said, suddenly feeling a need to be difficult. If he was going to be part of their ridiculous sketch they should have shown him the script.

"Jackboot of Imperialism, away! I am Sandino," she said.

Laughter spread, and one of the teenage conscripts who formed their personal guard bellowed she should take her trousers down and prove it.

"Get off, Johnny! Get off! Get off! You're encouraging them."

Sandino then was seen to kick the stubborn Jackboot of Imperialism in the shins, only to be kicked sharply back. Next, Sandino lost her large hat and dark curly hair fell about her ears. The audience roared.

"Get off you bloody fascist." Tanya looked ready to kill him.

But Johnny stood his ground. He was not sure if it was hatred of Anselm or the woman in that ludicrous costume which kept him rooted to the spot.

"Sandino triumphs over the Jackboot of Imperialism," insisted Anselm's voice over the heavenly choir on the loudspeaker. He sounded worried.

"It's because I'm a bloody woman you're doing this, you fascist bastard. If I were a man it would be different. Get off this stage."

"Shan't."

"Are you pissed again or something?"

"No, I always dress up as a boot at this time of day, except for Wednesday. On Wednesdays I'm one of those natty little high-heeled sandals with a sexy strap around the ankle."

"You fucking sexist!" screamed a hatless, androgynous Sandino, kicking Johnny purposefully between the legs, and for a moment the boot rocked forward and steadied itself with an awful groaning sound. One of the soldiers was laughing so much he started to weep. In the audience only Capitán Fernandez did not appear amused. The voice of Anselm interrupted on the loudspeaker again. He was sending in reinforcements.

"The Virgin Mary and the Socialist Phoenix, the expressions of the natural innocence and indomitable will of the people, aid the heroic Sandino in removing the Jackboot of Imperialism. Hurrah!"

"Booo," cried the audience. *"Viva El Zapato!"* "Long live The Boot!" went up the ironic cry.

Catherine, followed by Dr Annie dressed in the red-feathered costume of the Socialist Phoenix, ran onto the stage area and, taking up positions in front of the boot, began to try to push Johnny off the "stage".

"Johnny please," said the Virgin Mary. "Please be reasonable. Think what effect this is having on the poor children." But Johnny shoved harder and the petite Socialist Phoenix fell backwards giggling into a fake cooking fire to which one child had added real coals. Only the dampness of the feathers saved Dr Annie from serious injury and with a genuine shriek and trailing smoke she made a run for the river. To the added delight of the crowd she was closely followed by the anxious Sandino who put an arm around her smouldering lover and glared back at the audience. Soldiers on the bank whistled and shouted rude comments at the pair.

"Please, Johnny, for me?" pleaded Catherine.

"If you're nice to me."

"I promise."

"All right then." With a last stamp on the children, most of whom were ecstatic at having witnessed a battle of the gringos, the Jackboot of Imperialism departed to wild applause.

"At last the love of the Virgin Mary overcomes the Jackboot of Imperialism with the help of the people," said Anselm, barely able to contain his anger. Johnny had never seen the priest so annoyed. The stocky figure was heading towards him. But as Johnny let the boot drop Capitán Fernandez ducked around the corner of the huts and stopped Anselm in his tracks.

"What is the meaning of this?" he challenged in English, gesticulating towards the river. This time his temper was not blunted by translation. "I was told the purpose of these Perfect English plays was educational and religious."

"It is," said Anselm tetchily. "We have to iron out a few technical and casting problems."

"Technical problems? First you make a laughing stock of Sandino, our national hero, by having him played by a woman . . ."

"But it is for children," protested the priest. "Surely it does not matter if women take men's parts."

"It may not matter in your sewer of a country but it does here," said the bristling *Capitán*. "I find it impossible to imagine our blessed Sandino's parts taken by a woman. I consider it deeply insulting to have him portrayed as a pervert. Perversion has no place in our revolution."

"Perversion?" said Anselm. "What perversion?"

"That . . ." The angry soldier pointed to the mud-spattered figure of Sandino kissing and hugging a hysterical Socialist Phoenix, trying to soothe Dr Annie's singed behind. One of the guards on the bank had exposed himself and some of the Indian women threw stones at the couple. "That is perversion," pronounced Capitán Fernandez confidently. "Where did you find your helpers, priest? Which asylum?"

Anselm for once did not have an answer.

"Don't you realize this is a model settlement?" continued the *Capitán*, aware he had the advantage. "The other villages are nothing like this. They hate our guts. They don't need the slightest excuse to ridicule Sandino and Socialism. Just whose side are you on? All of these so-called dramas are to be submitted to me in the future. All men are to be played by men, all women are to be played by women and there is to be no funny business with birds or big shoes. Now perhaps you can give some lessons in your Perfect English without seriously damaging our revolution." Anselm was about to say something when the *Capitán* turned on his heel and strode angrily away, taking a swipe with his own boot at the plywood one now being broken up by the children. Johnny made himself scarce.

The next week was spent teaching from the glossy American

text books which the young ones loved. In Johnny's free hours, Benjamin took him fishing in the creek and, paradoxically, he spent more and more time with Catherine. She was one of those who would still talk to him. Indeed, after his rebellion as the Jackboot of Imperialism, she seemed to have new respect for Johnny.

Soon they were set to move again. In a carefully scripted ceremony which Capitán Fernandez had approved beforehand Father Anselm, dressed as Sandino, lectured the children. He handed out certificates of Perfect English and the large red and white enamel sheriffs' stars. The children were told to pin them over their hearts. The only puzzling thing was that even though all the children were of the same ability and had passed the tests, not all received the enamel badge.

"Who actually gets the badges is no big deal. It's the message that counts," insisted Catherine.

Johnny wasn't convinced. "I had two Creoles in my class, and they didn't get a badge even though I gave them higher marks than the rest. It just seemed a bit unfair, that's all. It's divisive as well. I would have thought good Socialists would have wanted everyone to have a badge. Look at that little girl's face. I've a good mind to go and get her one."

"Don't interfere, Johnny. Anselm is mad enough with you as it is. He said the whole project is hanging by a thread. That stuffy officer Fernandez came to see him again and told him he was unfit to be a priest. We were all trying to comfort Dr Window. Her butt still hasn't recovered from being set on fire."

They both laughed. He took her hand.

"When I came out to the Coast I really thought things were going to get better. You all lay on a splendid welcome for me, but I go and get drunk on that hideous Old Momotombo muck and say awful things. Then I'm seen talking to an old Creole, who does not exactly love the Sandys, just before a Contra attack, while my sole contribution to the defence effort is to spew over that Capitán Fernandez chap. Undaunted, I personally rescue another known Contra and to cap it all, I wreck Anselm's play. I didn't mean to do it, even if at times I find our perfect priest hard to take. I wouldn't be surprised if he thinks I am a saboteur planted by British Intelligence. But I do want to help . . ."

She kissed his cheek.

"To be honest, Johnny, I haven't enjoyed a play so much since Cambridge. But Anselm means well. Try to imagine yourself in his position."

"If the boot was on the other foot you mean?"

12

Johnny did try to be part of the Perfect English plan. I must give it a chance, he told himself, I must see it through. He sincerely prayed for guidance. But even the most blinkered optimists like Anselm and Bob noticed the sullen resentment of the villagers, who offered up their children as if they were going to be sacrificed, not educated.

At the village of Pakakawas, which Benjamin told Johnny meant "the river of the magpies" in Miskito, he was put in charge of the infants' class. As he gave out the brightly coloured exercise books he wondered how much use they would be after Perfect English disappeared into the jungle to the north. Most would be pulled apart in days or stamped into the red mud. A more thoughtful child might hide one away. But after a month or two there probably would be nothing left to show they had been in Pakakawas, except for the Perfect English badges. Johnny had to admit those were a good idea. The children loved the large, gaudy talismans, often promising to keep them for ever. It also became increasingly clear that their shell-shocked parents, displaced from their lands in the far north, fully supported those Miskito Contras who were waging their guerilla war against the Sandinistas, even though they were often caught in the crossfire.

"What do you want to be when you grow up?" Johnny asked one snotty-nosed child, who continually disrupted his class.

The boy sniggered.

"Do you want to be a fisherman? Is your father a fisherman?"

"My father fights with the rebels. My father fights the Sandinistas. My father kills Communists like you," came the defiant reply and the boy bunched his tiny fists. After that, Johnny endeavoured to be more diplomatic. It was not the Miskito children's ability to speak good English which impressed him (after all the area had been a British protectorate for several centuries), so much as their total rejection of Spanish. None of them had Hispanic names, their parents preferring old fashioned British ones. In this class there were three Alberts, two Nelsons and one extremely shy boy called Drake Wiggins.

"Now Rose, could you read the book to me?" Johnny said to a pretty seven-year-old who had the longest pigtails he had ever seen.

"Mr John Jones is a good man. He goes to church on Sunday. But other men sit next to him in church who are not-so-good." She hesitated and giggled. At that point in the book the not-so-good churchgoers were illustrated as devils.

"That's excellent Rose. Go on."

". . . who are not so good. When they have finished in church they play golf. They drink and eat. But Mr Jones is a good man. Mr Jones goes and helps the poor." The spotless Mr Jones was pictured prowling what resembled a poor part of Los Angeles, clutching groceries. The not-so-goods, shifty-looking types, were seen staggering into the club bar and getting drunk with glamorous women.

"When Jesus asks what they have done with their lives, only Mr Jones will be able to give the right answer. The other greedy men are cast down because they do not help the poor."

The illustration showed the golfers being marched towards a door marked "Hell" by neat, corporate angels who wore their wings over business suits. Perfect English, being a thoroughly modern Catholic organization, spared the infernal details.

"Please," said Rose. "Please Johnny, are there people like Mr Jones?" Her brow was furrowed. Her classmates, mostly indescribably filthy boys, laughed uproariously. One, for some reason, got out his penis.

"Yes, of course, Rose. Put that away, Armstrong."

"Where?" she asked, interested. She wore a generations-old

blue cotton dress which beating on the rocks in the stream had turned almost white. In a few years she would be married and have children. It might help to know the whereabouts of the good Mr Jones. Her face was hopeful. What on earth was he expected to tell her?

"What is golf?" demanded one of the boys as he hesitated.

"Golf is a game," he answered with relief. Rose's face fell and she became a picture of disappointment. But Johnny had no way of guaranteeing Mr Jones, just as he could not tell them where to find God, Jesus or St Peter. It was a Miskito trait, he found, to ask the exact geographical location of these obviously attractive and powerful personalities. When he did not reply, he was informed that the local Moravian pastor always knew. The man more or less gave map references. According to him Jesus and His saints were in the free-fire zone on the northern border. The pastor was fiendishly clever and on the side of the rebels. The only way they could verify what he said was to join a Contra war party, and that might get them close to the Almighty sooner than they thought. The Contras, the children told him, took recruits as young as twelve.

"How do you play golf?"

"With a sort of stick and a ball," Johnny said, picking up a bamboo blackboard pointer and taking a swing at a stone.

"Oh yes, we do that."

"What, out here?" he asked, somewhat perplexed. The idea of suddenly finding a lost golf course in the middle of the Central American jungle, put there by Aztecs who had met Scottish buccaneers, was too much. "Not golf with a small white ball?"

"No, with a chicken. A live, male chicken."

"You hit the chicken with the stick? I mean the club?"

"Only if you lucky." Armstrong stuck out his little chest.

"But how do you get the chicken into the hole?"

When he said this they all looked at him as if he had taken leave of his senses.

"You buries it," said Armstrong.

"Buries it, teacher. Aren't we talking English right? You buries it," added another.

"In the ground?"

There was a silence.

"Where else you bury something?"

"And then you hit it with a stick?"

"Only if you lucky."

Johnny decided somehow, possibly culturally, he must be at cross purposes with the class, who smiled at him angelically under the banana-leaf sunshade. There was only one thing for it. "Could you show me?" he asked.

"You buy the chicken?" said Armstrong.

"Yes," he agreed, "of course." He hadn't a clue what he had let himself in for when half the class pitched into a flock of chickens and caught one. He was teaching the younger children in the open air while the older ones used a large hut as a schoolroom and there was nobody else about at this end of the settlement. The impish enjoyment was contagious. Rose and another girl fetched a stout wooden club from one of the huts as he watched fascinated to see what might happen.

"Now what do you do?"

"We bury the chicken," explained Armstrong, who had dug a small hole with his hands in the earth. The surprised bird was interred up to its neck and started to make an alarmed cheeping noise. Rose then tied her kerchief round Armstrong's eyes and spun him round and round while another boy handed him the stick. The chicken fell silent, as if by magic, while the blindfolded Armstrong listened like a hunter. Before Johnny could stop him he had brought the club down only inches from the fowl's head. He passed the stick and kerchief to another boy with the aggrieved air of a professional just over par.

"This is how we plays golf," said the child expansively. "When you hit the chicken you take it home and eat it . . . Only good Mr Jones I think would share it with the poor."

All at once Johnny noticed Father Anselm had been watching the spectacle.

"Johnny, I know these children are brutalized by the conflict, but that does not mean we have to join in their brutality." He stalked off, not waiting for a reply.

"Is that Mr Jones?" asked Rose.

"I used to think so," admitted Johnny. "Believe me, Rose, I really used to think so."

The next morning, Johnny learned raiders had come in the night. A guard had been knocked unconscious, probably with a machete judging from the ugly scalp wound. He was left for dead beside the small, mangrove-choked estuary on which the village stood. Among the things they discovered were missing was the extensive Perfect English medical kit, although it did not need anything from it to convince them Dr Annie had become ill. She tried to put a brave face on it at first as a concerned Tanya dabbed her forehead with water and brought her boiled milk. But by afternoon she was crying out, despite taking Catherine's aspirin tablets. The pain was in her stomach and it was not getting better. It looked serious even to Sarah, their medic.

"She's started to throw up," said Catherine. "What is it?" The Perfect English medic did not answer, but glanced pointedly at Anselm.

"What is it Father?" repeated Catherine.

"It's probably nothing to be concerned about. Probably just a bad bout of Montezuma's revenge."

"Is it, Sarah?" said Tanya apprehensively. She had come over to where they were talking, at the other end of the hut, in low whispers. "Why were you feeling her stomach? It is serious, isn't it?"

"It's appendicitis," said Sarah simply.

"A suspected appendicitis," corrected Anselm.

"And there's absolutely no point in becoming hysterical," she said, seeing the sudden flush on Tanya's face.

"What can you do?" asked Johnny.

Tanya looked as if she were about to break down, but there was another low moan from Dr Window's camp bed and she went across to her.

"Can't you do something? What happens if it bursts?" inquired Johnny.

"If it bursts Dr Annie dies," replied Sarah quietly. "But even if I had the operating kit from the pack, I doubt if she would survive surgery out here. It would become infected immediately. The soldiers say they can't spare us any drugs. They've been relying on us."

"Do you mean she *is* going to die?" demanded Johnny, stunned.

"We all have to die sometime," said Capitán Fernandez with a Latin finality. He had been standing quietly in the doorway. From the way he looked at Johnny and Bob it was clear whom he would have preferred the grim reaper to visit. "I have brought something which may help."

"Some morphine?" asked Sarah hopefully.

"No *Señora*. I cannot give you the drugs for my men. But I have brought you these." From the pocket of his jacket he pulled an elaborate rosary. Holy medallions flashed in the sunlight.

"These were my mother's . . . If the girl prays hard, very hard, she may still go to the kingdom of heaven." The *Capitán* lowered his voice. "It may be her perversions were committed in a state of ignorance."

"We were still thinking more in terms of this world, *Capitán*," said Sarah testily, but she took the beads.

Capitán Fernandez shrugged. "Your priest has not given me an answer on the other matter we discussed earlier."

"What other matter?" asked Catherine.

"We have Bluefields on the radio. I have to know if Father Anselm wants to attempt to summon a helicopter. I am not sure if they would risk one. The Americans have offered a million US dollars to anyone downing one of our Hinds, and to land here on the beach would be very dangerous."

"You knew about this?" Catherine said to Anselm and Sarah. "Have you thought about exactly what a delay could mean?"

"Yes, I have," said Anselm.

"And you are prepared to let someone die because you don't want to take the risk of calling a helicopter?"

"We could all die if I do call the chopper. The Contras might not just shoot it out of the air. They may watch where it lands and come and cut us all to pieces. Isn't that so?" The *Capitán* nodded reluctantly. He was obviously a Catholic of the old school, and the dilemma was painful to him. The sheen of guilt glistened on his forehead.

"Are you scared the army might order us all to evacuate, Father? You should have consulted us," said Johnny. "We would have found out about this sooner or later and then Dr Annie would have been on our conscience as much as yours. Or doesn't one life matter when it gets in the way of the new church?"

"That is a very childish and upsetting thing to say, Johnny, and I am certain you do not mean it," replied Anselm. "I suppose you would rather me risk the lives of the entire group?"

"If we cease to care about individuals we might as well. As far as I'm concerned it's tantamount to murder not to call for help."

"Lay off, Johnny," said Catherine. "It's better this doesn't get personal. Is it really that dangerous to lift her out of here?"

Anselm nodded. "How about you?" he asked Bob, who was frowning, trying to look a part of what was going on. "What do you think?"

"Me? Well, er, I think we have got to consider our Sandinista comrades' perspective . . . But I would hate anything to happen to Annie." He peered down at his Nike trainers. His revolutionary ruthlessness did not extend to Dr Window, to whom he had talked lyrically of proletarian sacrifice.

"Call the helicopter," said Catherine.

At the other end of the room the pretty Marxist academic moaned again. "For God's sake do something," shouted Tanya.

"Do you want me to radio for help?" asked Capitán Fernandez anxiously.

There was an uncomfortable silence.

"Yes, go and call it," said Anselm finally.

"You will take full responsibility? You see, if I call it in and things go wrong it would be very bad for me. Very bad, you understand. You must fill out an authorization. Afterwards, of course."

"Yes, anything, but could you radio now, please? There may be a helicopter in the vicinity," urged Catherine.

"So I have your word, priest?"

"Yes," said Anselm. The reply sounded like the hiss of a snake. The officer strode out of the hut.

After all their arguments about it, the helicopter thudded in unopposed from the sea like a belligerent dragonfly to set down on the firm sand at the river's mouth, sending dust and even small plants flying in every direction. The villagers had all come out to look at the beast while the Sandinista guards on sentry duty surrounded the settlement, probing the jungle for the first sign of attack. To Johnny, the squat war machine appeared invulnerable with its pods of rockets and bristling machine-guns. Two men gingerly carried Dr Annie on a stretcher along the narrow path to the beach and into the waiting aircraft. For a moment Tanya stood at the door under the turning rotors as if about to climb aboard and then took a step back, waving at the unsmiling crew, who, like Anselm, probably knew just how much of a risk they were taking.

The helicopter's engines began to howl, and Johnny shut his eyes as half the beach seemed to be hurled in the direction of a stand of palms under which they were stupidly sheltering. A large green coconut missed Bob by inches but he did not notice. He was watching the helicopter with evident awe as it lifted only several feet clear of the ground then flung itself at full power back out over the sea. A soldier crouching in the cargo door had a rifle in his hands. The aircraft banked about a mile off shore and swung along the coast out of range of any machine-gun fire from the jungle behind them. Then it was gone and they were alone again. If such a machine – according to Bob a flying piece of artillery that could obliterate a town single handed – fled with such speed, it did not bode well for the safety of their group or the soldiers with them.

"Are you okay, Johnny?"

It was Anselm.

"Yes, I've just got a bit of sand in my eye. More of a mote than a beam, Father."

"I pray that Dr Annie is going to be all right, but I hope you can appreciate my anxieties. I was not trying to be callous. Do you understand?"

"I'm beginning to, Father," Johnny said, looking at the bank of haze to the south where the Hind had just disappeared.

13

The helicopter rescue of Dr Window should have been a cause for rejoicing, but ten minutes after the aircraft's departure the radio crackled into life and they heard a faint transmission from the Hind many miles to the south. Capitán Fernandez could not decipher the whole message, but certain phrases were clear enough to them all.

"Everything is on fire . . . the village is burning . . . I cannot go to help . . ." the pilot kept repeating in Spanish.

Then contact was broken. A village, probably one they had visited, was destroyed, the inhabitants massacred. No one referred to it directly; no one speculated out loud. But Perfect English left Pakakawas as soon as they could get themselves organized and struck north again, stopping at sullen driftwood settlements on the river banks where the people hated them on sight, offering them urine instead of water at a place called Saslaya; and in Rushwas someone threw a nest of jungle hornets into a hut they were cleaning out to use as a schoolroom. Father Anselm had carried the angry football out of the door on the end of a bayonet and dismissed it as a prank. Only the priest, as a veteran of Vietnam, and perhaps Capitán Fernandez could have known what the trek through the jungle was going to be like; the mud, the weariness and the fear of it all.

A worrying jungle sore covered Johnny's left shoulder. They had been travelling the rivers for too long and many of the soldiers had painful, ulcerated bites on their faces and bodies. Sarah, the medic, felt so ill she could not tend to them any more. The immense green barrier sucked the strength out of them and caused the light-headed weakness which grew day by day. Johnny did not become sick but the sensation was always there like a toothache. The jungle was forcing its way into him and trying to take over. Only their Miskito guides, who were a part of that jungle of ironwood trees and foul swollen rivers, went untouched, even thrived on the place. So, curiously, did Anselm.

At the drizzly presentation ceremony in Kayaska, several of the men of the village sat smoking on a log, sneering at the desperate rag-tag band of strangers who huddled around Anselm. The priest still insisted on going through the motions of awarding the Perfect English certificates and brightly coloured badges, which the children always prized. In that settlement, the twelfth and last in their programme, the teaching had been a fiasco. As in the other villages, English was these children's first language, but on their parents' orders they chattered away to each other in their Miskito tongue as an affirmation of apartness. Johnny had read how the Miskito had always preferred English to their own rasping Indian language, of which many of them knew only a few words, partly because English was more versatile and also since it annoyed the hated Spanish. But as soon as the servants of the Sandinistas arrived with their Perfect English programme, it became the language of the enemy and the Indians retreated into Miskito. Instead of bringing them nearer to the Sandinista revolution Johnny realized Perfect English was alienating the Miskito further, encouraging their nationalism. To the villagers, the badge presentation ceremony would be just another ridiculous game played out by the Sandinista stooges. A weary Catherine tried patiently to form the children into lines. She was not used to failing. Johnny had caught her on her knees praying a few nights before, her devotion increasing with fatigue.

"You have all done very well in this village. Better than in the other villages," boomed Anselm as it started to rain harder. Mothers began to take their little ones inside.

Catherine looked anxious. The group had been told specifically by Capitán Fernandez not to put on any plays in this settlement. Johnny thought the presentation was a farce. So did the villagers.

"All stop now it rain," said one, grinning broadly.

"No, wait a second," urged Catherine, standing up beside Anselm on the box he was using as a pulpit in the little clearing under a dripping mango tree. "All of the children get a big kiss with their badges."

"Do I get a kiss too, Spanish whore?" shouted a ginger-haired man seated on the log. One of the Sandinistas cocked his rifle.

"Come along, children. Come up here and get your pretty books and badges and pencils. I wish I'd had coloured pencils like this when I was a child. Every child on the Father's list gets a big red badge."

The Miskito troublemaker stepped forward.

"Are we all going to get a kiss, Sandinista whore? Where are you going to kiss me?"

Catherine turned to Anselm. All at once she had lost her poise. What the man said wounded her. Her shoulders sloped in resignation.

"Whore!"

Johnny could not stand the tension any longer. He had been leaning against a hut and now walked over to Anselm and Catherine. A young Sandinista followed him, trying to make every step seem casual.

The Miskito would not shut up.

"What are you going to do now, papist Madonna whore? Shoot our children like you shot them at Waspan when we were burying our dead? The dead of the bloody Red Christmas when you moved us from our homes and butchered our people? Who gives you Spanish the right to move a free people doing no one no harm? To move them from their homes and fishing grounds?" At the back of the crowd Johnny caught sight of Capitán Fernandez ordering his men into position around the huts. Unfortunately, so did the ginger-haired speaker. "That's it. That's your only answer. Kill us all. Shoot the children. Tell you what though, Miss Sandinista, if you do you'll never leave this river alive. Some plenty bad men near here. Very bad men . . ." He laughed. Johnny looked into the dark huts round them. Many of these people had shotguns and not all the village had turned up for the so-called ceremony. The rest could be anywhere. Had they gone to fetch the Contras? Catherine in her once-white cotton dress silhouetted against the trunk of the mango presented a perfect target.

"Come on, let's get on with it," he said, grabbing the box full of certificates and badges.

"No, don't," warned Catherine.

"You just watch me."

The children, many hugging their mothers' legs to hide, looked towards him. Directly in front of Johnny was a woman with a dark face and bushy fair hair cascading over her shoulders. She put her hands around her two girls' heads as he stepped over to them. Their hair was tied in old fashioned pigtails and he remembered, although they refused to be taught, both girls' eyes had lit up when he showed them the picture books.

"Now, you'll take one of these badges, won't you? If not I'll just have to throw them in the river." One child turned to look at the red and white sheriff's star. She held out her hand.

"Let me pin it on you."

"Don't touch her," snarled the mother.

Ignoring the woman, he quickly bent down and had the pin fastened before a defensive maternal kick laid him on his back. He got up hastily and passed a badge to the other little girl. In a rush all the children wanted one. Both the certificates and the badges were soon snatched away.

The crowd carried their bright booty back to the rancid huts. "Oh well," Anselm said. "I suppose we can't get things right all of the time."

They moved off to the safety of their hut. Johnny followed Anselm back out onto a tumbledown veranda, where the priest immediately began to record the irritating details of their failure at this village in his smart blue ledger. The Sandinista guards looked on suspiciously as the American crouched over his book, like a sixteenth-century Jesuit with his abacus – except Anselm had a solar-powered calculator to compute the scores on the simple aptitude tests they had tried to administer. Johnny mischievously considered asking the priest to work out how many Sandinistas could dance on the head of a pin. Yet he had one question.

"Father Anselm?" The soft invocation of his name linked to God was impossible for any priest to refuse.

"Yes, Johnny." A smile spread over the now-bearded face below a faintly ridiculous headband of twisted silk.

"I'm just curious, Father, about the awarding of the Perfect English stars. In the last village the only kids to show any improvement, or whose parents expressed interest, were not given stars. One child who wouldn't even talk and whose mother spat on us was given a badge and a certificate. Getting across the political message is all very well. But isn't it a bit of a contradiction if we award Perfect English badges not only to the enthusiastically imperfect but to the downright bad?" Johnny yearned to trip the priest up. To upset him. To pick a hole in his precious programme.

"We have to encourage the stubborn ones, Johnny. I award those things according to how hard they try, not on how well they do," said Anselm slowly. "Those children didn't throw the badges back in my face, did they?"

"No," Johnny admitted.

"So next time someone comes up river they might be more receptive to some education. All we are doing is preparing the ground, Johnny, making them a little more open to the ideas that are changing the rest of Nicaragua and most of the Third World. We can lead them to the church of liberation." He paused for a moment. "I think we have all gained a lot here, Johnny. I just fear we are losing you. . . ."

The next morning, a boy soldier crouched beside Johnny ceaselessly quartering the jungle across the river with nervous brown eyes, his rifle at the ready. The advance party of canoes had just left, taking Sarah, the sick medic, and half of their guard to where they hoped trucks were waiting to run them to Siuna and then on to Managua. The young Sandinista spat in the river for luck.

"My mother will kill me if I don't come home," he grinned. "She doesn't want to bury a coffin full of bricks. Here on the Coast no one ever finds the bodies."

Anselm called Johnny over to help with the packing. An immediate problem was what to do with the theatrical costumes. Johnny found a Perfect English badge on one and put it in his pocket.

"Are we going to take this home?" he asked the priest, holding up what once had been the Socialist Phoenix. It was a sorry sight. Those feathers not singed were covered in an inky black fungus. "I don't think it's much use to the enemy."

"Burn it," said Anselm bitterly. "I never want to see it again. The plays were a mistake. These people are too literal."

"I don't know. They certainly appreciate tragedy."

"Johnny," he said. "You know what the Sandinistas mean when they say someone is an objective Contra?"

Johnny shook his head.

"An objective Contra is someone who claims to be a Sandinista but whose attitudes and actions help the other side. Such a person needs watching. He is a dangerous man."

"Are you saying I support the Contra?"

"No, but out here your juvenile behaviour is not a joke. It only slows us down. If you want to get these boys killed, just keep on doing what you're doing. For heaven's sake, shape up."

"Heaven, Father? I thought paradise had been jettisoned with everything else that prevents the church becoming part of the revolution."

"I will make sure you never work in this country again, Johnny, or with any other liberation theology group," declared Anselm. Catherine walked quickly towards them from one of the huts.

"Spoken like a priest, Anselm," began Johnny bitterly.

"Shut up, both of you," snapped Catherine, breaking in on them. "You can argue all you want when we are back in Managua. The soldiers have picked up a message from a Sandinista patrol which has engaged a large Contra force not far west of here. They want us to get out as quickly as possible and make that rendezvous with the trucks." Johnny strained to hear the sound of gunfire but there was only the usual chatter of the forest and the splutter of outboards. "There is another problem," she added.

"What's that?" Anselm frowned.

"One of the pangas has been sabotaged. There is a hole in the bow below the waterline. It's useless."

Anselm sat down on a box and shook his head.

"What do we do now? That's the third canoe since we started. We won't have enough room. We should take everything that might be of use to the enemy."

"No problem," said Benjamin, the paddler, who had joined them. "My brother lives in this village and has an old panga. We can swop the outboard from the one that is sunk. But you must pay him, Father Anselm. It hardly takes any time to fix. I need another person to stay behind, to give weight to the front of the boat and help paddle if the engine fails."

"I'll stay behind," volunteered Johnny.

The priest looked at him and then put a hand on his shoulder. "I hope you realize the risk you're taking. Please forgive me if I misjudged you," was all he said. The remains of the Socialist Phoenix burnt fitfully on a fire the villagers appeared to be attempting to put out.

As she was about to leave, Catherine turned to Johnny, trying unsuccessfully to hide the fear in her eyes as she kissed him.

"I love you, Johnny," she whispered. "For God's sake follow as quickly as you can. I want to be with you always."

"Do you?" he said.

"Please, Johnny, I do. I really do. I want us to be together again." She kissed him once more and stepped into an overloaded panga. "Don't be long!" she shouted.

Johnny stood on the bank and watched until they disappeared round a bend in the river. Anselm was in the lead canoe, sitting cross legged in a yoga position. He could not seem to do anything without affectation. Johnny still suspected he had tried to take Catherine away from him, luring her with the ornaments of simple faith and revolutionary commitment, but really his motives were no different from the whisky priest who tempts a village woman with a bottle of spirits and a few cigarettes onto a filthy mattress. Politics was Father Anselm's whisky. You could almost smell it on his breath.

It took longer than expected for Benjamin to transfer the engine to his brother's canoe and then to load it with the remaining supplies. On the bank nearby a little girl was busy with one of the Perfect English picture books. "She's my niece," said the paddler with a proud smile. The six-year-old did not look up, but continued colouring a long American car orange. The typical American family she had crayoned brown, and a fire hydrant had been turned into a palm tree. The only other scribbled change was to give the man of the house a rifle. Eventually she turned to Johnny.

"I go to America one day. My mother says . . . Please do not let the Spanish soldiers kill us." But as he tried to find the words to reassure her she returned to her labours unconcerned. She waved goodbye when they left.

Johnny was relieved when they set off. It was dangerous for a long canoe winding its way through that maze of channels, but soon the whole absurd adventure would be over – and Catherine had said she wanted to be with him always. He sat in the front of the panga, a rifle across his knees. He turned to the paddler, who grinned at him. Johnny felt the Perfect English badge in his trouser pocket and fastened it on his shirt front. It was a hot day, and but for the ever present danger of running smack into a Contra patrol he might have settled back and enjoyed the changing green mystery of the jungle. He was almost hypnotized by the banks slipping past and the low buzz of the engine, when a tremendous explosion came from behind, sending birds flying in panic across the river and monkeys shrieking to the tops of the trees.

A second, smaller explosion was followed by automatic fire. Benjamin stopped the engine and listened as the shooting went on and on. Then came a silence far worse, as if everything in the jungle were hiding . . . and waiting.

Benjamin restarted the outboard, and before Johnny could object had swung the canoe around and was heading back to the village. Kayaska was burning. It was obvious from the hideous black pall of smoke rising above the forest. The paddler appeared utterly devastated, and Johnny remembered how fondly he had looked at his niece as she coloured the pictures in her Perfect English book. Just before the long bend which led up to the settlement, Benjamin cut the engine again. Johnny said a prayer. There was little else he could do as their canoe nosed stealthily forward, propelled on by the clean, powerful strokes of the paddler.

Sweat had begun to run from Johnny's hand onto the butt of his rifle. After the steady progress of the engine the paddling seemed desperately slow. Near to Kayaska the jungle was as noiseless as a tomb. His eyes searched the purple shade between the trees on both banks, trying to spot the first sign of ambush as they inched closer. They pulled round the final bend. The huts were hidden by a stand of trees, above which the smoke still billowed. Why should the Contras burn a village where so many supported them? It did not make sense.

The settlement was clearly visible now. All the houses were either burning or had been reduced to twisted skeletons. Bats roosting in the mango tree had been put to flight by the explosions and wheeled like demons around the ruined huts.

"Keep down, Johnny," came a hoarse whisper from the back of the boat. "We get out when we reach that tree." Before the village's jetty a tree grew out over the water. Johnny surprised himself by leaping deftly onto the bank, as Benjamin secured the canoe and stepped out too.

"Johnny."

"Yes, Benjamin?"

"Follow me close."

The Indian ducked under some trailing branches and was inching through low bushes to the spot where the settlement's pigs had been kept. Blood seeped out of one huge sow while piglets still suckled her teats.

They rounded the side of a burning hut and looked at the clearing they had left only a short while ago. Johnny blinked. Now there were bodies underneath the mango tree. The Indian turned to him.

"I go out there," he whispered. "If they shoot, you stay out of sight. Hide good. I got to go out there. I have to find my brother's family." No sooner had he spoken than he was edging towards the tangled heap of limbs, moving with the slow fluidity of a chameleon. Johnny screwed himself into as small a ball as his six-foot frame allowed and watched in a mixture of horror and admiration.

Through a gap in the smouldering wood wall he was crouched beside Johnny saw the bodies of a whole family. One man had been caught by a burst of fire and was propped against a hut, his elbows forced in by the impact and his tortured fingers frozen over a shattered chest. At first glance his wife appeared to be protecting their two children with her body, until Johnny noticed the pool of bright red under them. A burning shard from the roof fell and began to splutter on her back. He shuddered and shifted his position slightly to see more. One of the children, a boy, was bent under his mother. The other was a girl. Both had been shot. The boy was still wearing his Perfect English badge. Then a cry came from the clearing.

It was a cry of anguish, not a request for Johnny's uncertain help. Benjamin was standing over the pile of corpses. Slowly he put down his AK 47 and dropped to his knees sobbing, pulling the limp body of his niece towards him. He wept, a long, high-pitched despairing wail, and began to mumble to the child in a language Johnny did not understand. He smoothed the child's hair out of her eyes, talking to her as if she were still alive, and among the flood of Miskito words Johnny could hear him repeat in English over and over again, "Forgive me, forgive me."

Suddenly the paddler dropped the little girl's body and turned towards the trees. Johnny leant out from his hiding place and tried to see what, or whom, Benjamin was staring at. There was a movement at the other side of the village.

"No!" cried Benjamin. "It's me. Don't shoot. Why did you do this? You promised!" Then a burst of fire knocked him off his feet, his body quivering as it joined the other lifeless forms. It seemed the attackers wanted to sanitize the village of every untidy human. Johnny remained frozen for a second, and then began to edge backwards. The evening light reflected from the bright red of one of the children's badges in the clearing. A twig snapped close by and immediately Johnny felt a sharp point in his back.

There was laughter as he jumped and he forced himself to look round into the beaming face of a fair-haired Miskito.

"Time you go and join your friends, Spaniard."

14

Every nerve in his body was concentrated on the sharp point of the knife breaking the skin of his back and urging him painfully forward. But the scene in the clearing almost made Johnny forget his own predicament. A tall man in a faded red coat trimmed with gold brocade was poking at the bodies of children with a silver-topped Malacca cane. The creature hopped nimbly over the corpses like some dreadful russet carrion bird. The warriors emerging from the jungle had no uniform. Large, fierce Miskito, they looked more like the pirates they were descended from than farmers or fishermen. Several wore captured Sandinista combat jackets but the rest were dressed in the most brightly coloured clothes, in open defiance of the laws of camouflage, and more than one savage individual boasted a yellow scarf bound round his head. An immensely fat man had a purple waistcoat and a gold earring. Johnny was being propelled towards the red-coated figure, who raised his head.

"I find this Spaniard. I kill him, Highness? I told to bring any white folks to you before killing . . . " The knife point twisted against Johnny's back, making him cry out. "He wears the badge so we kill him?" The voice was gruff and insistent but the one he addressed as Highness, who stared at the Perfect English star, seemed scarcely the sort to disobey. His features were more negroid than Indian or European, yet the closely set eyes were blue and as expressionless as a reptile's. His skin was light and freckled while his hair was long, curly and fair. He embodied every disparate physical trait of the Miskito and, judging from the carnage, every wickedness.

He took a pace forward so he could look down into Johnny's face. A silk scarf hung from the leathery neck over a white shirt and in the belt of muddied trousers was stuck an automatic pistol. A strong hand tore the badge off Johnny's shirt and the thick lips spread into a grin, showing a mouthful of bad teeth.

A bony finger indicated what his raiders were doing. What he pointed to made Johnny begin to mumble a prayer. Men were enthusiastically seeking out the children. Nearby, one pulled a little girl, still clutching a doll, from under her mother whose body had failed to protect her from a burst of automatic fire which had killed them both. The Perfect English badge shone clearly on her chest. First, the man carefully detached the star from the thin fabric of the child's frock and laid it on the ground. Next, taking a sharp knife from his belt, he dangled the body like a rag doll and severed an ear from the head with one stroke. As Johnny watched, his mouth dry with terror, the man wiped the knife on his trousers and, picking up the badge, threaded the ear on the pin and put it in a blood-stained canvas bag. Johnny felt steel touch his own ear and instinctively cringed as those around him howled with laughter. Then the leader in the red coat spoke.

"We are Palmerston. Prince of the Miskito. Are you American?"

Johnny tried several times to answer but what he had just seen done to the child and might any moment happen to him had made his body revolt. Eventually he swallowed and said:

"I am English, your Highness."

"Kneel," Palmerston growled.

Johnny knelt. The tip of a blade still teased his earlobe.

"Where are the others? Where is the American and the girl teachers? Where are they?" He seemed to know a lot about Perfect English.

"They have gone, your Highness. They are far away up river." Or so he hoped. Johnny suddenly thought he would never see Catherine again. He was going to die for something he no longer believed in.

"We read your thoughts, Englishman. English and Miskito very close. We see you know our sister, Queen Elizabeth of England. Palmerston visits her often. We can fly to any corner of the world in a second. We talk to her in her bedroom. We friends. I love my little sister Elizabeth ..." Around him there was a chillingly respectful silence.

Johnny looked at the earth and tried to stop himself shaking.

"We see in your mind you are not a Communist like the Sandinista Antichrist. We ask my little sister Queen Elizabeth if you are a Communist. She says no. She talk across the oceans. My brain is a shining telephone. She says Palmerston must receive Englishman. She and her fancy man the Duke of York. But she no longer loves him. She only wears her walking-out frillies for Palmerston."

"But he was wearing the star, Highness. The mark of death," said Johnny's captor.

"It is also a mark of innocence in this case. Why should this man mark himself for death?" protested a handsome young Miskito who stood at Palmerston's right hand. Johnny couldn't believe his good fortune. "We must ransom him," continued his defender anxiously.

Palmerston seemed to be torn for a moment between the advice from his royal sister across the sea and the more immediate pleasure of killing Johnny. Suddenly he stooped down and picked up an ear unpierced by a badge. He forced it under Johnny's nose.

"You eat this, we let you live, Englishman."

Johnny looked at the bloody fragment with mounting horror.

"No!" he shouted, from sheer revulsion.

"Ha, ha!" Palmerston threw back his head and laughed. It was an ugly sound, like a body being dragged across gravel. "Englishmen only eat roast beef. This one comes with us. We give him to our nephew Jeremy. We wish it," he said with a leering grin, and popped the child's ear into his own gaping mouth, chewing it like gum.

Johnny passed out.

When he came round an evil smelling black bag was on his head and his hands and feet were tied. From the sound of an outboard and a strange bouncing motion he knew he was in a boat. At first he thought they might drop him over the side. Strong hands manhandled Johnny onto what he realized was a stretcher and he was taken indoors. He heard the sound of steps fading on a wooden floor. Someone was untying him, and pulled the bag off his head.

"My name's Jeremy. I'm called after a famous Miskito king. You really have the most lovely hair . . . What's your name?"

"Johnny Morgan."

"Morgan? That's lucky. The first governor of Miskita was Sir Henry Morgan. It may mean you live longer," said Jeremy, patting Johnny's hand.

Johnny instinctively pulled away. The room had the ephemeral quality of a junk shop. He had been deposited on an old leather couch. There were purple plastic anenomes on a Formica teak table and pictures of body builders on the walls. Jeremy smelt strongly of Chanel No. 5. Johnny feared the worst.

"Don't worry, Johnny, I'm not going to ravish you. It's my uncle who's the real beast. I was educated in the United States, thank you very much. I may occasionally be consumed with a passion for my fellow man, but never a passion to eat them like he does. Did you see him munch that ear . . .? Drink some of this rum, Johnny Morgan, you'll feel better. Palmerston is very strong on old Miskito customs, of which eating people is just one. He actually believes if you gobble up your fellow man you take his strength and will live for ever. I hope you don't think I'm a savage too, Johnny." Jeremy's deep blue eyes gazed longingly into his. "What's wrong Johnny? There's no need to be frightened of me."

"The village . . . They were your people. I don't understand why you killed them all."

"My uncle hates the other Indian Contra groups. He thinks they are Communists. He believes the poor Miskitos the Sandinistas resettled from the north are all spies. A few months ago he wiped out several of their villages. The Sandys came looking for the culprits and caught his brother. This may shock you, but a deal was made that we should actually massacre certain settlements for them. To someone like my uncle it was hardly a problem. You could say he has a taste for it."

"Do you mean that was not the first village?"
"No, I think seven or eight have been visited in that way. Perfect English villages." Jeremy chuckled. "The only perfect English around here now is on Miskito gravestones."
"The villages we taught at?"
"I think you are beginning to understand."
Johnny looked at the young man incredulously.
"For reasons best known to themselves, ambitious individuals among the Sandinista in fact wanted Palmerston to wipe out villages, or so they told his brother. But they only wished particular key settlements destroyed and selected families killed. The problem was to find a way of communicating to us which ones to destroy and who to kill. Then they hit on your programme, by which they could mark the children of the families they wanted eliminated by that badge. So you see, we get a bounty for each badge logged with proof of the victim's death. Of course, my uncle never saw further than the dollars."
"What do you mean?"
"The Sandinista plotters obviously want to stir up opposition on the Coast, not contain it. The kinsfolk of the murdered Miskito are eager to avenge their brothers, and the war on the Coast escalates. Next, we are surprised to find an American army team wishes to photograph these villages and the badges to make it look like Sandinista troops massacred the Miskito using the education programme as a cover . . . By then I think plotters in the government in Managua are playing big politics to discredit their present leadership so they can seize power. Brutes who will take a stronger line with the troubles here. Brutes who are more pro-Soviet. That is why I spoke up for you. No one who knew the deadly significance of those badges would be caught wearing one."
"You mean Perfect English has helped . . . ."
"Yes, Johnny. In a way you murdered those children. Perfect English gave out those pretty sheriffs' stars which killed just as surely as pulling a trigger. We have a guilt in common, you and I."
Johnny leant back on the couch. The garbled message about the burning village when Dr Annie had been airlifted

out in the helicopter now made sense. He was numbed. Johnny had given the badges to all the children in the last village and they all had died. Tears ran down his face and the young Miskito let him weep. Utter panic began to take hold of him. How had ordinary German teachers and priests who handed out yellow stars to Jews felt when they discovered what the emblem really signified? That its purpose was death? How could he ever rid himself of such a sin?

"Don't cry, Johnny. Remember, the Spanish priests didn't blame themselves for bringing measles and spreading death with every Mass."

"Who was behind this?" he asked angrily after many minutes. "Was it Father Anselm, our priest?"

"Someone must have known," said Jeremy, offering a handkerchief. "Our informant, Benjamin, said the Father awarded the badges. I only heard with whom the deal was made in Managua. I am telling you this because I believe the Sandinista plotters will now want to eliminate us. Perhaps you can aid me . . . I have to escape this nightmare."

"Who gave the order? Do you know the name?"

"We don't know his full name. Drink up. I want to show you something, or rather someone, that may confirm what I say. Please do exactly what I tell you and I will help you." He took Johnny's glass. "As I explained, we don't know the top man's full name, but he calls himself Bliss. Have you heard of him?"

15

"Follow me," said Jeremy when Johnny had recovered somewhat, leading him outside. A rivulet ran down one edge of the settlement; in the water stood several large inflatable rubber craft and a half-submerged wooden launch. Camouflage netting was slung from the jungle canopy. The rest of the encampment looked like a breaker's yard. Houses were built from sections of boat, roofed with sailcloth or the odd piece of corrugated iron tied together with banana sisal and patched with palm leaf. A stinking midden ran down from the houses into the rivulet, and a vulture that had negotiated the camouflage netting hopped away from it in uncharacteristic disgust. Here and there the jungle had tried to return, poking its way through the ships' timbers, bits of decking and a discarded slot machine. In front of a building with a cross, which Johnny supposed was a church – although he could hardly imagine any of Palmerston's crew listening to a sermon – was a powder-blue Ford Thunderbird, without its wheels, resting on four piles of stones and oily rags. Although rusting, and with no place to go in the roadless forest, the automobile seemed somehow tidier and better maintained than anything else in the rubbish-strewn vicinity. A glossy black monkey was picking fleas from its long tail on the car's roof.

"That is the official limousine," said Jeremy. "Isn't it dignified? If you are lucky his Highness will take you for a ride in it. It is a shame there are no highways to drive on. We have to carry it around on our backs. My uncle got it from a merchant ship we forced onto the rocks."

Jeremy continued down a muddy path, stepping over boat chandlery and, strangest of all, a rusting pile of kitchen scissors. Johnny grazed his knees on a propeller drive shaft unhelpfully dumped across the track. On a small creek to their left, men stripped to the waist were loading several black inflatables with boxes and provisions. Beyond them the channel became wider, and on an outcrop of sandstone covered in ferns and small white orchids more Miskito were scraping the decks of a blackened old tugboat. There were several recent bullet holes in its otherwise jaunty bridge. It looked indestructible. Here and there was a twinkle of gleaming brass and on the wooden rail near the stern Johnny made out a maker's plate. On it were the words, "Harland and Woolf, Belfast".

"I wouldn't have thought you could get such a large boat up here," he said as they approached the tug. On the foredeck a group of Indians were repairing a powerful winch. In contrast to their surroundings, everything on the boat was painted, polished and generally in its place.

"This is my uncle's equivalent of a Royal Yacht, except we have to keep changing her name," remarked Jeremy, patting the side of the boat. "It's his pride and joy and surprisingly useful. Very fast and strong, while the hull is so thick it's practically bullet proof. We use it to drag captured boats from the shipping lanes. She's a treasure. We fix no armaments to the deck so if she has to run for international waters we can dump anything really incriminating over the side and head for a friendly port. That way we have no trouble with the American fleet. We tell them it's a salvage vessel, which is partly true. We have no problem getting her up here. She has a shallow draft, and we are nearer the sea than you think."

Johnny dodged to avoid an oil drum thrown carelessly into the jungle from the high-sided boat. The crackling blue flash of welding made him blink. The creek opened out onto a lake, or it could have been a lagoon as mangrove grew around the edges. All manner of small craft, from fishing trawlers to pleasure yachts, were putrefying among the rotting vegetation.

They continued walking along the septic shoreline, but Johnny's mind was no longer on the scenery. Who had betrayed them in the Perfect English group? Who had been Bliss's contact on the inside? Johnny could not help but think it was Anselm. Had the American priest been party all along to the plan to destroy the villages? It was true he had high-ranking Sandinista contacts and Perfect English could only be consolidated if his friends gained power. Had he somehow been convinced what he was doing was part of a just war against the Contra? Was there no sin he wouldn't stoop to for his church of liberation?

Jeremy stopped at a hut and opened a surprisingly stoutly built door. Inside there was a foul-smelling room where two guards stood by a steel cage. It stank of urine. In the corner of the cage was a huddled creature which, before his eyes became accustomed to the gloom, Johnny thought was some sort of animal on a bed of filthy straw.

"Here is another meddler in the affairs of our state," said Jeremy. His tone had changed for the benefit of the guards, one of whom jerked a chain attached to a metal collar around the man's neck. There was a whimper of pain.

"Stand up," commanded Jeremy, reaching into his pocket and taking out a damp packet of Chesterfields. "Here you are." The bearded captive shuffled across the dung encrusted floor of his cage towards the cigarette which Jeremy dropped as the man stretched out a battered paw. He seemed pathetically grateful as he scrabbled for it among his bedding. Jeremy gave him a light.

"What did he do wrong?" asked Johnny in a whisper. His throat tightened. He did not want to be put on a chain in a cage.

"He helped bring us those pretty new inflatables you saw, and many guns. He arrived quite unannounced one day, which was his first mistake. Palmerston did not find the brutes with him so interesting. They are now dead. This one is a US Naval intelligence combat photographer. He came here to take pictures of the atrocities for his government and now he is in danger of becoming one himself." Jeremy cupped a hand to Johnny's ear and whispered. "They also brought a freezer for my uncle and now two of them are in it."

"But what did they do *wrong*?"

"Exactly what I said. Palmerston decided they were spies, too. It doesn't matter to him that they are employed to do such things in a professional capacity to assist us. If that isn't biting the hand that feeds you, I don't know what is. But then, my uncle has quite an appetite."

"You mean to say their crime was to supply you with guns?"

"Yes."

"But surely you need guns? Surely you need the Americans to supply you with guns in the future?"

"I'm afraid that to my uncle the mere fact we occasionally need these munitions does not excuse the American temerity in thinking they can just waltz in and start interfering. This idiot made the mistake of telling my uncle how they were both fighting for democracy. Palmerston loathes democracy. Miskita is a monarchy and the Americans have never been forgiven for pushing you Brits out at the end of the last century. But worst of all our photographer here quibbled when Palmerston asked him to pay for the privilege of taking pictures of the massacred villages. He claimed a deal had already been struck with this man Bliss in Managua, who appears to be playing both sides. As you can see, it was the wrong thing to say."

The Indian guards made some approving grunts. The American's right eyebrow had begun to quiver."

"Tell my guest your name," ordered Jeremy.

"B-B-Brooks. James B-B-Brooks from Baltimore. I'm only a photographer . . ." The chain jerked again and the poor man got back to his feet. The entire side of his face had begun to twitch violently. "Why are you doing this to me? We were trying to help you."

"What do you know of the Perfect English programme working for the Sandinistas, Mr Brooks? What do you know of Father Anselm? You know what will happen if you lie. We have just captured my friend Johnny here. I'm trying to educate him. He's an *Internationalista*. I'll leave you with him, Johnny. We'll be outside when you have finished. The air is stale in here." Both guards followed Jeremy out of the door.

Johnny watched Brooks in silence for some time as he crouched in the cage, which was less than five feet high. A hole in the timber floor took away the filth.

"How long have you been here?"

"I'll tell you anything . . . anything," the man pleaded, bracing himself as if expecting the neck-jarring tug on his collar. He rocked his head from side to side and began to pace the cell like a wild animal in a zoo.

"Weeks," he said at last. The voice was a whisper. "I have lost track of time. I wish they would be done with it and finish me off . . . They made me watch as the others were killed. We thought Palmerston's was just another Contra group, but he's no freedom fighter. He's nothing but a total psycho, a thief and a murderer . . . who's on whichever side that suits him. Help me, will you?"

"Do you mean have a word with him? I'd like to do all I can but in the circumstances I don't think it would do much good coming from me." Johnny was most anxious to keep as far away as possible from Palmerston. He could still see those bad teeth chomping on a child's ear.

"No, I don't mean that," agreed Brooks, desperately. "It would be no good. The man is worse than the devil. No, take the chain and hook it onto that big nail on the beam above you. One swing will break my neck and they'll not be able to do anything more to me. It will be instantaneous. It will snap my spinal cord. For God's sake, help me put myself out of this misery."

For a moment Johnny thought he had misheard.

"Please. . . ."

"I'm sorry, I can't."

"Please. I'll tell you anything, just do that for me. They will kill me soon, slowly, as they killed the others. It was horrible. You're my only hope."

"Suicide . . . it's a mortal sin," mumbled Johnny, half to himself.

The eyes under the matted black hair were pleading. Puffed grey lips like squashed mushrooms creased into a bitter smile. He had been repeatedly beaten. But even on such a face a flicker of amusement could still show.

"You're a Catholic?"

"Yes."

"Well I'm not. My parents are Christian Scientists. I would

help you if you were in the same position. It's nothing to do with your faith. It's human decency, a question of mercy."

Johnny picked up the chain and, hauling it through the bars, reached up to the beam. He held the link near the nail and kept it there. His hand was steady.

"Tell me about Father Anselm."

"Maybe I have heard the name . . . But they make us work separately. I wouldn't have information on someone working on the project inside the country . . . ."

Johnny pulled back the link of chain from the nail and the man began to talk faster.

"The CIA has agents in all those educational programmes . . . Infiltration is a matter of policy. We'd have someone inside this Perfect English group, I'm sure. These church and literacy groups are a way into countries that won't entertain the Peace Corps."

"And Father Anselm?" said Johnny.

"I'm sure I've heard his name mentioned but that's all. Help me, will you?"

It was no use. If he pushed it he was certain Brooks would tell him anything. Truth had probably been a stranger to the intelligence agent even before he was tortured. Now it was useless. Johnny dropped the chain.

"Someone told me about a priest working for the Company. It might be your Father Anselm. Christ fella, put the chain on the nail, please . . ." But Johnny ignored him. He had done enough lately to risk his immortal soul. Anyway, there was something about Brooks that reminded him of Anselm. He was sick of being conned.

"Wait!" screamed the agent, summoning all his strength. His voice petered out and he fell on his knees and begged. "Kill me, please. Look on me as an enemy. You were working with the Sandinistas. Well, I'm on the other side. An American supplying the Contras. Do it! Sins have to be suspended in a war, otherwise conflict would be impossible."

"No," said Johnny simply. "I'm not on anyone's side any more." He turned his back on the prisoner and walked out.

Escape was all that mattered, at the earliest opportunity. He could do nothing for Brooks.

Jeremy touched his elbow. "Do not worry," he said gently. "That will not happen to you. I have just been told Johnny has friends among the Miskito. Come with me." The smiling half-Indian, half-European features hardly conveyed reassurance. An argument was going on by one of the boats nearby that was nearly sinking under the weight of equipment and stores loaded on it. The encampment appeared to be on the move.

Jeremy drew him to one side. "We are going in to my uncle now. After seeing Brooks I don't have to warn you to watch what you say. He may tell you about a trip we will be making tomorrow."

Palmerston's dwelling was mainly composed of a rotting wooden prefabricated builder's shack, the type which came ready to assemble in a crate. Joined to it, forming an elaborate porch, was the bridge of a merchant ship from whose cargo hold the shack may have come. Paint peeled from the metal. Next to this "palace" was a flagpole on which the Union Jack hung like a wet dish cloth.

"Don't worry, that's not in your honour. Palmerston regards it as our flag as well. Sometimes he claims the Atlantic Coast is every bit as British as Guernsey or Gibraltar. He makes me write letters to your Foreign Office on occasion. We never seem to get a reply. Now," Jeremy continued, "you are going to meet a friend." Johnny prayed Catherine had not been captured.

As he stepped into Palmerston's domain the first thing he noticed was a smell of mothballs and, standing in the nautical ante-chamber waiting to be received with Jeremy, he spotted an ornately sculptured church font, full of green oranges, by the door.

"Remember always to say 'yes' to him," added Jeremy as they went in.

The room was as cluttered as Jeremy's, but mainly with old and what must have been valuable furniture before the mildew had started to eat into the delicate marquetry. Several cases of startled-looking stuffed owls stood on the tables, no doubt the life's work of some Victorian naturalist, parted from their owner by one of Palmerston's ancestors. The trunks and old military chests were probably crammed with enough treasures to satisfy a small museum. The windows were covered with thick curtains and the light came from oil lamps. Uniforms heavy with medals and a Viceroy's hat with ostrich feathers were being laid out on a green velvet sofa by two pretty maids. A picture of Charles II, the Miskito's first benefactor, hung over the marble fireplace. Like everything else in the room, except for the guards' M 16 automatic rifles, the portrait was a talisman against progress and the outside world, which threatened the river-gypsy life of the Miskito. Copying Jeremy, Johnny took a pace forward and bowed. The Prince of Miskita was sitting on a tall, high-backed chair, almost a throne, with a sly, satanic smile on his lips. Johnny's fear was rekindled by the man's dreadful eyes. Then something brushed his leg and made him look down.

"Gabriel!"

The unmistakable head lolled for a moment against his knee and strong arms hugged his left thigh. They then propelled the creature's trolley over to Palmerston's chair and spun it to face Johnny. Several other men were seated around the room, possibly the prince's senior retainers. All were dressed in the same manner as their demented leader. It was uncanny, and no doubt his imagination playing tricks, but there was a chill in the air in that dark parlour. The crippled preacher he had seen in Rama sat on a stool. Then Gabriel spoke.

"If I may speak, I would like to say that I thank the English boy for my life. I don't think he has any idea how useful he has been to us . . . poor thing. Our nephew Jeremy tells me you are descended from the privateer Henry Morgan, who once governed the Coast. That is good. I believe in predestination, Johnny. I believe you were predestined to help us."

"Thank you, Gabriel, but I only pulled you out of the sea. Anyone would have done that."

"No one else seemed eager to try, my boy. Your papist friends would have left me and the preacher to drown in the depths of the ocean. It was most fortuitous. Can I tell him what I was carrying, brother?"

"Brother?" mumbled Johnny, forgetting himself.

"Yes, Johnny, Palmerston is my brother. You have friends at court. We are going to ransom you." The devil in the red coat scowled.

"Tell him. It can do no harm now."

"It was a map," smiled Gabriel.

"A map?" asked Johnny, puzzled.

"A map which showed the villages Perfect English was going to teach in. I had picked it up with an advance payment of dollars which I concealed in a secret pocket where the leather here joins my board. We knew your route north exactly and the time you intended to spend in each village. Soon we shall have enough dollars to make us strong again and we will no longer need to make deals with the enemy. We are the natural leaders of our people. In any case those villages should not have accepted education and aid from the enemy."

Gabriel paused. Johnny felt Jeremy willing him not to say anything. He wanted to scream at his own stupidity. Yet a wrong word could put him in the cage with Brooks.

"I'll wager you saved me because you thought I was a poor cripple," continued Gabriel. "I'll bet it made you feel very Christian. But that is what Perfect English is all about: dispensing charity to the poor and needy . . . helping the wretched of the earth. Well, you certainly have helped solve some poor souls' problems, though not in the way you intended."

Johnny hung his head. He had to stay alive, if only to revenge himself on Anselm. He now knew why the priest made such a careful show of being so anti-Contra. The map must have come from him. He had been very wrong about Gabriel. But what the little monster said next made Jeremy gasp and Johnny feel far more uncomfortable.

"Johnny has also struck another blow for our cause, brother. When I was in Managua, I heard that an *Internationalista* of the Perfect English group actually ate the last remains of Sandino. A strange rumour. Our contacts tell us it is true. The boy who did so stands before you. Do I not speak the truth, Johnny Morgan?"

He hesitated, remembering what Jeremy had told him. He

guessed that answering in the affirmative applied to Gabriel, too.

"Yes," he gasped.

"Good," said Palmerston. "Very good, Englishman."

"Tomorrow we go to our annual gathering of the river peoples and you will come with us," added Gabriel, smiling. "It has always been known as the Garden Party, from the old times. All of the Coastal Miskito families will be there. Many no doubt to accuse us of crimes they think we have committed. Word of the massacres has spread. But there may be news of your friends. The girls of Perfect English . . . haven't you wondered what has happened to your friends, Johnny?"

16

A Panamanian flag rustled from a small mast at the stern of Palmerston's tug in the gentle breeze of the tropical dawn. The boat had been christened *La Tortuga*, the turtle, for the trip, only one of many name panels that could be interchanged on her bows. For a moment Johnny had quite expected to see the skull and crossbones, but everything about their voyage to the meeting of the river families had been covert and anonymous. They had travelled by night. For hours men had been making ready a variety of weapons and the sound of metal clipping smartly into metal, of guns constantly being stripped and tested, could be clearly distinguished above the engines as Johnny spent the time on deck, forbidden to go below. The sky was reddening and he could hear the scream of macaws and the chatter of monkeys in the mangrove. If he listened very hard he could make out the gruffer engines of a flotilla of Palmerston's smaller craft loaded with men making headway inshore. Heavily weighed down, they could not risk the choppier seas beyond the reef.

"He has not brought his state limousine," said Jeremy, coming up behind him. The smell of rum was on the young man's breath. "Usually he brings his Ford Thunderbird and the other families carry him around on the beach. But now they will be angry about what he has done to those villages. That is why we look like a war party. Before the troubles these occasions used to be great carnivals. When I was sent to school in the United States I told my teacher about them and that my uncle was a pirate. She said I was a liar."

"How long were you in the States?"

"For four years, until 1979 when the fighting started. Then I had to come back here. My mother, my father and my grandfather were caught in one of the villages massacred by the Sandinistas. It was ironic. Unlike Palmerston, they had given up piracy. They were all for making peace with the Sandinistas, for negotiating autonomy. After Grandfather's death Palmerston claimed the title and gathered around him all that old regalia you saw in the camp to add respectability to his thievery. That is why I want to get away. Away to join one of the proper rebel groups. I want to fight for a recognized Miskito homeland." The last words he whispered.

The engines changed their pitch slowly and then stopped altogether. Jeremy peered at the coast. Just to the north was a long strip of beach rising up to a low range of hills or dunes behind which through a gap in the shoreline was a lagoon, or so it appeared. Many captains had no doubt come to grief when the land turned out to be quite different from what they imagined, their hulls sticking fast in the sand or holed by the razor-sharp stacks of the coral reefs.

"There is an old fort through those trees. Do you see it?" said Jeremy. "If you look carefully you will catch sight of a ruined wall. Look, someone is flying a flag."

Sure enough Johnny could just make out what must have been a squat, pepper-pot fort of the type the British once built all around the Caribbean. The sun was getting up now.

"By the way, Johnny, I have to take your picture." Jeremy brandished a Polaroid camera. "It's lucky Mr Brooks had this in his bag among his other equipment. It is for the ransom. Let us go to the stern." Johnny followed, stepping past a half-naked Indian putting bullets into a magazine. He wore a cowrie charm around his neck, the ancient and the modern in incongruous but perfect harmony.

"They want you to write a letter, too," Jeremy said loudly and then his voice dropped again to a conspiratorial level. "When we get ashore there will be a big meeting. Palmerston will be asked about the villages. You, Johnny, may be interrogated by him before the audience. Follow the way he leads or it will be fatal. If he says, 'Is the sea black?', answer, 'Yes'. There will be nothing you can do. If the other families turn against him there could be the most bloody battle. Probably none of us will get out alive. He is taking a great risk."

"Why are you helping me? I mean, thank you for helping me . . ."

Jeremy smiled.

"If you are ransomed I hope I can accompany you to Honduras. Then I will forget to come back," he said, taking a photograph. "So please say the right things."

They waited in silence. "Oh, that's a nice snap," added Jeremy as the picture popped out.

Johnny wondered how much a doubting Catholic *Internationalista* was worth on the open market. Once contacted, his mother would be frantic with worry and his stepfather crisply efficient. It would give him great pleasure to demonstrate to his errant stepson the power of Mammon. To go home in such circumstances would not be an attractive prospect, although anything was better than Palmerston's hospitality.

As if on cue, Palmerston appeared on the bridge and greeted one of the men from the wooden boats which had come alongside the tug in the difficult swell. The metal wheels of Gabriel's trolley clattered over the deck planks towards his brother. Immediately they started to argue.

"Do we go ashore now?" Johnny asked.

"Not until all our smaller boats have landed and made sure there is no ambush waiting for us," said Jeremy. "This Garden Party could be very dangerous. Then we will wait until Palmerston is certain he is the last family head to arrive. After that we will wait a little longer, just to rub in the message that he's boss. Ceremony is always slow. I imagine it is exactly the same in England."

"Aren't you frightened the Sandinistas might find you?"

"The only danger is right now, as our boats land and, of course, when we leave. This old tub can lie off the coast and pick up any approaching ships on her radar and no patrol boat can see what is happening at the other side of the sand spit. Anyway, if there was an attack from the sea the families could escape into the jungle. We have been using the same spot for a hundred years and there has never been trouble from outsiders. I would not hope for rescue if I were you.

Anyhow, if the Sandinistas found you still alive they would think you were our spy."

Eventually both of them were allowed to go ashore, although Palmerston and Gabriel remained implacably on the tug. Johnny and Jeremy lowered themselves unsteadily into a large longboat with a steep prow, which was driven by two outboards. On the craft's wooden seats dirty, dishevelled men from one of the other families watched Johnny with suspicion as he followed Jeremy into the waist-high surf and waded ashore. The beach was empty, but under the trees were more men with guns.

"We are not going to tie you up or anything like that, Johnny. There are probably three hundred men the other side of those trees, any of whom could track you through the jungle. But if you are smart we can both get to Honduras."

What Jeremy said was brought home painfully when a rifle barrel was jabbed into Johnny's ribs. His assailant chuckled and he stuck close to his protector as the path wound around boulders and clumps of wild pineapple beneath the tamarind and palm.

Suddenly they were out in the open again under the strengthening morning sun. Figures teemed on the beach of a large lagoon and groups of men immediately hailed Jeremy.

"Is your uncle too afraid to show his face?" they taunted. Tents had been erected and tables were loaded with food and drink. It was the tail end of a party which had obviously begun the night before. On the sand men lay with that empty-eyed look when drink has worn off and the sun has come up as both headache and anticlimax. Johnny now saw the reason for the extensive military precautions Palmerston had taken: every man had his rum flask but he also had a gun. Hostile stares came from four men guarding some boats tied up at a long stone jetty. One clutched a captured Kalashnikov. Their old craft were studded with tar patches and in the stern of one was embedded a large piece of shrapnel.

"Man-nak-is-má," said Jeremy.

"Paesa."

The greeting over, Jeremy spoke in English again, much to Johnny's relief.

"Here is a cousin from the British Kingdom."

The guard spat into the fire near to where he was squatting. On the sand were a number of monkey corpses. One had been skinned and looked like a dead infant. Flies swarmed around it. Johnny turned away and walked on.

"How on earth can you live like this?" he said when they were out of earshot.

"How could you eat Sandino?" replied Jeremy tartly with a wicked grin.

Several hours later, Palmerston and Gabriel deigned to come ashore and take part in the large open-air meeting. One of the walls of the ruined fort had crumbled away, creating a natural amphitheatre. Someone shouted for silence and the proceedings began, in English.

A group of men in blue-green uniforms, who, Jeremy whispered, belonged to the Misura Contra group fighting with the Nicaraguan Democratic Front based in Honduras, called for an end to the lack of discipline of some of the families and to the piracy and self seeking.

"We have evidence that the so-called Prince of Miskita has been taking money from the Communist devils in Managua to murder our own innocent people resettled in villages by the Sandinistas. Further, that he has imprisoned and killed American agents, our allies, who came to him with military supplies, after failing to extort money from them. This is the sort of leader we can do without, brothers. We know these things from honest men among his own ranks . . ." There were catcalls and laughter at the suggestion that any of Palmerston's men were honest.

But now it was the prince's turn to speak.

He stood in his red jacket gazing hatefully about him, more like a judge who might hang them all than someone accused of a crime.

"How dare the Misura who live in American luxury in Honduras accuse us?" He paused, and there was a wave of approval. "We have killed no Americans. They have brought me no military supplies. We are Miskito. We are not the tool of the Americans." The simple lies met with cheers. Then to

Johnny's horror, Palmerston turned and beckoned him forward.

"Here is one of our prisoners. He does not work for the Americans. He is a teacher we captured in the pay of the Sandinistas. Is that not true?"

Johnny glanced anxiously at Jeremy who nodded.

"Yes," he said. It came out as a hoarse whisper.

"Loud," commanded Palmerston.

"Yes," Johnny repeated, to universal booing.

"The other American we have. Is he a CIA agent who brings me military things? Or is he a member of your group? Answer! He is a member of your group? Yes?"

Again Johnny looked to Jeremy who indicated he should agree.

"Yes," Johnny replied.

Palmerston dismissed him with a flick of his wrist and Johnny went to stand back with Jeremy. All around him he could sense enmity.

"It is true our other prisoner is American. An American called Brooks. He works with the Sandinistas. We found him in one of those villages you accuse us of destroying. We went to help and we discovered these men. It was they who led our people into the arms of the soldiers. It is the Sandinistas who are the murderers. What shall we do with this Brooks?"

The reaction was unanimous.

"Kill him!" came the reply.

Jeremy pulled Johnny behind Palmerston's chair as the shouting continued. The speech was clearly not what the young Miskito had expected.

"How shall we kill this man Brooks? In the traditional way?" boomed Palmerston.

"Yes! Yes! Death to all outsiders!"

"We have everything ready on the sea beach," cried Palmerston. "Brooks is there."

The vengeful crowd surged from the fort and through the trees. Johnny went with Jeremy, running and at times being pushed, along the twisting pathway until they stood on the beach looking out to sea.

A twenty-foot wooden boat with a long prow bobbed at

anchor and Brooks stood on the sand before it. He had all the frenzied stillness of someone who fears the worst and can do nothing. There was a hush of anticipation. Then the American agent glanced up towards Johnny and nodded recognition as he anticipated the fate he would have committed suicide to avoid.

All at once a man stepped forward and felled the American with a blow on the head from the flatside of a machete. Brooks lay immobile in the sand. Rapidly men bound ropes around his arms and legs, so tightly the limbs below them turned purple, and bore him shoulder high to the waiting longboat. There they held him against the prow as willing helpers passed the ropes on his hands through brass eyelets along the side to what appeared to be a wheel at the stern. His legs were likewise secured under the waves. The prow of the boat pressed into the agent's spine as a bucket of sea water was thrown in his face to bring him round.

"They're crucifying him," whispered Johnny, aghast. He could not believe his eyes.

"There is nothing I can do, believe me," said Jeremy. "It is a tradition that goes back to the Carib peoples. I told you my uncle was big on old customs. When they examined the missionaries' crucifixes they thought the priests carried them to ward off the death they dreaded most. So that is how the Indians killed the fathers. But instead of nailing them to a tree they fixed them onto the front of their pangas, usually when taken into battle. It became a magical ceremony to bless a boat and is said to be where the pirate symbol of the skull and crossbones flag comes from. The body is left to rot down to its skeleton. Sometimes death is quick. Nowadays, if ropes are used and pulled very tight, the man's back is usually broken from the speed of the boat's acceleration. Or, it can take ages. When Sandino operated on this Coast in his early days he executed people in this manner. In many ways he and my uncle are the same sort of political animal."

The engine of the boat burbled into life and the ropes wrenched Brooks's arms back as it lurched forward. Immediately there was a scream, followed by a cheer from the crowd on the beach. As the craft turned, the ropes pinioning the agent's arms were tightened. The crowd yelled in anticipation. Palmerston dropped a white handkerchief and the boat leapt forward again, pushing the prow into the man's backbone, sending his ear-splitting shrieks over the water. Then the engines were throttled back once more and the front of the craft sank into the sea, turning slowly, waiting for the signal to make another agonizing pass.

Palmerston raised his walking stick and the only sounds in creation seemed to be the idling engines of the two outboards and the faint wail of Brooks.

Palmerston dropped the cane.

The boat thundered forward under full power, and as it lifted its stem right out of the water, Johnny imagined there was a snapping sound, like the breaking of a heavy branch during a storm. For several minutes there was an ecstatic uproar while the boat sped round and round the bay with its new figurehead. Men who had jeered Palmerston in the fort now came up to him pledging their allegiance. The death ritual had taken away his guilt. Palmerston held up his hands.

"Death is the fate of all trespassers in this Miskita Kingdom."

The crowd howled its approval as the prince turned to Johnny.

"Tomorrow it will be the turn of the English boy. He has admitted his crimes. He helped the Communists. He must die. Prepare a boat for him . . . ."

17

They bound Johnny by his hands and feet to a tree overlooking the sea, in such a way that he could not sit down. Anyway, there was no question of sleep. Whenever he shut his eyes he saw the twisted, accusing face of Brooks in those last moments of torment. Johnny looked up at the stars and cursed the fact he had been lulled into believing their talk of ransom. He had been arrogant enough to expect they would keep their word, applying his own comfortable, liberal morality to men who were pirates. Now the monster in the red coat was going to kill him; all for teaching English. His fear gave way to complete panic. But no matter how hard he frantically pulled and tugged at his bonds they would not come loose. Again and again his eyes were drawn to an imaginary line between sea and sky in the darkness, where he would see the first pale glint of light. At dawn they would come for him.

The once hidden encampment on the lagoon had spilled over onto the sea-facing beach. Brooks's execution had been the signal for general drinking and merriment. His own guards were frequently offered bottles from wild-eyed men who staggered for a moment into the light of their weak lantern and then cavorted around fires on the sand, lit without a thought for Sandinista patrols. Screams and cries came from the trees behind him, and all at once a group of men sped by chasing someone as running fights broke out between the rival groups. Waiting for death in that place was the nearest thing to purgatory Johnny could imagine. Then before him stood Jeremy and another Miskito.

"Palmerston sends you some rum. He wants to see the prisoner. We will take him." The voice was calm and matter of fact.

"He told us to keep the boy here."

"I have a paper signed by his brother Gabriel."

For a second the guard hesitated, then he shook his head.

"We don't care if you have a paper signed by the Archangel Gabriel, do we mates? When Palmerston hears of this you will probably be sent to meet the angels. The English is your bum boy. We all know that."

Jeremy shrugged his shoulders. The gesture was followed by a gurgling sound made by one of the guards, who fell forward, a knotted cord around his throat. The one who had been speaking groaned and slumped against the base of a palm tree. Four more Miskito stepped out into the lamp light to cut Johnny free. All at once he felt he could not breathe and had to take long, slow gulps of air. The blood returned to his arms and legs in a surge of pins and needles, the welcome pain of freedom. Out at sea was the first grey promise of morning.

"Johnny, pull yourself together," Jeremy said, grabbing his shoulder as he stood there dazed. "We are going north to the border. To Honduras. I cannot let my uncle kill you."

To Johnny's surprise they led him onto the beach, picking their way through groups of drunken men. For some reason he thought they would head for the jungle. Around them more fires were being lit against the morning chill, all semblance of discipline gone. No one paid them the slightest attention.

"We must get to one of those boats," Jeremy said, pointing to three wooden whalers. A fourth anchored further out in the bay still had the body of Brooks hanging from its prow, silhouetted against the reddening sky. Alongside anchor ropes on the beach a party of Miskito guarded the launches.

"I have come to see my uncle on the *Tortuga*," said Jeremy, walking straight up to them. "I have the prisoner with me. Palmerston wants him." It was a mistake.

"Oh, he does, does he?" replied the man. "Well your uncle came ashore half an hour ago, so if he's here how could he want to see the prisoner out there?" The man held his rifle across his chest. "If you still want to see him, he went towards the old fort. He's in a fine temper about all these fires." The other men eyed Jeremy suspiciously.

"Well, I've been told to take this man out to the boat. That is my uncle's wish. Or do you want me to tell him how you have contempt for his orders? Come on, Thomas, you know me, don't you?"

But the man was not to be moved.

"I obey Palmerston," said the man defiantly. "When he came ashore he told me not to let anyone near these boats."

"But that does not mean me," said Jeremy in a more friendly voice. "What my uncle meant was this drunken rabble on the beach."

The man hesitated. "I will contact the tug boat," he finally conceded, producing a radio set like a conjurer. He picked up the handset. The other guards huddled round as if about to worship the mysterious technological god. Jeremy took his chance.

"Put down your weapons ... push them away. That's right . . ." One of Jeremy's Miskito picked up the rifles.

"Palmerston will hunt you down like a dog for this, traitor . . ." Then the man fell silent, his eyes fixed on something out at sea.

"Sandinistas," someone whispered.

Johnny looked in the direction they were pointing. Round the headland to the south, through the coastal mists, nosed the squat shape of a gunboat. Other men further up the beach had seen it too and began shouting.

"My God," said the man with the radio, turning around. "The Spanish are coming from the north as well. They have us from both sides."

"Come on," Jeremy cried. "We can break out if we hug the coast inside the reefs. Quick, into those boats before someone else has the same idea. If we take one each it will double our chances." At that moment they saw Palmerston striding up the beach. One of the guards they had disarmed yelled "stop them", and pointed in their direction. But the Sandinista gunboat to the south, which had been joined by several more, opened fire. Out at sea, the tug boat started its engines and moved away, gathering speed. Gabriel would be safely on board, and whoever had been dozing in front of the radar screen would not want to face Palmerston. Anti-tank rockets were fired from its deck and lit up the sea with an eerie red light as they snaked towards the pursuing craft in a shower of sparks. Shells started to fall. The last image Johnny had of the Miskito prince was of him standing on the white sand howling with rage and shaking his cane at the approaching armada.

Jeremy was already in one boat and heading out to sea. He waved Johnny towards another, where a man had started the engine. Johnny and three other Miskitos jumped in and they took off around the coast at full throttle. Behind them the scene had been transformed: pillars of flame and sand shot into the air, obscuring the jungle. Three gunboats were pumping shells into the beach from the south. The first one gave up chasing the disappearing tug and turned inshore, raking fleeing figures with its machine-guns. To the north, other Sandinista Marine boats opened fire. Johnny's craft followed in the wake of Jeremy's. A shell exploded in the water to their right, drenching Johnny. Another detonated inland as one patrol boat split from the main force and concentrated its machine-guns in their direction, almost hitting both launches as they dodged in amongst the rocks and shelving reefs.

They rounded another headland and found themselves in a bay of deeper water, buffeted by waves. It occurred to Johnny that they no longer had the protection of the coastal reef and the more powerful craft behind them could now use all its speed. It was bound to catch up with them. Sure enough, at that instant bullets thudded into the wood beside him and a Miskito fell, clutching his chest. The helmsman crouched low as they sped on, but the machine-gunner had his range and fired again. As splinters danced around him Johnny jumped, dropping into the cool blue waters, into sudden peace and silence. It could have been only seconds but he seemed to be down there for an age, in that calm world, before floating with the bubbles towards the sun, breaking the surface to see the engine of the launch he had been riding in explode in a sheet of flame, sending the craft crashing into the rocks. There was no sign of Jeremy's boat.

Slowly the Sandinista torpedo boat turned, gingerly retracing its path even in that deep bay, as if the captain had only just become aware of the dangers of the coral. The boat was coming straight for him.

"Please God," he said out loud. "Please don't let the silly bastards shoot me." It would be absurd to be shot by people he had come to help.

"Ayudame compañeros. Ayudame," he shouted and waved. "I'm on your side, you stupid bastards. Peace be with you, comrades . . . I'm on your side!"

To his horror, the turret gun fired and Johnny dived, coming up for air only when his lungs were bursting. He held his hands above his head as a sign of surrender and inadvertently sank again. As he came to the surface for a third time he realized the crew had thrown him a line, which he struggled to swim to, while the turret gun opened up high over his head into the tamarind trees by the water's edge. Contra rifle fire crackled back, and as he grasped the life preserver he thought he heard a helicopter.

They hauled him out of the water, the sailors of the Sandinista Marine, looking somewhat puzzled.

"Thank you. Thank you," he said in Spanish. "I was captured by the Contras. I am on your side."

But the men on deck still had their Kalashnikovs levelled at him.

"You are hurt," said one of the sailors, pointing. Johnny looked down. His shirt was ripped to shreds, exposing a gaping hole in his side, oozing dark red blood. There were other wounds in his thigh. The sight of his injuries seemed to trigger immediate and excruciating pain. He felt dizzy and extremely cold as they laid him down. An officer stuck his head out of the wheel house and eyed Johnny uncertainly. The sailors seemed embarrassed by his presence and caught off guard by his command of their language.

"You are an *Internationalista*?" one man finally asked. They were all crowded around him.

"Yes, I was a volunteer," he replied, as a youth dabbed

away at a wound with his red and black kerchief before applying a stinging field dressing. Another felt in Johnny's pockets and helped himself to a comb.

"He could be CIA," he heard one hatchet-faced young man say. A voice inquired again if Johnny was an *Internationalista.*

"Yes, yes I am," he managed to answer as the pain shot in spasms up his left side. Nothing seemed to matter anymore except staying conscious. He was becoming lightheaded and incapable of Spanish.

"On the other hand," he began in English, "you could say I was an *Internationalista*, but I failed. I cannot solve my own bloody problems, let alone yours. I'm not good enough to be a proper Christian and my conscience won't let me be a proper Socialist. Now I have lost my fiancée to a priest . . . I ate your national hero. I slaughtered villages full of children . . ." They gave him an injection. It left him feeling warm and aware and oblivious to his injuries.

One of the sailors crossed himself.

"I understand English," he boasted to his comrades who, thankfully, didn't. The boy assumed a priest's authority. "The gringo is possessed. I had a dog once who was possessed. Shortly he will foam at the mouth and die. Poor gringo," and they all took off their baseball-style caps and looked down at him sympathetically.

He lay against the patrol boat's torpedo tubes covered with a blanket the young Sandinistas had put on him. The battle was ended as soon as it began, with the Miskito fleeing into their friendly jungle, and after much argument back and forth over the radio, Johnny was taken south. He was ecstatic to see the gingerbread houses of Bluefields again. They stretchered him to the Ernesto Che Guevara Fire Station, where they dressed his side and gave him several more injections, producing a theatrically large syringe from an old Skippy peanut butter jar. A tired officer with a bandaged head wound came into the room and lit a cigarette despite the protests of the nurse. To Johnny's dismay it was Capitán Fernandez.

"I am to escort you to Managua, gringo, where, if there is

any justice in this world, you will face a firing squad. Those of my men who are not dead are in the hands of the FDN Contra, as are your associates. Probably in Honduras. I alone escaped. I thought it was suspicious when you stayed behind in the last village. Obviously it was to get in touch with your filthy Contra friends. Now I understand why you do many things."

"I was captured by the Contra, too . . ." Johnny protested. "Is Catherine all right? Honestly, it wasn't me . . ."

"You were captured by the Contra, too?" sneered Fernandez. "Then why aren't you in Honduras? I'll tell you why. It's because you were in league with that child-killing devil Palmerston, whom we have now dispatched to hell. He sent you to spy on us. But no more questions, worm. They will expect answers in Managua. Then I, Capitán Federico Fernandez, will dance on your grave." The *Capitán* grinned horribly from the end of the bed. Johnny was clearly wasting his breath with the irascible officer. He prayed Catherine was safe.

The airplane journey across the mountains was not painful in any physical sense. But the engines drummed into his brain and all he could think of was Palmerston. The man had exploited the traditions and trappings of the ludicrous Miskito monarchy in the same cynical way the Sandinistas embraced the new Catholicism. Both were used to dignify naked ambition and as a way of keeping the people in place; a little puff of opium for the masses. Naturally, the revolutionaries had welcomed the radical ideas of Father Anselm who insisted that the only true sacrament was to help the wretched of the earth. The Sandinistas claimed that everything the revolution did was to help the poor. Every jail and lock and strand of barbed wire was all for them. Perhaps such "good works" absolved the Sandinistas of having to stand before God. Of seeing themselves and all their accomplishments as fragile and weak.

The plane bumped and banked suddenly among the clouds and a string bag containing hundreds of oranges from a grower on the Coast burst, sending the fruit rolling around the floor. It was cheering that the best laid political and economic plans were always vulnerable to the Almighty's little jokes. Johnny drifted off into a narcotic sleep as an *Aeronica* official scrabbled about the bucking cabin of the twin engine aircraft, trying to round up the delinquent fruit.

"Has he been wounded? At the front? So they do have *Internationalistas* fighting alongside the Sandinistas, just like in Spain. He's not dead is he . . .? Can I take a picture?" Johnny came round as paramedics wheeled him to an ambulance outside the Augusto César Sandino Airport in Managua. The voice belonged to an earnest girl with plaited blonde hair. She bent over him. She even smelled innocent.

"Is he a hero? Did he fight at the front? Where *is* the front?" asked another.

"Sí," replied a bored official voice, as Johnny's stretcher was shoved inside and the doors slammed. "Everyone in Nicaragua is a hero," he heard one of the paramedics say as they drove off. The blonde girl would have been ideal for the Perfect English programme.

The old American ambulance hurtled to the centre of the city, its siren screaming all the way. Capitán Fernandez gazed expectantly out of the window. He had changed into his best fatigues on the plane. Johnny felt a jolt as the vehicle shot up the steep incline of the Tiscapa volcano, on which the military hospital was built next to El Chipote prison. There was an attractive bravado in building a city's hospital beside a volcano in a part of the world where such things can never be considered extinct. Too many had come back to life. It showed a national fatalism.

They wheeled him down endless corridors and the crowds of patients and doctors became fewer and fewer. He was taken through a locked and guarded door where Fernandez left him without even a last insult. A silent nurse pushed Johnny into a very large and light room, the size of an entire ward. His bed was in the corner looking out over mournful Lake Tiscapa, and he could see the little shoreside cafe where he had waited for Dr Window and the rest so full of expectation. As views went, it was not unpleasant, if it hadn't been haunted by the crater's grim associations with torture and violent death. For Johnny was just as certainly a prisoner as if he were in El Chipote next door. For a moment he felt a pang of fear. Perhaps this *was* El Chipote. Did the military hospital connect with the famous jail? He shivered. Along one wall were miscellaneous pieces of medical equipment. A dentist's drill stood by some flaking plaster. He hoped they were not going to torture him.

However, all that happened was a doctor came in and stitched his wounds under local anaesthetic. His injuries were not as serious as they had looked, but it seemed they needed to heal under armed guard. Then for a week a nurse brought him a selection of pills and made him take them. They left him suspended in a vacuum where he was hardly able to come to terms with that stark white room, let alone anything outside it. During the second week they lowered the dose and he became gradually familiar with every crack and crevice in the wall opposite. He wondered about Catherine, if she was all right. He tried to conjure up her image before him, but he had to be careful where he let himself wander on those pills. Once, as a vague feeling of guilt had returned, he imagined himself in the middle of a clearing surrounded by rotting human remains. The Perfect English badge gleamed in the sunlight on the blouse of a young Miskito girl who kept asking him "why?". He hoped he would be questioned soon. It would help to tell someone what had happened.

One day the nurse brought him several blank sheets of paper and a pen. She did not say anything, merely put them on a table beside the bed. The sheets were ruled off at the top and marked in red with the initials of the Department of State Security. The brownish, cheap paper must have been designed for confessions.

At times it all seemed like a horrible dream but the guilt intensified. Anselm had said they were in a state of Grace and free of sin while helping the poor, but Johnny could not imagine that covered what he had done. Anyway, he had lost his trust in priests.

All at once the thought occurred to him that no one would be blamed for the massacres. The Sandinistas were rid of refugees they did not want, the Americans had won a propaganda coup – although not with the photographic evidence they had hoped for – and the Miskito were at least rid of Palmerston. There was no morality in that political swamp land. No one was going to own up and take the blame, unless he did. It would be a relief to be punished.

He picked up the pen and began to write in his painstakingly rounded, childish hand. The sweeping curves taught by his mother in a sunlit drawing room looked incongruous as he paused and re-read what he had written. He was making his confession, addressed to the People's Tribunal, in order to bring things out in the open. Johnny wanted to own up to himself and also to God about what had happened. Otherwise he might as well never have been in Nicaragua.

Johnny did not stint. He wrote down each horrible detail. When he had finished he felt so much better. The dignity of the confessional was intoxicating. Strangely, the catalogue of failure had rekindled his faith; shown him the difference between God and man. By him on the bed lay the last page with his signature and above it a short and damning paragraph in what he imagined was the style of such things:

"I admit to objectively being an agent of the Contras and the CIA and deserve whatever punishment is coming to me."

18

"Peace be with you, comrade . . . Wake up sleepyhead," said a soft voice near his ear. Johnny was so surprised to see Dr Window that he tried to sit up too quickly and winced at a twinge of pain in his leg. She looked so lovely and English and normal in her pink and white Andy Pandy dungarees. However, as she stood up from kissing him he saw another individual coming towards him in a wheelchair, who from their short acquaintance was anything but normal or reassuring.

"Tom! How on earth?"

"Don't sound so pleased to see I'm alive. I have a good mind to sue you. I thought you said those mortars were friendly. The next thing I know, I'm scattered all over a mountainside. It took them weeks to find me and now I've been rebuilt by a team of Bulgarians. Fucking lousy job, but what can you expect from Commies? They wouldn't even make me bigger where it really counts."

"How did you get in? I thought I was off limits?"

"Blanca brought us," said Dr Window. "She seems to be in charge of you and was very concerned about that lunatic confession you wrote. She let me read it. You've been through such a lot. Poor Johnny." Annie stroked his hair.

"Well, I like that," interrupted Tom. "He gets shot in the ass or wherever and suddenly he's been through a lot. He hasn't even been operated on by that bearded folk-dancing troupe masquerading as surgeons."

"Please shut up, Tom, we have to talk like grown-ups," said Dr Annie. "I know you must have been upset at the time, Johnny, but that confession was a mistake. You were lucky Blanca got hold of it."

"I can understand why she wouldn't want it to go any further. She works for Bliss. I stand by what I said. Every word of it is true." He stubbornly reached over to the bedside table for more paper but it had been removed. If they'd lost it, he'd bloody well write it out again. He was hardly likely to forget the details.

"Let him be a martyr if he wants," said Tom. "But martyrs have to get themselves crucified for something, Johnny. Those are the rules. It's pretty ragged to be a martyr without a cause, just because you're outraged that no one around here is dumb enough to take the blame."

"Have you heard about the others? What happened to them?" A wave of anxiety about Catherine overcame Johnny's annoyance.

"Catherine, you really mean," said Dr Annie, with a smile. "She is in Honduras. How do you think she would feel if you were rotting in a jail here for twenty years? If that confession went any further, if you came before the People's Tribunal, God knows what they would do to you, or to me, Johnny. Some former cattle hand from Chontales is not likely to understand your finer feelings. Think about what could happen to Blanca. All that nonsense about being an objective Contra is so dangerous, quite apart from being silly. I don't know who put that thought in your head."

"Is she hurt? Is Catherine hurt?"

"We don't know. Only that Bob was killed in the ambush and the others were kidnapped by a Nicaraguan Democratic Front Contra group. There are still tremendous rows going on about what took place in those villages, Johnny, all of which has been censored here. Blanca told me a young Miskito called Jeremy gave a press conference yesterday saying the Sandinistas were responsible for the killings and naming Bliss. The Sandinistas have accused the US-backed Contras. It was very moral of you to put it down on paper, and historically commendable, but as a way of bringing the right people to justice it's a non-starter. Can't you see there is no way the Sandinistas can risk an open trial? Blanca has an alternative."

He sighed.

"You don't understand, Johnny," continued Dr Annie.

"Ever since they sent that helicopter up for me and the crew saw one of those villages burning, the powers that be have been putting together the pieces for themselves. Not everyone is rotten, you have to believe that. They really want to get Bliss and his cronies but it has to be their way. There has already been one secret hearing, and Blanca has put forward evidence on what was said to you in the Miskito camp about the link between certain Sandinistas and Palmerston. The rest of your confession is in the hospital incinerator. She's very fond of us, Johnny. The good news is that they are holding Bliss under guard."

"What does Blanca want me to do?"

"Apparently Bliss has demanded to confront all witnesses against him. If you're willing, they want to bring him along this afternoon. You only have to repeat what you said about Palmerston's deals with Bliss."

"What will happen to him then?"

She shrugged. "It's in the lap of the gods. Blanca said she could not be sure. The plotting seems to be quite a lot more far-reaching than even you uncovered, but then that's Nicaragua. Many top Sandys were involved."

"Let the confession go," sighed Tom. "It's not your fault you are a complete dingbat. But you have to help the exquisite Blanca put one over on this creep Bliss."

"What about Anselm? He must have been part of the plot."

Annie looked pensive. "I think you are influenced by your personal feelings against him, Johnny. It's Bob I feel so sad about. He was such a sweetie deep down. He loved being in Nicaragua. He adored the whole thing like a child with a new train set."

"Until someone from a rival line blew his fucking head off."

"Tom, please."

"Okay Dr Annie, but if this guy Bobby you have told me so much about had been looking out for himself instead of playing with his toy, he wouldn't be vulture meat now."

"I'm glad he didn't know what Perfect English was being used for," said Johnny.

"He did die a revolutionary," mused Dr Annie. "He once told me that he would not mind dying fighting against the

Contra. I doubt if he did any harm to them, though. He was a worse shot than me. But then Lenin couldn't shoot for toffee either."

There was a giggle from the wheelchair.

"Tom!"

The American was shaking with laughter.

"I'm sorry," he gasped. "No, I'm not. I was trying to think what the Sandinista Youth will sing around the campfire about Badshot Bob, the myopic guerilla from Bournemouth. His birthplace even sounds like a disease. They could name a battalion after him and put all the other Bobs in it . . . the real space cadets."

"Get him out of here Annie, before I throw something. I'll do whatever Blanca says."

"Thank you, Johnny," Annie said, kissing him.

"Peace be with you, comrade," smirked Tom. "If you're a good boy I'll introduce you to my Bulgarian anaesthetist. She's so mysteriously hairy in all the wrong places. But as you see, I've lost my heart to Dr Annie . . ." The blonde academic turned and blew Johnny another kiss as she wheeled Tom away. There never had been any accounting for the good doctor's strange tastes.

Johnny lay back in his bed. Perhaps the confession had been naïve of him. Pompous almost. He had not considered how it would affect others – Annie or Blanca, or Tom, whom he thought was dead. He had not even asked the foul New Yorker about his injuries in any detail. The American seemed a born survivor.

Blanca arrived in the early afternoon.

"How is my wounded soldier?"

"I'm not anyone's soldier."

She kissed him passionately on the lips.

"I'm so glad to be with you again, Johnny. I've been talking to Dr Annie. I hope she explained everything to you. They are bringing Bliss in now. If you could repeat what you wrote in the confession about his links with Palmerston, we will be grateful. He may say some hurtful things."

"What hurtful things?"

But there was a tap at the door. It opened and a woman stenographer came in. Bliss's assistant Alegría followed her. He nodded to Johnny, but for him that was tantamount to a friendly embrace. Then two guards brought in the object of the exercise. To Johnny's amazement Bliss seemed as cheerful as ever, bouncing into the room grinning from ear to ear. He was dressed in blue prison overalls and his hands were cuffed behind his back. The small eyes sparkled. After him came several men in business suits whom Johnny took to be legal representatives of some sort. Bliss's grin merely grew wider.

"The gang's all here," Bliss said, as the proceedings were declared open. The questioning was in English. The former CIA man had an advantage from the start.

"Now, did the Miskito, Jeremy, say to you that the man you know as Bliss told Palmerston's group to attack the resettled villages, to kill any child with a Perfect English badge and their families and then to cut off each child's ear, returning it with the numbered badge for later payment?"

"As I have said, that is the case. Yes." But they took Johnny over the same evidence at least ten times.

"Did he mention any other names?"

"No."

"And the man you know as Bliss is standing in this room? Please point him out?"

Johnny indicated Bliss at the end of the bed.

Blanca came over to him. "Now the accused will question you Johnny."

"You bet," said Bliss. "Remember I told you they'd get me, that the purges were coming? Well they're here, Johnny. We are standing right in one."

"Please ask your questions," snapped Blanca at her former boss.

"If he's up to it," chirped Bliss. "Did Mr Morgan know that his poor sweet Catherine was the one who supplied all the information on the Perfect English programme, the villages to be visited – the lot? That she was my informant?"

"But what about Father Anselm . . . I thought . . ."

"Poor Father Anselm," said Bliss. "Such a good man, and one of his disciples suspects him. Well, you were wrong,

Johnny. But didn't you have any suspicions about Catherine? Remember when you were first here? You were hardly together. Catherine kept coming to see me with details of the programme. She was so thorough. She even drew the maps that Palmerston followed and no one ever knew."

Johnny felt numb. "How did you make her do it?"

"It was so easy. I'd once met her father, so the minute she landed I brought her in for a security check. She was perfect, a beautiful spoilt brat. We said that with such a capitalist parent, who had once worked for the CIA in the Middle East after the war, she must prove her loyalty, her political integrity. We only asked her little things at first. To rat on other *Internationalistas*. That's how I knew all about you, Johnny. Then I started asking for more. She came to my house and I pretended one of my drivers was from the Ministry of Education. By accident she told us about the Perfect English badges. It was a godsend. Everything fell into place with what I had been trying to get off the ground on the Coast for my *comandante* friends."

The stenographer stopped typing and looked at one of the men in a business suit to see whether she should continue. He shook his head. The obvious embarrassment at the mention of the magic word *comandante* made Bliss even happier.

"We then instructed her that the Perfect English badges were to be given to the children of the most uncooperative Miskito, and she was to persuade Father Anselm to do this. We said we could then concentrate on them in follow-up schemes. Which in a sense we did . . . The strange thing, Johnny, was that I am sure Catherine did not believe a word of my bullshit. At first I think we appealed to her sense of intrigue. But what really hooked her was she didn't want to be just another bleeding heart liberal spreading a little learning. Catherine really wanted to help Nicaragua. She wanted to take sides. To be at the sharp end. It's quite amazing the evil one can make a good, committed person do. . . ."

"Bastard," said Johnny. "You're finished now."

Bliss laughed and nodded towards the silent stenographer. "I doubt it, Johnny boy. Now my name is in the American papers the Sandys cannot execute me without a trial. If they did it would not please their liberal friends in Congress. Yet if they put me on trial in order to execute me they will have to slaughter a good few of our ruling junta as well. Those important honchos will get their names known too. I'll make sure of that. Also, the people will hear officially for the first time that two gringos ate their precious Sandino. What's the irritation of my continued existence balanced against national shame and disgrace? I think they will let me go."

He paused. No one said a word.

"It was such a fine plan until you came on the scene with your doubts and jealousies, Johnny. You really have a knack for fucking things up. That's what my *comandante* friends wanted me to do, Johnny. To cause chaos on the Atlantic Coast. To start a Miskito uprising so firmer hands could take charge and put it down. What better instrument of chaos than a religious foreign aid group whose do-gooding, God-squad smugness blinds them to what is really happening? But then, Johnny, you decided to accidently eat Sandino and nearly got Perfect English chucked out of the country, spoiling my plans. You're always poking around Johnny ... asking questions ... getting in trouble. You should be in my business."

"But why did you do it?"

"Money, Johnny, money; what else is there? My *comandantes* promised to release my money, ill-gotten gains under Somoza I had not been able to transfer to Costa Rica from the National Bank. They also gave me full permission to screw the CIA for all I could get. The Company nearly crapped when I told them about the badges and the ears, and said I was in their good books again. As usual they went off half-cocked without thinking it through. Even if they had managed to take pictures of the ears, it would not *prove* who cut them off. As usual the US blamed the Sandinistas. But the Sandys turned round and blamed the US-backed Contras. Atrocity is all a matter of the politics of the beholder. If it weren't for you, Johnny, and that smart-assed nigger Jeremy, I would be in Costa Rica now, sunning my backside and raising a glass to free enterprise. And I still intend to, mark my words."

"Palmerston thought he could take everyone for a ride too,

and he died," said one of the suited men without emotion, as if commenting on the weather. "His mistake was to kill those American agents. Through our contacts in Honduras your precious CIA told us exactly where to find him and when. I would not like such friends."

"But that savage didn't get himself named in the *Washington Post* as the big Sandinista bad guy like I have," countered Bliss proudly. "If the Sandys ice me now, they will be admitting they're a bunch of child-killing, ear-chopping, no good Commies. What an outraged Señor Bliss has to do is face the international press and deny these vile imperialist smears, which have helped keep me alive. All I can say is thank God for Perfect English and the written word."

"Get him out of here," snapped Blanca.

"I'm so sorry Johnny," she said after all the others had gone. "I'm so sad you had to find out about Catherine this way."

Three days later Blanca switched on the light of his room in what seemed to be the middle of the night. She smiled at him.

"Goodbye, Johnny," she said. "I think it's best you go now, before anyone changes their mind. Here is your passport. Someone will be at the border to take Tom to the American hospital. They will look after you too, and Annie."

He grabbed her hand. "Are you going to be all right?"

"All right? I've even been promoted. Come on, get your clothes."

The ride to the Honduran border was uneventful and they were nodded through to the other side where they were transferred without formality to a large American ambulance. Johnny noticed his wound had stained the dressing slightly.

"They'll give us a bill for this if I know my fellow countrymen," said Tom. "Oh Nicaragua, I feel incomplete on leaving you. I think the Bulgarians have several pieces of me still kicking around in their fridge."

Someone switched on the radio.

"Here is a US Forces health tip to all you Joes. Hold that salt. Do you know more people die of heart disease in El Salvador than from political assassination? So hold that salt and serve your country. Now here's Elvis . . ." Johnny dozed until the ambulance came to a jolting stop. A large billboard announced their arrival at the American Field Hospital, Palmerola. Another sign said Weinberger Way.

Johnny felt angry, like a child who had been caught doing something wrong in someone else's home, and instead of a smacking only gets sympathy. Dr Annie was pensive too. For once Tom didn't say anything but went quietly as attendants took them to clean, private rooms which even had televisions. Johnny began to think of Catherine. He wondered if she was here. What would he say to her? Did she realize what she had done? There was no way she could have failed to hear the news, the accusations of the Miskito organizations that a man who called himself Bliss was behind the massacres of the villages. It galled him that Bliss was probably going to get away with it. Every revolution was undermined by such people but Johnny felt it deeply and personally that so evil an individual should go unpunished. Then he laughed out loud. They had made a Nicaraguan of him. He remembered how he had watched the procession on his first day, thinking the crowd might welcome those priests; then wondering why they could not forgive. Now he could not forgive Bliss. He was not sure if he could ever feel the same about Catherine, ever be with her without thinking about those children. He turned on the air conditioner, flipping a switch by the bed.

In the early evening, there was a knock at the door. A kindly looking man put his head around it. He was in uniform but had silver crosses on the collar of his smartly pressed shirt. He was an army padre. Seeming ill at ease, he stood at the bottom of the bed and cleared his throat.

"How is Catherine Hope?" demanded Johnny. "Nothing's happened to her, has it? Is she in this hospital?"

The padre nervously tugged at his hair. He was only in his early twenties but prematurely balding.

"She's fine, or what I mean to say is, much better. My name's Blair. Yes, she's here. She injured a leg."

"How?"

"The Contras mistook your group and their guards for a regular Sandinista column in the area. People all look the same in uniform. An English boy was killed. But Father Anselm threw himself across Miss Hope and she only received shrapnel in the leg . . . It will scar, of course."

"And Anselm?"

"He is asking for you. He's conscious – has been since they brought him in – but, well, he took some of the blast in his kidneys. These new fragmentation weapons never make a clean wound. I'm afraid he is dying. You can be sure everything has been done. In here we don't make political judgements. He wants to see you before he passes on. Do you feel up to it? I'll get the nurses and a wheelchair."

"Father Anselm is dying?"

"Yes, that's what I said. I may not agree with his form of Catholicism but he seems a thoroughly moral person. He gave his life for another."

"It's not fair," Johnny blurted out without thinking.

The young priest looked sympathetic. "The death of a friend never seems fair," he said. "I'll get the nurses."

"Where are the rest of the group?" Johnny asked as two nurses dressed in angelic white decanted him into the wheelchair. They insisted on him using one because of "regulations", even though he could walk on his own now. Father Blair put a forefinger against his brow. "Sarah, the medic girl, is helping us right here. She loyally stayed on to see Anselm was treated properly. Tanya, the one with the weight problem, has gone home."

They stopped at a door outside which sat a Marine guard, who stood up grudgingly and opened it before sliding back into his seat. Inside the blinds were drawn. Lights winked from banks of equipment around the bed. The dot of Father Anselm's heartbeat jumped on a screen. A nurse pulled back the bed curtain a little. Propped on the pillows was an emaciated face Johnny hardly recognized. Johnny had never seen the once muscular body at rest, yet now it barely seemed capable of supporting itself. The strong, tanned face had turned a yellowish, parchment white, while tubes crept out of his nose and mouth like plastic snakes. One arm across the bed looked bent and wasted. But the eyes managed a smile, even if the lips couldn't. The nurse removed one of the tubes.

"Peace be with you," the voice gasped. As Johnny wheeled himself to the bed, a frail hand took hold of his.

"Forgive me, Johnny. I want you to forgive me. I did not know. I didn't know about the badges. About the killing."

"I know. It wasn't your fault," Johnny said. The hand gripped him with a sudden frenzied strength.

"I was too proud, Johnny, and look at me: the revolutionary priest is being kept alive by his enemies. Why should I have presumed I could do anything? I was too proud. I trusted too much in man."

"We all did."

"But promise me one thing. Promise me you will stay with Catherine. That you will look after her. I've failed, Johnny. I should have seen the evil. But do not blame her."

"I thought it was you when I was captured."

"And I suspected you too, Johnny. But will you promise me?"

"Of course, Father. I will look after her. It may sound odd but this whole business has restored my faith, strengthened it. I don't have much faith in the works of man anymore."

Anselm's eyes smiled. "But we must keep trying, Johnny. We must keep striving for that earthly perfection. I failed, Johnny . . ." Suddenly the priest's breath became laboured and the bleeps from the monitor rushed close together. A nurse pulled Johnny's wheelchair away from the bed and out into the corridor. A few minutes later Father Blair followed. He was holding a small army Bible.

"He's gone, Johnny. It was as if he had been waiting to see you. His body had packed up. I read the last rites over him as he went into trauma. He refused them before. Said he didn't deserve them. He was a true Christian. You were very close?"

"We didn't get on terribly well."

The priest looked puzzled.

"Well, your Father Anselm certainly seemed a fine man to me," he fumbled. "One's best intentions can go very wrong, even with the Almighty on your side."

They wheeled Johnny back to his room and dressed his wound before taking him to see Catherine. He needed to collect his thoughts. It was strange, but Father Anselm's death and what he had asked Johnny to do made forgiving her easier. When he thought of the priest, weak and broken, receiving the charity of his enemies, it made his feelings about how she had betrayed them seem so petty and entirely human; like the shattered shell of Managua's cathedral, a bitter proof of God's greatness and man's stupidity. They had expected too much, Catherine most of all.

She was sitting up in bed with her hair falling around her lovely face, but there were deep dark lines under her eyes. Weights suspended her right leg above the sheet.

"You must hate me," she said flatly. "You know the truth now, don't you? I confessed everything to Anselm. What happened in those villages was my fault. I can understand if you never want to see me again. What I did was so horrible."

Johnny took her hand and kissed her tenderly.

"I don't hate you, Catherine. In fact, I love you more. Being in Nicaragua has made me realize just how precious life is."

"But Bliss used me to murder all those children. . . ."

Johnny stroked her hair. "He could have used any one of us. He chose you because you were the most committed to the revolution. He knew you would do what he wanted without question. But it was not because you were evil or anything, quite the opposite."

She started to cry.

"As soon as you can travel we will go home. To my home in England," soothed Johnny. He had been so afraid of losing her and now she had come back to him, though perhaps not in a way he had ever intended. For an hour she poured out her soul, minutely analysing her every motive.

"I was sick of being a marshmellow liberal aid worker, Johnny," she said finally. "I wanted to be a revolutionary. I wanted to be tough. So Bliss picked me for his greedy personal schemes. Some revolutionary." She looked lost and angry. "He had me for breakfast, Johnny. Can you begin to comprehend what it feels like?"

"Oh, I can," he murmured with a shudder. "Believe me, I can imagine it all too well."

EPILOGUE

He had stopped to look in a jeweller's in Wallingford. His mother had told him about it. The shop belonged to an old family friend. Johnny had promised he would pop in, now he was fully recovered, although he had wanted to buy the ring up in London, something very special. Catherine had been home in England six months with him and although her leg was almost as good as new, she easily became depressed. Johnny's family doctor had said it was something they both must live with, the natural price one paid for witnessing such things. The nice old man had offered him a cup of tea, though his surgery was full, and told Johnny he had seen a lot of it after the last war and Valium was no use at all. That was why Johnny was anxious to give her a beautiful engagement ring. To cheer her up.

But when he peered in the window there was nothing that caught his eye. He turned as it started to drizzle, and saw a man arguing with a parking warden across the road. The man was shaking his head and symbolically raised his eyes towards heaven. His gaze met Johnny's for a second and he seemed puzzled, then went inside a shop. The name was Tambey and Brown of Windsor (By appointment). There was no mistaking the strawberry-coloured birthmark. It was Arthur. Johnny hesitated for a moment and crossed over.

Inside the funeral parlour two people were being shown a varnished coffin on top of which was a large bouquet of gladioli. They looked up at him. Arthur frowned, then handed his customers over to an assistant.

"Come this way," he hissed as if Johnny were a tradesman. At the back was a cosy little office. Beneath a seascape was a drinks trolley and on a table *Sporting Life* rubbed shoulders with a coffin catalogue.

"Sorry about that, old man. Can't jaw about Nicaragua round here. Just opened this one. You do understand . . . What's your poison?"

"No thanks, a bit early for me. My stomach's still a bit off. I picked up a bug," said Johnny. Somehow it did not seem right to drink in an undertaker's.

"I thought it was you across the road. But I said no, it can't be. I hope you didn't consider I let you down in the auditorium, but there was nothing we could do. I'm glad to see you got out in one piece."

"Only just. We had a bit of trouble on the Coast."

"We have been out to Managua again to complete our work."

"Sandino?"

"Yes. We came home shortly after our last unfortunate meeting. Then a month ago they sent us some airline tickets. It seemed they had finally found a corpse the right size. It was all very mysterious."

"What happened?"

"Well, we came out of the Intercontinental on the first day and there was a crowd in the road. Someone had been knocked down. It was that fat little dago with the bad taste in clothes I remembered from the auditorium. A truck's brakes failed."

"You don't mean Bliss?"

"Yes, though in *Barricada* the next day they said he was in Foreign Press Liaison. He'd just been taking some correspondents to lunch and saw a child run out into the road after a ball. He bravely ran after the nipper, so it claimed in the paper, and gave his life to save the child. The foreign press didn't see it because they were finishing their coffees. One told me the man had kept remarking he was worried about his health. They asked the driver what had happened but he turned out to be a mute."

So Alegría had got him. Capitán Happiness had murdered Bliss in broad daylight, no doubt acting on orders for the common good.

"Well, we went to the mortuary to pick up our body to recreate Sandino, and it turned out to be Bliss. He was perfect. More or less the same size and weight and not too badly damaged. We did, if I may say so, a creditable job. Quite overtaken by enthusiasm until we sat down and had a think. It was a bit chilling to recall that we got our tickets three weeks before the man's demise, when he was still walking about. Probably just some sort of cock up, but it makes you think."

"It certainly does," said Johnny.

"Promise you won't tell anyone," added Arthur, suddenly nervous. "I mean, it's only supposition. Would you like to see some photographs?"

"Please."

Arthur unlocked the top drawer of his desk and took out an album. Picture after picture showed Tambey and Brown had lived up to their reputation, except they could not suppress Bliss's eternal grin.

"They are going to put it in the new Palace of Justice," said Arthur.

"How very apt."

Johnny accepted a drink from the undertaker after all, and then another. When he left he walked across to the jeweller's and bought the most expensive ring in the shop. The sky had cleared as he drove his car towards Catherine and the west. It was a lovely English summer afternoon; in fact very nearly perfect.